Praise for Michael Ledwidge:

'Michael Ledwidge has the gift – he knows how to involve us in the story from page one. The writing is sharp and the action doesn't let up'
James Patterson

'A gloriously pulpy, no-nonsense adventure ... Ledwidge knows how to keep readers' adrenaline pumping'
The Times

'I'm not sure how he did it – it seems to defy science – but Michael Ledwidge figured out a way to write a book using pure, distilled adrenaline. Michael Gannon is a fantastic protagonist, destined for the pantheon of characters we love to follow through countless adventures. Here's hoping for many more'
Rob Hart, author of *The Warehouse*

'Michael Ledwidge give us sharply drawn characters in a tense, fast-paced adventure that keeps the reader entertained from the intriguing start to the wild finish'
Thomas Perry, author of *The Burglar*

'The action is tense, the characters are surely drawn, and a wonderful sense of authenticity drives the story ... a high speed roller coaster that will carry you away'
T. Jefferson Parker, author of *The Last Good Guy*

Since 1999, **Michael Ledwidge** has been writing popular bestselling suspense novels that have delighted tens of millions of readers from all over the world. In 2003, he partnered with the world's most popular suspense master, James Patterson, to write over a dozen global bestsellers. In 2020, he reignited his solo career with *Stop at Nothing*, an action-suspense thriller so gripping that Forbes magazine dubbed him 'an author who has mastered his craft'. His newest pulse-pounding thriller, *The Vault*, is his twenty-second novel.

Also by Michael Ledwidge

Beach Murder
Stop at Nothing
Hard to Break
Run for Cover
The Narrowback
Bad Connection
Before the Devil Knows You're Dead

Cowritten with James Patterson

The Quickie
Now You See Her
Zoo
Step on a Crack
Run for Your Life
Worst Case
Tick Tock
I, Michael Bennett
Gone
Burn
Alert
Bullseye
Chase
The Dangerous Days of Daniel X

THE VAULT

Michael Ledwidge

Copyright © 2023 Narrowback LLC

The right of Michael Ledwidge to be identified as the Author of the Work has been asserted by him in accordance with the Copyright, Designs and Patents Act 1988.

First published in 2023 by Headline Publishing Group Limited

This paperback edition published in 2025

1

Apart from any use permitted under UK copyright law, this publication may only be reproduced, stored, or transmitted, in any form, or by any means, with prior permission in writing of the publishers or, in the case of reprographic production, in accordance with the terms of licences issued by the Copyright Licensing Agency.

All characters in this publication are fictitious and any resemblance to real persons, living or dead, is purely coincidental.

Cataloguing in Publication Data is available from the British Library

PAPERBACK ISBN 978 1 0354 0433 9

Offset in 10.9/13.7pt Bembo Std by Jouve (UK), Milton Keynes

Printed and bound in Great Britain by Clays Ltd, Elcograf S.p.A.

Headline's policy is to use papers that are natural, renewable and recyclable products and made from wood grown in well-managed forests and other controlled sources. The logging and manufacturing processes are expected to conform to the environmental regulations of the country of origin.

Headline Publishing Group Limited
An Hachette UK Company
Carmelite House
50 Victoria Embankment
London EC4Y 0DZ

The authorised representative in the EEA is Hachette Ireland, 8 Castlecourt Centre, Dublin 15, D15 XTP3, Ireland (email: info@hbgi.ie)

www.headline.co.uk
www.hachette.co.uk

For the Hahn family and in loving memory of Ian and James

PROLOGUE

NICE NIGHT FOR A STROLL

It was a nice night for a stroll.

Just as I passed the Waldorf Astoria heading south down Park Avenue, that was what struck me. How remarkably movie-set perfect the city was.

There's something special about summer in New York. Something romantic and enchanting. Especially at night. On a nice August evening in the afterglow of the hustle and bustle, the random window lights in the darkened skyscrapers above Midtown can suddenly seem like glittering constellations beckoning you to wish upon a star.

Staring up at those silver lights as I walked toward the MetLife Building's towering dark monolith, it was almost as if for a moment I could actually feel the night itself pulsing with the life force of the naked city's eight million people.

I stopped at the next corner and took a breath then looked down at the rivulet of blood that suddenly ran down the back of my hand and spilled off my ring finger and plopped like a tiny drop of spaghetti sauce onto the concrete beside my pink-and-white FILA running shoe.

Correction, I thought as I swiped my hand with the already bloody towel that I was hiding up the sleeve of the men's Brooks Brothers raincoat I was wearing.

Make that soon to be 7,999,999.

Then I finally walked through the Helmsley Building's tunnellike east pedestrian concourse and crossed empty 45th Street, and I was there.

I pushed through the MetLife Building's heavy revolving doors.

There was a security guard behind a little desk at the top of the left-hand escalator, a very large middle-aged Hispanic gentleman with a shaved head. He looked up from his phone as I carded through the turnstile toward the elevator banks.

Had he noticed anything amiss? I thought warily as I checked the lobby marble behind me for blood.

I didn't see any, but I did suddenly feel quite weak and hot as if a fever were coming over me.

I thought for a moment about asking the nice bald man to call me an ambulance.

But by then one of my blood-free fingers was already on the call button, and the elevator dinged open, and I tottered in and hit 54 instead.

My desolate office suite was the third one down the right-hand corridor from the elevator. After I closed its door behind me, the city lights through the north-facing window illuminated the same two things that were in its center the last time I'd been there the week before.

An industrial shredder and a glossy black cello case.

"The tools of my trade," I said as I threw off the coat and headed straight into the executive washroom.

There was a first aid kit behind the sink mirror, and I took it out and very painfully undid the makeshift duct tape and paper towel dressing I'd used to staunch the bleeding. After I emptied a bottle of hydrogen peroxide over my bloody left forearm, I took out my phone.

"Siri, internet search, gunshot wound," I said.

A click later, the internet informed me that without any major arteries hit, a through-and-through bullet hole was just like a nasty puncture wound.

Nasty puncture wound, I thought as I bandaged and gauzed and taped everything back over again.

I closed the mirror and stared at my pale twenty-four-year-old, graduate school valedictorian face.

"The title of my upcoming *Dateline* episode," I mumbled.

Or would it even be *Dateline*? I wondered as I headed back into the empty office. *American Greed* maybe? A crossover episode?

Suddenly cold, I threw the raincoat back over my shoulders for warmth as I headed to the window. I leaned against the wall for a bit, and then found myself sliding down it until I was just sitting there, staring at the lights of storied, moneyed Park Avenue below.

Money, I thought. Money, money, money.

They say that money is the root of all evil.

But that's not really true. Money is just a tool. Like a hammer, money is just something you use to do things.

And like a hammer, money is a tool that is mostly used to do practical and useful and helpful things like build coffee shops and farms and schools and hospitals and roads.

Sure, hammers sometimes end up cracking someone's skull in every once in a while, but is that really the hammers' fault? They don't say hammers are the root of blunt force trauma murders, do they? No. They don't.

And they don't put hammers on death row.

In the one English class I took in college, I remember Shakespeare saying something about the fault lying not in the stars but in ourselves.

Maybe I should have taken more English classes. It turns out that Shakespeare guy knew his stuff.

Because in the end, I had only three people to blame for the things that had happened to me.

For the decisions I had made.

For the things I had done.

Their names were me, myself, and I.

I found that out the hard way. Boy, did I find that out.

Because what started out good went bad quicker than a New York minute.

And then got uglier and uglier and uglier.

But the worst thing about it was that I was the one who set it all in motion, no one else.

As I sat there bleeding, that's what really got to me the most.

I thought I was cleverly building a way to get all the things I'd hoped and worked for, a way to finally realize my dreams, to make everything right.

It was only when it was too late that I realized that the only thing I'd been building was a trap.

Then I fell straight in.

PART ONE

SUMMER IN THE CITY

1

In New York City near the southwest corner of 63rd Street and Madison Avenue, there is a restaurant called Stella's and when everything started, I was sitting in one of its coveted lime-green velvet booths.

It was coming on ten at night, and I was drinking a lemongrass daiquiri. In all my years on the planet up to that point, I'd never touched lemongrass or daiquiris. Until that summer. That summer it seemed like it's all I drank.

"Should I get you ladies started on a new one?" asked our waiter.

Our waiter was named Tommy, and he was a fortysomething Italian guy with slicked back hair who had the vaguely menacing solemn look of a *Sopranos* extra. But intimidating demeanor aside, he was always exceptionally nice to us. And when I say us, I mean my work cubicle mate, Priscilla Hutton, who was sitting across from me.

Priscilla and Tommy were actually old pals as she had been partying here at Stella's since her Birch Wathen Lenox private high school days.

I did some high school partying myself back in my small town in Kentucky. Just never at a place that had nine-thousand-dollar bottles of champagne on the menu and a VIP room described in *New York* magazine as "Hollywood East."

"The answer to that is yes, Tommy," Priscilla said. "My friend and I need two fresh jolts stat. If that's okay with you, Faye."

Sometimes I wonder about that question. I wonder about what would have happened if I'd gone back to my apartment instead of accepting.

Or even more importantly, about what wouldn't have.

"I'm game if you are," I said, smiling.

The second drink order surprised me. We usually had only one polite drink at the end of the week here, down the street from our job, and then parted ways.

It was part of our unspoken deal. I hooked up Priscilla by handling all of our incredibly high-pressure work stuff, and Priscilla hooked me up by letting me hang out with her a little.

Even though I was totally carrying her, it was a good deal on both ends because Priscilla was gorgeous and rich and knew everyone in New York. She'd actually been in society pages like *Avenue* magazine ever since high school, each time tan and perfect in an effortlessly stylish outfit that she just threw on after a day spent surfing or skiing or at the spa.

Priscilla was also one of those people who had that voice, that eastern establishment rich person voice, that some call Transatlantic or Boston Brahmin or Locust Valley lockjaw. Not a ton of it, not a pretentious amount, just a sophisticated hint, an elegant tinge, just enough.

It made her sound like a young Lauren Bacall or Bette Davis or someone. I loved just listening to her. It made you feel a little special just to hear her confide in you, as if only for a few moments, you were in the privileged people club, too.

I really didn't even know why Priscilla had applied for, let alone accepted, our summer internship. It was extremely hard work, and she was kind of a ditz, so why not just take the Instagram influencer route? I often wondered.

I think it had something to do with her father's business, some defense contractor aerospace company in Connecticut that made airplane parts. Maybe she needed some finance experience to become an executive there? Not that she had told me any of this, but I did have internet access.

She even pretended to be my friend. She shared fashion advice with me, which was a sorely needed lesson. And she also told me all these incredible stories about her days in prep school and Yale and Palm Beach and the Hamptons.

At least at the office. When she was in the mood.

"But another?" I said as Tommy left. "That's okay, Priscilla. I know you have things to do. I should be going."

"No, not yet. I owe you big time, Kemosabe. If you hadn't remembered to recheck the Westland account for me before it went to the treasury team, that Aiken would have dragged me up the stairs of the boiler room by the scruff of my neck."

It was true. She had screwed up big time. One of our biggest hedge fund clients wanted $130 million wired into their Cayman account, but Priscilla had boneheadedly put in the account numbers of a completely different fund instead. Getting a number wrong here and there wasn't a problem. Sending money into another fund's account was. If it had gone through, the money could have instantly disappeared without a trace with no way to unwind it, and our client could have been out $130 million.

"Oh, that," I said. "Don't mention it. Anytime. I was looking for something to do anyway."

That's when Priscilla looked at me, and we both completely lost it.

Oh, we laughed then all right. Practically until the lemongrass came from our nostrils.

Looking for something to do, I thought, shaking my aching head.

That was a phrase I used way back in the normal life I led before I accepted the summer internship at the venerated Wall Street private investment bank, Greene Brothers Hale, nearly three months before.

Our musty-smelling windowless basement office a few blocks down Madison Avenue really did look like a boiler room or maybe something out of a Dickens poorhouse. Only with computers and phones on our cheap desks instead of dusty ledger books.

And out of these electronic torture devices, all day—for pretty much twelve hours straight from eighty-seven different pissed-off, stressed-out directions at once—came numbers.

The stress and anger directed our way was due to the fact that the numbers represented money. Profoundly massive amounts of money from hedge funds or institutional investors or just really, really rich people. This money either needed to be placed into our bank's fat cat VIP client accounts or taken out of them and sent other places, places like the Cayman Islands or Switzerland.

You'd think this given task was simple enough like we were mere bank tellers, just moving around much larger sums.

But you would be wrong.

Each incoming or outgoing bank transfer had to be placed in its proper slot. Each one processed through a verification process wrapped in an amount of red tape to make your eyes bleed. Emails with these numbers had to go to the proper people for due diligence verifications. All in the proper order. Yesterday. Or else.

It was the volume of the orders. It was staggering. The air traffic controllers out at Kennedy airport had less to juggle.

Or maybe it was the unhinged wrath of the psychopathic traders and other finance people on the upper floors of our building who kept calling down to see if the transfers had cleared.

Where the hell was the money? they wanted to know. *What the hell was wrong with us? Did they actually have to f-ing come down there?*

Every morning when I sat down and looked at my newly filled inbox of waiting orders, I thought about the Greek hero, Sisyphus, cursed to eternally roll his rock up that hill.

In envy.

Was he a summer Wall Street intern, too? I would wonder.

And did I mention all of this labor and misery was being extracted from me *gratis*?

That was the kicker. Since it was an unpaid internship, we were only doing it for the *possibility* of *maybe* getting a full-time entry level job as a junior investment analyst.

My skin was being flayed *for free*.

As I sat there that Friday, attempting to cool my smoking brain with rum and lemongrass syrup, I couldn't help feeling like I'd been duped.

Because I thought I was going to be a swashbuckling Wall Street pirate.

Instead, I'd been shanghaied and thrown into the slave galley to row.

2

Still in the middle of enjoying our punch-drunk Wall Street intern gallows humor, we both turned as someone suddenly appeared before our booth.

The men who lined Stella's famous zinc bar usually ran older, fifty- or sixtysomething Hollywood or European types, their wrinkles smoothed away with plastic surgery, fake tans, and impeccable clothes.

But with his tousled strawberry blond hair and beard, the cute twentysomething guy standing by our booth looked more like an aging frat boy than a millionaire.

When I noticed he was very thin, I thought maybe he was a model. Though he wasn't really tall enough. Everybody was someone at Stella's. It was an ironclad rule. Well, except for snuck-in stowaways like me, of course.

"May I?" he said, sitting down next me.

As I reluctantly scooted over, I turned to see that Priscilla's face was as puzzled as my own.

"And you are?" Priscilla said.

I was taking in the guy's vacant expression and glassy eyes

when I noticed that the sleeve of the suit jacket he was wearing was opened up from the wrist to the elbow. Then I caught a whiff of body odor and inched away like you do when a homeless person sits down next to you on the subway.

"I'll have one, too, please," our strange new visitor said to Tommy as he arrived with our fresh drinks.

"You again?" Tommy said, peering daggers at him. "Didn't I tell you not to come back in here?"

"Oh, my goodness. Gareth?" Priscilla suddenly said wide-eyed.

"In the flesh," the guy said, rolling his eyes. "Wow. Finally, Prissy. Took you long enough."

Priscilla squealed as she leapt up and hugged him.

"You know this guy?" Tommy said.

It was my question, too.

"Yes, of course, Tommy. He's with me," Priscilla said, shooing Tommy away as they both sat again.

"Gareth, when did you start with that beard? You almost completely fooled me. Gareth, this is Faye, my work buddy. Faye, meet Gareth. You know how Jamaica has Usain Bolt? Well, Park Avenue has Gareth Haynes. I'm not even kidding. How many school track records did you set?"

"Four but who's counting?" Gareth said with a laugh.

"He came in first in states in the thirty-two hundred," Priscilla said. "What was your time again?"

"Eight forty-one dot forty-two," he said. "It was the high school state record until last year."

"Thirty-two hundred?" I said.

"It's the two-miler," Priscilla said. "I'll never forget that race. It was neck and neck until the last half mile then he dusted them."

"Those were the days, Prissy, huh?" Gareth said. "Remember coming back from that meet on Randall's Island when we plotted with Mr. Ken to take us to Florida for spring break?"

"Mr. Ken!" Priscilla laughed. "World's best school bus driver! He would have taken us, too. And the other time, when he squeezed the bus through the McDonald's drive-through on the West Side? The look on the woman's face! If Mr. Ken wasn't the best thing about that stuffy institution, I don't know what was."

"Well, you still look terrific," Gareth said. "As always."

"So do you," Priscilla said. "Last time we met was what? Two years ago? Thanksgiving weekend at that place in the meatpacking district. You were at... UCLA film school, I think."

He passed a hand through his prep school hair and kind of gave it a flip as he laughed again.

"That didn't last long. Went to Tulane Law after that and that lasted even less time. I did some surfing. I was in Morocco for a while. You ever been?"

"No," Priscilla said, putting her lovely chin in her hand. "But I took a day trip to Algiers the last time we went to Ibiza. What wonderful people and the food was amazing. It must have been beautiful. The Mediterranean is so serene."

He nodded.

"Then I was back out in LA, and now I'm back here. I'm not sure if you heard. My dad's not doing too hot."

"I did hear. Scarlet told me. I'm so sorry," Priscilla said.

"Yeah, me, too," Gareth said, suddenly standing.

"Wait. Can't you stay?" Priscilla said.

"Ah, I won't torture you anymore," he said. "I was just walking by, and when I saw you through the window, I knew I had to pop in and say hi, Prissy. You were always so...nice. Those Mr. Ken days really were such good ones, weren't they?"

"The best," Priscilla said. "But where are you going? You have to stay for a drink."

He looked at his phone.

"Can't now, Pris. But I'll be around. We'll catch up next time, okay? I promise."

"You better," Priscilla said, smiling.

But he didn't go. Not right away. He stood there for a moment, looking at her. There was an expression on his face, a kind of sadness. I noticed the same sad wistful look on Priscilla's face, too.

They'd been in love, I suddenly realized.

"Nice meeting you," he said quickly, turning to me.

"You, too," I said as I watched Priscilla watch him leave.

He laughed as Tommy stopped him by the door. Then his laugh turned into a wince as Tommy seemed to seize and squeeze his wrist. He almost knocked over the Wait to Be Seated sign as he broke free, stumbling out onto the sidewalk.

"Now that sucks," Priscilla said after knocking back half her new drink.

"About his dad?" I said.

"No, about Gareth," she said, twirling her straw. "His parents threw him out. The whole family has basically disowned him. He's a...well... He's a drug addict."

"No way," I said. "That's terrible."

"Terrible is the word," she said. "Been in and out of rehab a bunch of times. I'm surprised he's still alive. I heard they even cut his trust fund down to hardly anything in a last-ditch effort to convince him to get clean again. I'm still close with his little sister, Scarlet, who was in my year at school."

"Wow," I said quietly.

She tapped at the rim of her glass as she shook her head.

"He invited me to the prom. I would have gone, too, except someone else had asked me the day before. He was so funny and talented. One of the best athletes in the school's history. Not just track either. You had to see him play basketball. Even without all of his family's money, he would have had the world at his feet."

"His family?" I said.

"The Hayneses. Real estate," Priscilla said. "They own Smith & Haynes, the biggest luxury real estate service company in Manhattan. Their agents sell and manage almost all of the luxury apartment buildings on the Upper East Side and half of the office buildings in Midtown. S&H are also the go-to brokers in Greenwich, the Hamptons, and Palm, of course. The family is actually a huge private client at our bank. Imagine? All that property and Gareth probably sleeps on the street. Drugs can be so destructive."

As she went to take another sip of her drink, Priscilla looked over at me and seemed to sit up a little, to catch herself as she suddenly wondered if talking out of turn to an outsider was wise.

Then it was her turn to check her phone.

"Well, I must be going, too, Faye," she said as she lifted her Louis Vuitton clutch. "Cheers to you. Thanks again for the save. By the way, how the heck did you even notice my mistake? You looked over my shoulder at my screen for like a second."

"I remembered the number," I said truthfully.

"The client's routing number that I got wrong?" she said, raising a perfectly arched eyebrow.

"I sent money to that same Cayman account the first week. That's why I knew it wasn't the Westland one."

"You remember routing numbers? No! Really? Come on. What do you do? Like memorize them? How?"

"Piece of cake," I said with a wink as I lifted my glass.

3

Buzzing hard on top shelf rum, I headed out into the sultry summer night and walked to the corner and headed west. A block up past all the billionaire row town houses, I crossed Fifth Avenue and followed the Central Park wall to Central Park South and made a right.

As I walked west, I smiled as I took in the scenery, the glittering Sherry Netherland princess tower, the famous FAO Schwarz toy store, the majestic Plaza hotel. For how grueling work was, you couldn't knock its über-fabulous *Vogue* magazine photoshoot backdrop.

As I approached Sixth Avenue, I saw one of those romantic horse and buggies by the entrance to the Central Park Drive right by the three-story-tall black granite and bronze statue of Simon Bolivar on horseback.

As everyone who has googled him knows, Simon Bolivar was a great liberating hero in the vein of George Washington who in the early 1800s led South America's fight for independence from the Spanish Empire.

And at the base of this legendary mounted hero's statue, sitting on a bench, I found my hero, Cavan Fagen.

Who also had a horse, come to think of it.

As I got closer, I laughed as he lifted the acoustic guitar at his feet and began to play the intro to *Pretty Woman*.

"Pretty woman, would you like a ride?" he sang, eyes closed, with a lot of extra gusto. "Pretty woman, in my hansom cab?"

"Why, yes, I would, sir," I said, stopping and petting his horse, Lily, who was harnessed to his carriage at the curb. "What's the price?"

"No more than this," my drop-dead-cute, black-haired boyfriend said with even more extra corny drama as he lay down his guitar and hopped up and embraced me.

"Get a room," said a homeless woman rattling by in the street with a baby stroller full of empties as we were still in the middle of making out.

"I'd love nothing more, madam," Cavan cried out at her back in his Irish accent. "If only I could afford one!"

Of the two extremely lucky things that had happened to me that summer, scoring my summer internship with Greene Brothers Hale was actually second in line.

Because meeting and instantly falling in love with Cavan Fagen was the cherry on top of the cream.

I'd met him on the subway as I was heading to my orientation. I got turned around on the Six train, and Cavan, who was on his way to work as well, saw me staring at the map behind his head and stood and showed me where I had gone wrong.

It was a week later on my lunch hour that I bumped into him again here at the Bolivar statue. From the moment we met on the subway when I noticed how mischievous and sparkly his blue eyes were, I was pretty smitten. But when our eyes connected again for the second time through the hot dog vendors and day-tripping camp kids, I knew that Cupid and the fates must have conspired.

True love didn't mess around. No way. Not in NYC in the summertime when you were on your own for the first time.

Now almost three months into the summer, bumping into him had basically become the purpose of my existence.

Let the sea keep all the other fish, I thought as Cavan helped me up onto the carriage's jockey box.

Just out of graduate school and being from a very small rural Kentucky town, there were a lot of things that I hadn't figured out about life yet.

But one thing I had figured out, to the mitochondria of my cells, was that I was head over heels in love with Cavan Fagen.

I want to be with you forever, you kind and wonderful upbeat hilarious talented man, I telepathically told Cavan as he settled in beside me.

Whatever it takes.

4

"So?" I said as we both got comfortable behind his horse, Lily.

"So?" Cavan said, looking at me perplexed. "Whatever do you mean, pretty woman?"

I punched him on the arm.

He frowned.

"The answer's no, darling. Lots of bills in the mail this morning at the ole Bronx villa. But no green card."

I closed my eyes.

No, come on, I thought. Just no.

It was the one glitch. Of course, there had to be one.

Cavan hadn't come to New York from the Emerald Isle to be a charming hansom cab driver or even a busking sidewalk singer, which he was also amazing at.

After a Yank uncle of his had gotten on with the NYPD, it had been Cavan's lifelong dream to become an American police detective. He had scored perfectly on the test, but there was one little problem. He wasn't a citizen yet. You had to have your green card before you could start at the academy.

It usually took between four and five years to get one, and

Cavan, being on his fifth year now, was super hopeful. But then again, of course, there was another problem.

In his frustration with not getting on with the NYPD, he had applied for other first responder jobs everywhere. Even back in Ireland. And wouldn't you know it, the Dublin Fire Department had sent him an acceptance letter. He was to report for duty in Dublin right after Labor Day.

So, unless his green card came in the next couple of weeks, he would be leaving.

Which was monumentally unacceptable.

"That's okay. There's still time," I said.

"We're running out of that, little darlin'. We have to start being realistic."

"We will. If your green card doesn't come, we go immediately with Plan B," I said.

I had, of course, devised a Plan B.

As soon as I was permanently hired at Greene Brothers Hale, I was going to get an apartment for us. Cavan's housing costs taken care of, he could still wait for his green card.

I had it all worked out. I knew exactly how much money I would be offered, and I'd even started looking for apartments. Problem solved.

"You and your plan," Cavan said, folding his arms.

"What's the issue? I'm going to make it happen."

"That's the issue," he said. "Have you ever considered that *I* might want to wear the pants in our little romance here? That maybe I don't want to be a kept man. Haven't I told you ten times, Patrick, my boss, is selling the cab this October. I'll be out of a job. Penniless."

"You can still help pay the bills. You can busk."

"Busk on the subway?" he said, throwing up his hands. "That's a plan? Or maybe instead, I could look for empties like the enterprising lass who just passed here. My busking days are over, Faye. I need a real job. What about you coming to Dublin? Come with me like we were talking about. Greed is good in Dublin, too, these days, Miss High Finance."

"I can't," I said. "Not yet. I'd have to work at GBH for at least a year or two before I could transfer to another bank and besides..."

Cavan tsked as he folded his arms again.

"I forgot. Your sister."

"Come on," I said. "Don't say it like that. Caitlin is coming up, but there's going to be plenty of room. I have it all worked out. It's going to be fine."

"I don't know about that," he said. "But enough grim talk. How was work today? How's my friend, old Ivy League A, doing?"

He was referring to Priscilla.

"Don't be mean. She's fine."

"Uh-huh. I'm sure she is. Because of you. With all the carrying her around, you'll be able to bench press a city bus soon."

We both turned as a figure stepped by on the sidewalk, clapping and laughing and mumbling to himself. It took me a second to register that he wasn't on his phone. Then another to notice the reddish-blond scruffy beard.

It was Gareth Haynes.

As he passed by the Bolivar statue, I remembered the sad long-lost-love look he had given Priscilla. Now he was out here in the dark by himself looking pretty wasted.

As we watched, he stopped on a Central Park bench another half a block west of us and closed his eyes. Instead of falling asleep, he began rocking ever so slightly back and forth.

"See that?" Cavan said. "On the nod, they call that. It's the junk makes 'em do it for some reason."

"That's just terrible."

"Have you never seen a junkie before?" Cavan said as he saw me watching him. "Stick around. This park here starts filling up with all sorts right around now."

I shook my head.

"It's not that. I know him," I said.

"How's that?"

"Gareth is his name. He stopped by at Stella's. Priscilla knows him. He's actually really rich. Or his family is. They are the biggest real estate brokers in Manhattan. She's friends with his sister."

We watched as Gareth swayed back and forth some more and then lay all the way back with his feet up on the bench.

"Well, I'll say one thing for your Gareth there. He's a well-dressed bum at least with that jacket. Probably buys his crack pipes at Tiffany's. Real breeding there. You can tell."

"Oh, leave him alone, Cavan," I said. "His parents threw him out. Plus his dad is sick. I really feel sorry for him."

"See, that's your problem right there, lass," Cavan said, putting an arm over my shoulder. "If you want to survive in this town, you have to toughen up and stop feeling sorry for everyone. You're like Lily here."

"I'm like your horse?" I said. "Why, what a romantic thing to say to a girl."

"Listen. This is a dog-eat-dog city, Faye, and Lily and you need to stop acting like you're the beggin' strips. Lily here, for example, is always stopping to let people pass in the crosswalks. Always letting the cabs cut her off. She's skittish as a cat. She could be in the Kentucky Derby, pulling ahead at the final turn. She could, but no. Here she is, a four-legged taxi. Because why? Like you, she's too nice. No killer instinct."

"Don't you listen to him, Lily," I called down to his poor horse. "You're perfect."

"Sir? Excuse me, but is it too late to take a ride?" said a voice.

We turned toward the street. A pudgy sweet-looking old black man was waving as he helped his even pudgier elderly wife over the Central Park South crosswalk.

"I hate to bother you," the old man said as he arrived. "But the play let out later than I thought, and I promised my wife. It's our anniversary you see, and well…is it too late for a ride?"

"You're right. It is too late," Cavan said, leaping down.

The old man's face fell.

"Except in cases of anniversaries, of course," Cavan said, opening the cab's door with a theatrical bow. "Permission to board, granted."

"What were you saying about being a pushover again?" I said as Cavan helped me down.

"Very funny, funny girl," Cavan said, squeezing my hand.

"Funny girl now?" I said. "What happened to pretty woman?"

"You're all of them, lass," he said in my ear as he hugged me. "And more. Now text straight when you get home."

I am home, I thought as Cavan hugged me goodbye.

5

It was just after midnight when I made it back to my apartment that night.

It was in Chinatown in an old gray plaster building on Mott Street sandwiched between a grimy fish restaurant and a video arcade.

During the summer, I had learned that there were actually at least two types of weird in NYC. You had your regular legless homeless guy on a skateboard on the N train sort of weird. And then you had haunted house in Chinatown weird.

The arcade I lived beside was case in point. It still had all the classics, I saw, as I walked past it from the subway station on Canal. Inside, Galaga, Space Invaders, Joust, Pogo and many more retro electronic delights—from the '80s, or was it the '70s—flashed and bleeped and blooped from their ancient smart-car-sized consoles.

Even at this hour, the arcade was going strong with its door open wide. Though no one seemed to be in it. No one ever seemed to be in it. And yet like a public park or something, it never seemed to close.

I stared at it warily as I walked around a giant greasy Hefty bag full of fish guts into my building.

Come to think of it, the arcade couldn't close, could it? I thought, looking at it as I passed. It didn't even seem to have a door.

Living beside a greasy fish restaurant was bad enough, but the arcade was...an almost surreal enigma. How was it possible that it even existed? I often wondered. Was it a portal of some sort? A time machine back to 1981?

My third-floor apartment, if you could technically call it that, was a studio with a plywood divider down the center of it. I called it The Box. I had the Box's left side and my roommate—some really nice German girl named Petra, who was trying to become a Broadway actress—had the other.

One of the perks of the internship at Greene Brothers Hale was free housing in a new NYU dorm. The pictures of the rooms in the package they sent looked like something from a luxury hotel.

Unfortunately, by the time I sent my acceptance, all the units had been filled, so they had given me a housing stipend of a thousand dollars a month instead.

Having only been able to pull off the unpaid internship by using every penny in savings I had, plus a lot of begging and borrowing, I had searched high and low and found this sketchy arrangement here in Chinatown for $650 a month.

I wasn't complaining. The extra $350 came in very handy.

And to be honest, it was actually not that bad when you considered my room back home in Eastern Kentucky coal country consisted of the top bunk bed in a single wide trailer.

How I had gotten from there to an internship on Wall Street was a rags-to-potential-riches story for the ages because my academic career had not started out promising at all.

Especially when in junior year of high school, I'd started hanging out with this boy down my country road named James who was what my grandmother referred to as a troublemaker. But he was a funny, nice-looking troublemaker who convinced me pretty easily that riding around all day in his daddy's old pickup truck drinking beer and singing Blake Shelton songs was much more fun than attending school.

At the end of the year, I had failed every class except for gym. Though I could belt out "Sangria" to bring the house down.

For punishment that summer, Gramma, who'd been raising my little sister and me since we were about six and eleven, forced me to get a job at the tire store in our tiny flyspeck town of Ester.

This, as it turned out, was to be the greatest thing Gramma would ever do for me in my life.

My boss, Mr. Baker, was quite a unique individual. Though he was large and bearded and had a bit of a biker look to him like many of the other locals, he was actually part preacher and part bookworm.

From the moment I started my shift, he would sit in his office all day listening to classical or Christian music while he read the Bible and Civil War history books and did crossword puzzles.

One day, when he noticed how I had tallied up a set of Michelin LTX all-terrains in my head without using the computer, he brought me into his office for a meeting.

"Faye, you're smart," he had said.

"That right?" I had said. "Could you tell that to my guidance counselor, Mr. Baker? Because she says I need to repeat junior year."

"You're smart," he repeated. "Some people are smart because they have an active imagination, and some people are smart because they have a great memory. You seem to have a steel trap in there, Faye. And a memory for numbers is even rarer. Let me take a guess. At school you liked math and were pretty good at it."

"Yes," I said.

"And in the other classes, you never did your homework but

you remembered everything the teacher said, so you still did pretty well on tests. Am I right?"

"How'd you know?" I said.

"I was the same way. That's why tomorrow is going to be a big day for you."

"It is?" I said.

"Yes," he said. "I'm going to teach you how to play chess."

And so he did. It only took me about a month to play him to a stalemate and by the end of the summer, after I beat him for the first time, he told me the Plan.

"What you're going to do this September, Faye," Mr. Baker said, "is not go back to high school."

"No?" I said. "You're taking me on full time?"

"Yes. Not only that, you're going to get your GED. Then what you are going to do is apply to that community college down in Pikeville. When you are there, you are going to get straight As, do you understand? Straight As. After you get those straight As that prove how smart you are, you are going to apply to the University of Tennessee at Chattanooga where you will be awarded a full-boat academic scholarship in mathematics."

"What?" I said, gaping at him. "How on earth is all that going to happen?"

"My brother is a tenured math professor there," he said. "That's how."

"Why would you do this for me, Mr. Baker? We're not even family," I said.

"Because you're smart, Faye," he said. "Smart's rare. Maybe the rarest thing there is on God's green earth. Plus you're good, too. I see the way you take care of your sister. Smart plus good equals light, Faye. And this dark old world needs light as bright as it can get it. That's why you need to get on out of here to Chattanooga and quick."

Mr. Baker had been right about one thing. I was smart. Smart enough to follow his incredibly wise advice, that is.

Because it had worked. I did exactly as he said, and not only did I get straight As in community college with the help of Mr. Baker's brother, I followed that streak all the way through Chattanooga and graduated as valedictorian with a degree in Advanced Math and went straight on to its graduate school and got my MBA.

That's why when the dust settled, I had not one but two offers for very promising summer internships. One from Morgan Stanley to work in Atlanta, and another for a bank I had never heard of before called Greene Brothers Hale in Manhattan.

GBH as it was referred to by those in the know, I quickly learned, was one of the oldest and largest private investment banks in the world. I didn't even know what a private investment bank was, but it only took me the time to read the part on its Wikipedia page where it said it had three-trillion-with-a-T under management for me to call the recruiter back and sign on.

Even though the GBH internship was incredibly grueling, as I threw on my Mandelbrot set PJs and settled into my slot in the Box that night, I had a giant smile on my face.

Because not only was the Plan still in full working operation, I had found the love of my life, Cavan, now to be a part of it with me.

As I lay down, I thought of the sweet way he had made that old couple's anniversary even more special.

Cavan couldn't be mean if you put a gun to his head, could he? I thought with another smile. He wouldn't know the first step how.

Smart plus good equals light, Faye, I heard Mr. Baker say in my head as I closed my eyes.

"God bless you, Mr. Baker," I whispered as I fell asleep.

6

The apartment I went to look at that Sunday afternoon was way uptown around Columbia University at 121st Street and Morningside Drive across from a park. As I arrived, I saw that the drive curved there back toward Amsterdam Avenue and so did the charming prewar building itself.

The broker standing out in front of it was younger than I thought she would be and well put together in a cream cocktail dress and pearls, and her hair seemed expensively colored.

I stifled a smile as I looked at her Louboutin satin mules that looked suspiciously like the knockoffs I had bought off the sidewalk down on Canal Street.

Ah, a go-getter like myself, I thought.

Playing the part of a money-is-no-object young professional Wall Street woman on her day off, I was wrapped in meticulously devil-may-care casual Fendi athleisure wear that I had bought three Canal Street sidewalk stalls down from the fake Louboutins.

Though I was new to the blood sport of NYC fake it till you make it, I liked to think I was catching on quick.

"Sabrina?" I said.

"Faye?" she said with some kind of accent as she gave me a faint smile.

"That's me," I said.

"Super. Let's go inside," she said.

They say that you fall in love with a place within the first five seconds of walking in the door, and that's pretty much exactly what happened.

There was exposed brick, walnut butcher-block countertops, and an en suite bathroom in the bedroom. The front of the apartment had a curve in it and looked out over the park. In the living room, there was a spiral staircase that led to a tiny loft.

"Would it be okay to film?" I said, taking out my phone.

"This won't be for TikTok, will it?" Sabrina said in her Eastern European accent.

I laughed.

"No, for my sister. But now that you mention it, maybe TikTok as well. If I start a dance routine, please feel free to join me."

"No," Sabrina said, smiling. "Not on Sunday. On Sunday, dancing is extra 5 percent on commission."

I went up the spiral staircase.

"This is like an unofficial second bedroom," Sabrina said. "It could be removed if you want."

"Oh, no. I would leave it," I said as I came down.

"So, what do you think?"

I stood by the window, looking down at the leafy trees in the sunny park across the street. It would be snug as a bug in a rug, but we could do it. We really could. It would be a start.

"Three thousand, right?" I said.

"Yes. With a one-month deposit. One-year lease. If you give me the deposit, we sign today."

I sighed. The cost wasn't the issue. GBH gave a $10K signing bonus once you were officially hired. The problem was that the decision of which interns would be hired wasn't supposed to happen until the end of the summer.

"This is a problem?"

"I want the apartment, but I can't sign today. Will it go quickly?"

"How long do you need? A week?"

"A month," I said.

"Things are a bit slow right now. It might still be here. Where do you work? Midtown?"

"Yes."

"Finance?"

"Yes."

"I will tell the landlord your situation," Sabrina said. "But don't worry. If it's gone, I know other one bedrooms just like this for three thousand."

"I love your shoes, Sabrina," I said as she gave me her card back outside.

"Thank you," she said. "I like your leggings. Fendi, right? And your accent, where is it from?"

"Down south," I said. "You?"

"I am from the south as well," she said, smiling. "South Poland. So much juggling and running around for one so young. Finance job and getting nice apartment. I know just how you feel. Breaking into Manhattan is not easy, is it?"

I knew what she meant, but the way she said it in her accent made it sound illicit. Like breaking into a house.

"No, it's not, Sabrina," I said. "Not even a little."

7

After the broker left, instead of heading straight back to the subway, I took out my phone and crossed the street into Morningside Park and sat on a bench.

"Hey," I said to my sister, Caitlin, when she picked up.

"Hey," she said.

"You see the video I just texted you?"

"No," she said. "I just got out of the shower."

"Showering at three in the afternoon?"

"Gramma woke up and needed the lawn mowed or the world was gonna end. Give me five minutes. I'll call you back."

"Four," I said as she hung up.

Gramma, I thought, picturing her on the trailer's "front porch," complaining about everything. She'd been nice to take us in. Hell, no one else would. Caitlin and I had been in grammar school at the time. I guess even Gramma, as mean and selfish and thoughtless as she was by nature, couldn't figure out a way of getting out of that.

But to say that we were even remotely a priority for her would have been lying. She drank a lot and popped pills. On the weekends, she drank at a nearby honky-tonk bar, and strange men would come back with her. One night, one of them tried to climb into bed with my sister until I hit him with an aluminum baseball bat a couple of times.

If that weren't bad enough, Gramma would forget to get a new propane delivery during the winter and the trailer would get as cold as a meat locker. Many times, she left for days with no food or money for us.

On the bus to school that first year, a boy said Gramma was a hooker, and I about strangled him with the strap of my backpack. She certainly wasn't grandmother of the year, that was for sure, but she wasn't that bad.

Despite all the craziness with Gramma, Caitlin and I had started out our lives in just about the happiest most normal family on earth. We weren't originally from the Appalachian hollers but from Walhalla, South Carolina, down in the Blue Ridge foothills.

Our dad was the head mechanic at the Ford dealership in Lake Keowee, and we lived in a new four-bedroom house in a subdivision. We wanted for nothing. Spent our early childhood at the town pool, bouncing in our backyard trampoline, racing all our friends down the steep hill of our cul-de-sac on anything that would roll.

Our pretty mom didn't even work at an outside job. There was no need to. She spent all her energy on the three of us and the house. She kept our granite countertops clean as an operating table. Kept all of us right in line with everything, with school, with church. In dreams, I would be back with her in our beautiful house's upstairs sunny laundry room folding sheets.

But then she died of colon cancer, and life immediately started getting shakier than a dollar store wheelbarrow.

Dad, who had been a good provider but probably the quietest person I'd ever met, didn't know what to say or do. Only eleven, I started cooking and shopping after the funeral, and then two months after that, Dad was fired when his drug test came up positive at work.

Not long after that, there was a For Sale sign on our front lawn, and we moved up into the Kentucky coal mine mountains where my parents were from. Or, I should say, escaped from. Their town of Ester in Pike County was a very poor almost lawless area with a lot of drugs and desperate people who poached deer to get through the winter.

Up there, Dad had basically dropped us off at Gramma's trailer and left to go live with his older brother who we had never even met. When he was arrested a few months later, Gramma wouldn't tell us what for, but I figured it out by listening to her gossip on the phone about it to my aunts.

He'd been pulled over with a ton of prescription pills in his car, and when he fled from the cops, he ran over a middle-aged woman who was out jogging and killed her. He got nine years in a plea deal plus five more when he was involved in a prison fight.

The one time we visited him at the state penitentiary in Eddyville, he told us never to come back. To forget he was our father.

I knew that was bull and that deep down he loved us, but he couldn't say it.

I didn't even blame him really for being such a hopeless mess. He and Momma had been inseparable. Our mom had really been an incredibly strong person and had been carrying him, taking care of him and keeping him in line. Suddenly without her holding him up, it was like he lost one of his legs and gravity took back over and he fell.

I myself had gotten into trouble up in those hollers, hadn't I? If my personal fairy godfather boss, Mr. Baker, hadn't seen my potential and come up with the Plan, I'd probably still be in trouble.

And the area was worse now if that were possible. Not a week before, a high school teacher nearby over the state line in West

Virginia was actually shot down in some kind of drug deal gone wrong. A high school teacher!

That's why the Plan now included getting Caitlin out of there and up here with me where I could help her get her life going the same way Mr. Baker had helped me fix up mine.

Caitlin needed her chance, too. To do what, we hadn't quite figured out yet. Getting her up here was job one.

So that was my little secret that the folks down at Greene Brothers didn't have a clue about. I acted like I was like the other interns. Normal, middle class, a rah-rah STEM-loving, college-educated young woman who, when I wasn't building my career, was devising entertaining, socially conscious posts for my Instagram.

But I wasn't. That was a ruse. I was older than my years. I'd been hungry. Cold. Hopeless. I had seen real evil, had to actually fight it in the dark with a baseball bat.

But the bonus there was that by knowing real evil, I also knew what real good was, too.

That's why I knew, to my bone marrow, that Cavan and I were destined for each other. Even before the first date, I could tell how good and pure he was, see the light in him.

Mr. Baker had said that smart was the rarest thing in the world. But in my opinion, good was even rarer. I had found a ten-ton mother lode in Cavan. I think it was because he was a rural person, too. He'd grown up on a cattle farm in Meath with three brothers and two sisters and two parents who taught him how to work hard and how to love and care about people.

That's why I was taking Cavan and running. We were going to be together forever, amen. It wasn't even a question.

Because from the beginning, that was really what the Plan was about.

My tastes were simple. Getting ahold of some simple safety and stability and joy again. I wanted a house, not made out of aluminum, with a door with a good lock on it. And Cavan inside of it to make me laugh and to share my life with.

Everything else was a means how.

In my heart, I knew what I wanted was my momma's life, her gleaming countertops, the sparkle in her eye when she heard the hum of the garage door.

If acting like the female version of Gordon Gekko for a year or two was the price of getting it, so be it, I thought as I felt my phone buzz.

"Bring it on," I said as I hit accept.

8

The Six train I caught that Monday morning from Canal Street ran express to 42nd for some lucky reason, so I got up to Midtown early enough to get in a little exercise.

As usual when I was running early, I got off at Grand Central Station.

Out of so many cool, only-in-New-York things that my internship came with, I thought commuting through Grand Central had to be one of the coolest of all.

With its stately Old World marble Main Concourse bookended by its famous arched cathedral windows and topped by its colossal 125-foot domed ceiling, it looked more like an opera house than a train terminal.

Crisscrossing through it, I always felt instantly sophisticated as if instead of heading toward my cubicle, I was hurrying to find my balcony seats above the orchestra pit before the curtains rose.

On one of our first dates, Cavan had actually taken me to a swank bar called the Campbell Apartment that was up a flight of stairs off one of the terminal's labyrinth-like corridors. I still hadn't forgotten the surprising speakeasy class of the place. Taking in the Money Honeys and Don Draper look-alike clientele listening to Sinatra as they sipped highballs in its moody yellow sconce glow, I thought, now this is the type of New York I'd signed on for!

Once I scored my full-time appointment at GBH, I'd already decided that it would be where Cavan and I were going to celebrate.

I smiled as I stared up at the golden sprawl of stars painted across the barrel vault of the terminal's famous Sistine Chapel–like ceiling.

Cavan and I were going to be moving into the Campbell Apartment once things started to roll.

I waded along with the morning rush-hour crush into the Lexington Avenue passage and grabbed some Starbucks. The exit spilled me out onto Lex across from the Chrysler Building, and I went up to 45th and made a left around the post office.

Half a block up the narrow side street by the back loading dock entrance of the post office, I saw there were several mailmen out on the sidewalk, laughing and goofing around. Having made this walk before a few times, I knew what that probably meant.

Bingo, I thought, as one of them smoothed his baggy mailman shirt over his beer belly and made a kissing sound.

"Morning, beautiful," he said.

As he said this, in the traffic beside him, a white Escalade with dark-tinted windows started dropping trap beats.

"Looking good, *mami*," the mailman continued, bopping his head to the beat as I crossed alongside him.

That was NYC for you, I thought, pretending I was deaf as I widened my berth.

One second it was Ol' Blue Eyes swing and the next Uncle Murda was in da house.

Then we both looked up as a mail truck shrieked to a stop up above on the elevated roadway that goes around Grand Central.

"Hey, Papi, catch!" said the young Hispanic mailman who leapt out of the truck.

I halted as the heavy bag of mail he suddenly dropped off the overpass landed down onto the sidewalk in front of us with a dusty thud.

"Hey, whatta you crazy?" Papi hollered up at him. "Gonna kill somebody! Drive it around, dummy. Sheesh. How many times I gotta tell you!"

Seeing my escape, I stepped out into 45th Street between the tailgate of a traffic-stopped grumbling dump truck and the bass-pumping Escalade.

"So sorry, miss," Papi called at my back. "These summer interns, ya know!"

Oh, I knew, I thought as I hurried up to Madison.

I knew all about them.

As always as I made the right-hand turn around the corner, my eyes zeroed in on GBH's offices way up on 60th. Not that they stood out. Quite the contrary. If an office building could be called demure, the offices of Greene Brothers Hale was it.

Among the vertical strata of twenty- and thirty-story glass office buildings that lined both sides of the avenue, if it stood out at all, it was because it was one of the few stone prewar ones left.

Even the entrance of the old beige stone, plain-Jane, twelve-story building was low-key. Off to the north side of the building, it didn't even have any markings except for a utilitarian brass address plaque that said 653 Madison on the pale limestone above its doors.

But the lobby inside was a different story. Newly redesigned by some famous Dutch architect, the dramatically low-lit chamber of glowing white marble flowed past a spacious concierge desk to elevator banks the color of old gold.

Coming in off the gray dusty avenue, its stark aggressive antiseptic whiteness was always a bit of a surprise, like entering a modern art piece.

Or maybe a spacecraft airport, I thought as I finally pushed inside. Next stop, planet money.

"Good morning, Marvin. I brought you a present," I said as I took out the second coffee from the cardboard holder I was holding and placed it on the concierge desk.

"Not only a southern beauty, but so generous, too," GBH's most likable security guard said, throwing up his hands in comic shock.

Pale, bald, five-foot-nothing and eighty if he were a day, Marvin was actually more like GBH's unofficial mascot than a security guard. Though Marvin was barely able to lift the radio on his belt, some of the curmudgeons in upper management had tried to get him to quit several times and even offered him a handsome buyout.

But to no avail. The sweet funny stubborn little old man was in the building service workers union and wasn't budging.

"Faye, what do they want me to do? Move to Florida?" he had confided to me. "I still live in the apartment I was born in on the Lower East Side. This is all I have. They'll have to carry me out."

Why this character had taken me under his hilarious little wing from the moment I arrived, I didn't know, but I loved it. I had never had a grandfather let alone a comic Jewish one.

We both turned as the doors revolved behind us. The tall sixtysomething man who hurried in through them was wearing a beautiful dark suit and had styled white hair, and eyes the shade of crystal blue they use to dye cleaning products. The caramel-colored leather briefcase he was carrying looked as soft as velvet, and it had an equally expensive-looking umbrella niftily tucked in beneath its shining brass buckled clasps.

Being that sharply put together didn't seem possible, I thought. He looked like he'd just stepped out of a Ralph Lauren ad.

Oh, my goodness, I thought as I suddenly realized why.

It was the GBH's managing director, Arthur Dabertrand.

Investment banks have a strict hierarchy from intern to analyst to associate to vice president then finally up to the managing director who runs the whole shebang.

Dabertrand had missed our orientation, but there was a picture of him shaking hands with a Saudi prince on the landing page of GBH's website.

"Marvin," he said in a confident voice, nodding to me as he passed.

"Mr. Dabertrand, here let me get the elevator for you," Marvin said, immediately walking along the glowing marble with him toward the golden elevator doors.

"Another walk-off for Judge? He just doesn't quit," Marvin said, hurrying alongside GBH's king of the jungle.

"I know, Marvin. You had to see the stadium. Ripped the roof off," Dabertrand said. "I'm so glad I came back early from the beach."

After Marvin beat him to the call button, I swallowed, starstruck, as Dabertrand turned his perfectly tanned and powerful and distinguished face toward me.

"Wait, you're… Don't tell me. You're Thompson, right? No, sorry. Walker. Faye Walker, right?"

"That's right, sir," I said, trying to stay upright in the presence of a man who had his thumb on more than the GDP of most countries.

"I wanted to tell you how impressed I was—we all were—with your taking over duties for Alexander when he couldn't get back. I thought we'd be bottlenecked, but there wasn't even a hitch. I did my own time in the boiler room, so I know it's not easy. That's extremely impressive, Faye. Truly. Good job."

"Thank you, sir," I said, trying not to blush and failing.

"Alexander, there you are," Dabertrand said as my boss, Alexander Aiken, came in through the revolving doors behind us. "We were just talking about how well Faye here did your job when you were out. And she beat you in here, too. An intern, no less. What are you feeding her down there?"

"Oh, it's not me. It's the new recruiters you hired, sir," Aiken said with a beaming smile I'd never seen on him before. "All of the interns this year are incredibly talented."

I stared at my boss. Short, fit, handsome, and forty with retro black glasses and a perpetual scowl, he reminded me of an aging Clark Kent who, perhaps poisoned by kryptonite or something, was embittered because he could no longer become Superman.

I didn't get along with my snippy boss. I tried, but he just wouldn't let me. Which was strange because I was his best, most reliable underling. Sometimes I suspected this was *why* we didn't get along.

And no surprise, not a foot in the door, and he'd managed to both kiss ass and take the spotlight off me in the same breath.

"Well, good then," Dabertrand said, dandily snapping a cuff before he swung his fabulous umbrella and briefcase into the elevator. "Let's keep up the good work and hit the ground running today. Who does the race go to again?"

"The swift, sir," Aiken said cheerily.

My boss waited for the elevator door to close before he turned back to me with his instantly returned scowl.

"After you, Walker," he said, opening the boiler room door on the other side of Marvin's kiosk.

"Oh, look. I'm getting a call," I said, pulling out my phone. "Be down in a sec."

"I think he likes you," Marvin said as the door to the stairwell closed.

"Aiken? My boss? Are you crazy?" I said as I put my phone away. "He hates me."

"No, not him. Forget him. The big cheese. Dabertrand."

"You think?" I said, smiling.

"I know," Marvin said, winking. "You're doing great, Faye.

Don't tell the other interns, but you're my favorite. I'm rooting for you."

I was still smiling as I gave the sweet little man a peck on his bald head.

"Don't tell anyone either, Marvin. But you're my favorite around here, too," I said.

9

It was actually a fairly light morning for a change, and we were all down in the windowless slave galley, standing and stretching right before lunch when my desk phone chirped.

"Walker, put me on speakerphone. Now," Aiken demanded, from where he was upstairs at a meeting.

Aye, aye, jackass, I thought, hitting the button.

"Listen up, people. It's lunch at your desk time. Just got word from Bluepoint Holdings they are shifting management and are about to let the investors know, so we are anticipating a mother lode of redemptions incoming."

Groans and eye rolls immediately emitted down the lane of low-walled cubicles from our eight-member team of galley slave interns.

Bluepoint Holdings was one of the biggest hedge funds. Blue-*whale* Holdings, we called it.

"Give me a break! How many we talking, boss?" said a brave voice two cubicles down from me. I turned to see it was Kenny McPhee, a cocky handsome jock and Philly native who had been second-string quarterback at Duke.

"Who said that?" Aiken cried.

Even without Aiken in the room, Kenny ducked his head down as if scrambling from a blitzing linebacker.

Besides me and Priscilla and McPhee, there were three other girls and two other guys. The three other girls—two debutantes from Boston and one from Venezuela, all of them very pretty and very snotty—had all gone to Dartmouth. One of the guys was a handsome Asian Indian guy named Pernod from MIT whose dad had helped found PayPal and the other was a nice very quiet white guy named Mike who had been a champion college hockey player and the salutatorian at Cornell.

"We're talking upward of five hundred, people," Aiken said. "Five hundred wires. All of them same day. I repeat same day. So, brace yourselves."

The whole basement crew all stared at each other in horror.

Five hundred redemption wires meant five hundred investors were going to be cashing out of their hedge fund investment and needed to be cut checks by six o'clock.

This task in the time allotted wasn't just going to be difficult.

It was going to be impossible.

It was the level of documentation that would need to be collected from the investors. We would have to obtain AML (anti-money laundering) documents and KYC (know your customer) documents as well as tax forms, FATCA (Foreign Account Tax Compliance Act) regulatory forms, bank reference letters signed from the investors' banks to verify the accounts that the funds would be wired to.

We would have to figure out what AML documents we needed from investors based on their entity type. Trusts needed trust deeds, from LLCs you needed formation documents, operating agreements, disclosure of beneficial owners. Once you saw what tax and FATCA documents were missing or incomplete, you would have to blast out emails to them to follow-up. Tracking down the investors over the phone alone was a nightmare as some were in different countries and time zones and spoke different languages.

Then once all of this data was gathered, it had to be reviewed with a fine-tooth comb to ensure it all met our requirements. What was really fun was any new anomalies had to be updated in a slow and inefficient system database before the wires could be uploaded.

Then once you finally uploaded the wires, you had to call in favors from the treasury team to review them and push them out to the investors for you in time for the 6:00 p.m. cutoff.

We'd once done three hundred, and it was a breathless nonstop scramble of being on the phone and following up with people internally and externally all day long. The whole time with Aiken and the hedge fund client breathing down our necks to move all the money.

"Psst. Faye," said a voice as we all slumped down into our office chairs with our hands over our mouths.

I looked up. It was Priscilla.

"How can you still be standing?" I said.

"Listen, Faye. You didn't see me," Priscilla said as she lifted her bag.

This one was a Gucci. Company guidelines were strict about not dressing too flashily, but since it didn't specifically mention bags, I guess Priscilla thought it was okay to sport one that cost the same as a new minivan.

"I didn't see you where?" I said.

"If Aiken comes down, I already left for lunch," she said.

"What, are you crazy?" I said. "You heard Aiken. He'll kill you."

"I'll handle him," she said, checking her phone. "I need an hour. It's important."

I stared at her curiously. Aiken had just told us that a new dump truck of rocks for us to break was on its way, and she was going to what? Pick at some Dover sole with mumsy at a supper club? Maybe get her highlights touched up?

I could see the other galley slaves already looking over suspiciously.

If she bailed on us and made us carry her now in our time of need, she wouldn't just have Aiken to worry about, I knew.

Or maybe she was done, I thought. Like with the navy SEAL testing. People couldn't take the punishment anymore, so they rang a bell.

Was that what this was? Priscilla ringing the give-up bell?

"Are you sure, Priscilla?" I said, wide-eyed.

She nodded.

It's your funeral, I thought.

But it wasn't.

There was going to be a funeral all right. But it wasn't going to be Priscilla's.

10

Madison Avenue was all but deserted when I finally pushed out of GBH's lobby around nine o'clock that night. And just as I made the corner, to add insult to my aching mental injury, it started to rain.

I groaned as the drops started pelting down upon the dusty concrete and my completely bare head. I thought about Arthur Dabertrand and his English briefcase with attached dashing umbrella.

Masters of the Universe thought of everything, didn't they?

"We galley slaves not so much," I mumbled.

Yeah, who was I kidding? I thought as I dodged a passing homeless guy pushing a ten-speed laden with recycling bags of empties up the sidewalk.

I ducked under the eave of a boutique florist.

As an unpaid summer intern coming on the end of July, I couldn't have even afforded a *used* umbrella at that point.

But that was okay.

I winced as I put my bag over my head and began jogging eastward.

My beyond overheated brain was in dire need of a cooldown anyway.

My soaked-through shirt had started to stick to my back by the time I finally arrived at 58th, where Cavan was parked alongside the Plaza Hotel with Lily. He hopped out of the stagecoach-like cab, where he was keeping out of the rain. I smiled as I saw he had on the top hat he sometimes wore.

I had always hoped my Prince Charming would come, I thought as he started frantically waving me over. Though who'd have thunk he'd be dressed like the Mad Hatter.

"Look at the state of ya! Get in here," he called as he threw open the batwing door.

Even Lily looked concerned as she turned around and took in my bedraggled, soaking condition.

"Hey, you, taxi horse dude! I need to get down to Rockefeller Center and quick," a dapper-looking young blond frat-boyish kind of guy in black tie yelled as he came running down the steps of the Plaza.

"Off duty," Cavan said.

"I'm in a rush. I'll double whatever you charge. I'll triple it, bro."

"It's okay, Cavan," I said. "I can go."

"Ya deaf, bro?" Cavan yelled back at him as he ushered me inside. "Off duty!"

I let out an enormous sigh as we settled in. I always liked it when we sat in the coach. It had a square rear window instead of a heart-shaped one, but it always made me think of the last page of *Cinderella*, where she's waving bye-bye to her mean ugly stepsisters.

"Oh, Cavan, I'm sorry. You didn't have to lose a fare."

"No?" he said, staring at me with deep concern as he helped me onto the black velvet-covered seat. "Have you seen yourself? You look mind-blown."

"Mind-blown?" I said as I rubbed my temples. "That's because I am, Cavan. My brain feels like I sprained it or something. Honestly, I think I might have broken something in there."

"Overworked the gray matter calculator a bit today, did they? Did you eat?"

"No," I said, crying a little. "I forgot. There was no time."

"I figured," he said as he handed me something. "That's why I got you a treat."

It was half a sandwich. Half of a *gargantuan* sandwich. The scent of the corned beef almost made me feel alive again as I tore the foil open.

Was there really any doubt why I loved this man? I thought, closing my eyes and actually moaning a little as I tucked into the juicy stack of butter soft corned beef that was about the size of a pop-a-shot basketball.

Did Prince Charming himself even think of these things?

"Mmmur mmmmur mur," I got out.

"Yes. Uh-huh. I got a big tip this afternoon, which is the reason for the largesse. Just chew now. Eat, Faye. Eat. Live."

As I did as ordered, he took a beach towel out of his knapsack and draped it over my soaking head as if I were a boxer who just made it back into the corner.

"No wonder you want to be a first responder, Cavan," I said after I quickly made the sandwich disappear. "A second ago, I thought I wasn't going to make it. You've brought me back from the dead."

He lightly touched my forehead as he handed me a bottle of Gatorade with my napkin.

"You're right. You do seem back from the dead. Barely. Your noggin feels like a hot stove though. So, what happened?"

I told him.

About the five hundred redemption orders we had received at lunch. Which turned out to be *only* four hundred ninety-three. About how incredibly *not* possible it was.

"So how many did you get done?" he said.

I took another swig of Gatorade before I let out a long breath.

"All of them," I said. "Every single one. With five minutes left, we had four to go, but we did it."

Cavan shook his head.

"Is that right? Now, how many did you do personally? No, wait. First let's see how many were your share. Four hundred ninety-three divided by the eight in your team is..."

"Sixty-one point one," I said.

"Stop," Cavan said. "No decimal points, Miss Calculator. Just round off. We're cooling the brainpan down, remember? Okay. So, sixty-one was your share, but since you're you, I'll times that by three. What's that? A hundred eighty?"

"One hundred eighty-three," I said, my eyes closed as I leaned my forehead against his shoulder.

"Did you do a hundred eighty-three?" he asked.

"Two hundred seven," I whispered into the nape of his neck.

He immediately broke up laughing.

"Stop shaking," I said. "Please. It hurts when you laugh."

"Two hundred seven!" he cried. "By the love of all that's holy! Two hundred seven. Were all the others dead?"

"No, everyone was going crazy," I said. "They were trying as hard as they could. It was a madhouse."

"Wait a second," Cavan said, taking out his phone. "Wait one little itty-bitty second. When did these orders come in again? Lunch you said?"

"Right before lunch. We had to eat at our desk."

"I knew it!" he said as he scrolled through his screen. "I knew it!"

"Knew what?" I said.

11

"Darlin', I hate to blow what's left of your mind there, but your intrepid man-about-town boyfriend has a little something to show you," Cavan said.

He queued up a video. The screen showed a traffic-filled avenue in Manhattan. It didn't seem like Fifth or Midtown. The buildings were older and smaller and brick except for one glass-fronted building.

"Where's this?"

"That's the new courtyard Marriot down on 34th and 10th," Cavan said. "I dropped off a couple there and was waiting while the husband went to a cash machine for that big tip I was telling you about."

He thumbed the play button.

"That's when I saw this recordable moment," he said.

"Priscilla?" I said as I saw her come out from underneath the hotel's awning.

"And look at the time there," Cavan said.

It said 1:35.

What the? I thought. She'd finally made her way back to

the office around two. That's where she had to rush off to? She was down at a hotel on 34th and 10th Avenue in the middle of the day?

As I thought about this, I realized what Priscilla had said about Aiken was odd yet true. When she slunk in at past two, he didn't even come out of his office. He hadn't said a word to her.

"And now for the hold-your-hat shocker," Cavan said. "Would you feast your eyes at who her companion is. Wait for it."

As Priscilla made the curb, a white-haired man stepped out of the hotel doors and stood beside her.

A handsome older man in a beautiful dark suit swinging a beautiful leather briefcase.

One with a dashing umbrella slid under the shiny brass of its clasps.

No, no, no, I thought.

"That's impossible," I said as I watched in stunned disbelief as Managing Director Arthur Dabertrand and Priscilla climbed into a taxi. "That is NOT possible."

"One last highlight," Cavan said. "Warning. This one is, um. You'll see. Just try to keep the corned beef down."

The cab actually came right at where Cavan was filming from, and he zoomed in at the back window as it stopped at the red light a car length away. Through the back window, I saw Dabertrand lean in almost on top of Priscilla. I almost threw up as I saw him do what I didn't want to see him do.

The sick, grandfatherly bastard had his hands all over her as he licked and bit at her earlobe.

"Either I'm blind or that's little miss Ivy League A, am I right?" Cavan said. "Or is it Ivy League something that rhymes with *A* but starts with an *L*?"

I watched jaw-dropped as the cab pulled away on the phone screen.

"What's the expression?" Cavan said. "The rich aren't like you and me? She likes 'em older, huh. You crunch her numbers while she what? Cruises the old age homes for a little afternoon delight?"

Then it dawned on me. What it meant.

What it *really* meant.

Don't you worry about Aiken, I heard Priscilla say again.

My hand went to my still open mouth.

No, I thought.

No.

12

I got in early to work the next morning. Very early. As I exited Grand Central, Lexington Avenue was practically still dark, and when I cornered past the dim post office even the 45th Street mailman "Mornin', Mami" crew hadn't yet arrived.

Up on Madison I saw Marvin from two blocks away. He was out in front of the building, talking and laughing with a maintenance worker who was still hosing off the sidewalk as I arrived.

"Faye, what's wrong? You couldn't sleep? Early bird catches the worm, but this is ridiculous," he said.

He was right. I couldn't sleep. Not a wink. But getting into why with Marvin was not going to happen.

Not today.

I faked a smile as I handed him his coffee.

"Who does the race go to again?" I said, quoting the biggest scumbag I knew as I pushed in through the brass door.

Downstairs in the windowless slave galley as I tossed my bag under my desk and sat, I knew I was just being paranoid.

That I was the top intern was not even a question. Though Cavan made fun of me for doing more than my fair share, there was a method to my madness. From the second I had gotten to Greene Brothers Hale, I had one goal. To make myself indispensable.

Why? It was simple.

I had no other choice.

My resources were not just meager, they scraped at the top layer of the bone. The other interns who were going to be let go had options. Parents. A basement in a suburban house. Try again next year.

Not me. I was never returning to Gramma's trailer so that meant what? Living on the street? Moving in with Cavan who already had two roommates in an illegal apartment in Woodlawn in the Bronx?

I folded my arms. I didn't know. I had bet it all on this internship. All that I had. I was all in. Not getting it was one of those event horizon scenarios where the outcome of something is a complete enigma, literally inconceivable. As black and unknowable as the dark side of the moon.

As I thought on this, my eyes kept glancing over at the pebbled glass door of Aiken's office.

Why hadn't he said anything to Priscilla when she came in late? I kept thinking. Why? It was the dogs that didn't bark that told the tale, right? And he was a barker all right. Why hadn't that little junkyard dog barked at her?

Because he knew, I thought as I sat up.

He knew what I knew.

I had asked around. Marvin especially was useful for telling me what was what. Even the $2.23 that his coffee cost me was a calculated investment.

Out of the eight interns, only two would be picked. One of them would be McPhee. That was a given. GBH was founded by a Duke graduate and recruited heavily from Duke. It also hired Division One NCAA athletes. McPhee was both.

And the other slot was for the brightest and best. That was to be me because I was, hands down, demonstrably the smartest, the quickest, the hardest working.

I had proven it, hadn't I? I had crushed it over and over again. It was because I was quickest on the draw. The others could add in their head. Well, besides Priscilla. But I could do it faster. The others were good at remembering numbers, but I could remember several digits more. When Aiken had missed a flight back from Florida, I was voted to step in as team leader. Unanimously.

I unfolded my arms as I thought about this. And then my legs seemed to stand me up all by themselves, and I stood there staring at Aiken's office door.

No. Don't do it, said a voice in my head. *Sit back down.*

I didn't listen.

I came down along the cubicles and took a deep breath and creaked open Aiken's door.

Quickly I crossed to his desk and swirled his mouse and typed in the password he'd given me to access his control databases when he was away.

Before I clicked, I held my breath thinking that he could have changed his password.

Then I clicked and his screen lit up like Times Square in the unlit room. The first thing I noticed on it was that GBH's internal message program was already open along the bottom.

I clicked it open wider and went immediately to the sent folder.

And then I swallowed.

Hard.

I saw that a message from DABERTRAND was already there along the top of the left side.

That aggravating swirly circle thing appeared and spun for a bit when I clicked on it.

Round and round it goes. Where it stops nobody knows, I thought staring at it.

Then I knew where it was going.

Hey responding to your query, Dabertrand's message read. I spoke to the boys. No one wants to deal with a third analyst. Walker is great. Sharp. But no dice.

Boom.

Something inside me exploded, and the jarring hard smack of it reverberated through the center of me like a touched-off nuclear bomb. How I stayed standing was a mystery.

There it was, confirmation.

Wow. I was sure Walker would be such a natural fit, my boss Aiken had typed, actually pulling for me.

Final was Dabertrand's curt coldhearted reply.

I felt a stabbing pinch in my chest as I read it a second time, and my hands covered my mouth as I closed my eyes.

13

"Hey, everybody. Let's raise a glass to Faye," Priscilla said.

It was after work and we were at Stella's again.

It wasn't just me and Priscilla but our whole team this time, and we were packed into one of the huge lime-green circular booths in the VIP section in the back.

I took in the whole scene as our entire boiler room team dutifully obeyed Priscilla's order. From where I sat at the booth's end, I looked into the face of each of my teammates.

Already two drinks in, their happy Ivy League faces were even happier than usual, weren't they? Their blissful perfect vapid smiles lit up like the Fourth of July. In the candlelight, I noted that everyone had showed. Of course, they had. This was their natural habitat, not mine. They wouldn't miss a night at a place like Stella's for all the world.

The surprise dinner after work for our team had been Priscilla's idea and treat. A way for her to smooth things over with all of us for covering her butt during the day of the five hundred redemptions.

But I knew what it really was. After peeking at Aiken's computer, I knew everything now.

It was sheer unadulterated guilt. Priscilla knew she was taking what rightfully belonged to me.

Or were sociopaths capable of guilt? I thought, glancing at Priscilla across the table as everybody began to whoop and holler.

"Faye! Faye! Faye!"

Or maybe this was my consolation prize, I thought, pretending to laugh as I stared at my drink.

Maybe this was a last meal for the condemned, the second-place set of steak knives I got to take with me as I was booted out GBH's door.

"She's not kidding, Faye," McPhee said, topping off my glass from one of the two pitchers of margaritas he'd ordered the moment we sat down. "You were a machine."

I looked at McPhee. Really looked at him, pretty much for the first time. He was as effortlessly good-looking as Priscilla, wasn't he? Sandy haired and tan and square jawed, he had a sort of laid-back pro surfer thing going on. Of course, he did. Because life was a breeze for the McPhees of the world, wasn't it? Life was just some tasty waves and a bong hit or two between the fish tacos as your success and bank account always went in one direction. Straight up. To the moon.

I wondered if he'd been told as well. I thought he had. Hell, they'd probably told him during the interview back at Duke that he'd be a shoo-in. They'd probably handed him a contract and a fat signing bonus right there in the restaurant before they took him in the limo to the strip club.

"Faye! Faye! Faye!" he started chanting with the others and then even Tommy, the waiter who was taking our orders, joined in.

"Hey, come on, guys. Give me a break," I said, the aw-shucks smile on my face studiously practiced.

I looked over at Priscilla beaming back at me.

I had after all learned from the best.

I looked at her perfect orthodontist-brochure teeth as she laughed at something Tommy was saying to her. At first, I had actually felt sorry for her. Sleeping with the boss was beyond sick especially when he was old enough to be your father. But your grandpa? That wasn't just sordid. It seemed…deeply criminal.

But as I watched Pricilla throughout the day, and I had watched her very, very carefully, I didn't see an ounce of trauma. If anything, what I saw along with her usual poise and beauty was a sense of self-satisfied contentment, a spa day glow of accomplishment at a job well done.

Everybody hooted and clapped again as Aiken himself finally showed up a few minutes later.

"Quiet, people," he said in his stern drill sergeant work voice as he sat down next to me.

I looked at my sad Clark Kent of a boss. It was funny the way things worked sometimes, wasn't it? Out of everyone, I thought he was the one to look out for. But as it turned out, he had been the only one to go to bat for me.

Yeah, it was funny all right. So funny I forgot to laugh.

"Walker," he said.

"Name's Faye," I said, holding up my glass.

"Walker," he said again, only with a small smile this time.

That small smile did it for me. The genuine pity in it.

I could take a lot. In fact, I had. More than anyone sitting at that table. I had seen the kinds of trouble they had never even heard of.

But even I had my limit.

I placed my untouched drink carefully down on the immaculate linen before me.

Then I looked into the perfect faces of the giant booth full of beautiful people, who I had thought for a very naive and stupid moment or two had actually been my friends.

"If you would excuse me, Alexander, I'd like to use the ladies."

But as he scooted out of my way, I didn't head for the ladies.

The tears were already streaming down my face as I passed the bar and headed out the open door.

14

One time when I was a little girl in that first year after my mother died and we'd been abandoned to the darkness and craziness up in the Appalachian Mountains of Kentucky, my little sister, Caitlin, had gotten lost.

It was around sunset, and we were playing down by a creek that ran along the back of the property where the trailer park was. We were having a contest to see who could find the most tadpoles and place them in the plastic margarine containers we'd brought with us, and when I looked up, she was gone.

At first, I didn't think much of it. Like myself, Caitlin was a bit of a dreamer when she was little, prone to playing games with herself and wandering off.

But then it got dark.

Up in the hollows of the mountains, especially in autumn, night falls like it slipped on something, and when it did and I hadn't caught up with my little sister or even heard her cry out to me, a sense of dread began to free-fall through me.

I can't say why it was even more terrifying that *she* was lost. Maybe because she was smaller than me or that I was supposed to watch out for her. Something my mother on her deathbed had made me promise that I do.

In ten minutes, I was convinced my sister was dead and gone forever. In the next five, I thought now it was going to be my turn. When I finally made it back to the house an hour later, I prayed and begged God to please, please, please let her be there. He could have anything. He could take me instead.

It had all been in my crazy head, of course. Caitlin had merely gone back to the house without telling me.

It was the sense of spookiness of the twilight or maybe just the fairy tale strangeness of the mountain forest when I turned to find her not there that had triggered the awful thought inside of me that she had wandered off forever.

As I came out onto Madison that night in Manhattan, that same horrible little-girl-lost-in-the-woods dread instantly returned.

I was at a loss all right. For words, for thought.

As I walked and cried, I thought about Mr. Baker, his selfless help to me, his hopeful plan. I thought about all my professors. The pleased look on their faces as I sat in the front row absorbing their lesson plans like a happy sponge.

To them, it was all about merit, wasn't it? At school you did what you were supposed to do to get the gold star. Then you were on to the next task and the next gold star.

And I'd been all over it. Like Ms. Pacman back at the Chinatown Mott Street arcade that I slept above, I'd been gobbling up the gold stars laid out before me like they were going out of style.

But there was a limit now, I realized. A place where the gold stars ended. I was standing there now, staring into its brick wall dead end.

People talked about a glass ceiling for women, but that wasn't it. It wasn't a glass ceiling for women, I saw now.

It was a *class* ceiling. For everyone.

There was a class that you had to be born into. The truth that professors in their ivory towers probably didn't even know. Or were maybe paid by endowment donors to keep their mouths shut about. The real truth about real life.

That in the real world—at least up in its highest chambers where the big money moved the big gears—merit meant jackshit.

Up in those C-level executive suites, no matter how good you were, the golden to-the-manor-born wheat got separated from the servant-class chaff. No ifs, ands, or buts.

Priscilla Hutton was case in point. She came from a good family. One with *peerage*, don't you know? Priscilla was a debutante. For a person like Priscilla, losing out to other people—especially nobodies like myself—wasn't an issue. Not a factor in the equation.

When you were talking the real money, the real club that had a hand on the reins of the world, there was only one rule.

Whatever the hell the Park Avenue insiders like Arthur Dabertrand and Priscilla Hutton wanted, they got, and the devil take the hind.

I looked up at the Midtown towers as I crossed Fifth Avenue. For some reason, the neighborhood didn't seem so storybook romantic now.

I was just another sucker, wasn't I? I thought. Another rube to be used and abused and chewed up and now came the spitting out part.

To top it off, Cavan wasn't at the Plaza. And when I arrived back at the Bolivar statue two long blocks up, he and Lily were gone from there as well.

All alone I stood, rooted to the corner of Central Park Drive. As I looked at the taxis gliding into the park and at the glittering million-dollar hotels across the street, I felt it then in my heart like a sharp cold sting. How this was going to be it now. That I would lose Cavan, too. That I would never see him again.

I was on my own again, wasn't I? The stupid plan. My ridiculous expectations. Where had they led me? Nowhere. Wandering around in the dark again like a silly little fool.

I was numb as I headed back to Lexington. I came to my subway pit in the sidewalk and went down the dirty stairs and pushed through the greasy turnstile and sat on a grimy bench in the smelly heat.

I'd just missed a train, and the station was deserted except for some homeless person cackling to himself on another bench across the two tracks on the uptown side.

When I began to come out of my stupor of feeling sorry for myself, I realized that my neighbor on the opposite platform bench wasn't just any homeless crazy person.

I shook my still spinning head.

"You have got to be kidding me," I said.

It was Priscilla's friend, Gareth Haynes.

As I watched, he stopped talking to himself and closed his eyes and began rocking ever so slightly back and forth.

I remembered what Cavan had said about me feeling too sorry for people.

Well, I didn't feel sorry for him this time.

Spoiled rich kid, I thought, watching him on the nod. Everything there on a damned silver platter. But he was too selfish, too decadent and disgusting like Dabertrand and Priscilla.

To hell with him, I thought. And Dabertrand and Priscilla and Madison Avenue and lemongrass and this horrible evil city. They could have it. They could choke on every dirty filthy corrupted unfair cheating square inch of it. For all I cared, they could—

It came to me then.

Staring at Gareth, swaying and rocking back and forth, I stiffened, then suddenly sat up ramrod straight as all at once it came to me fully formed.

A tingly sensation started at the back of my head as butterflies swirled in my stomach.

The same thing happened sometimes when I played chess

and I got in the zone and could see all the pieces and the moves ahead of time.

As I stared at Gareth, what I could do presented itself before me like an itinerary.

Each thing to the next to the next to the next. It was a solution, a solution to everything.

Literally everything could be taken care of, I realized as I stared at Gareth.

At least maybe.

"Plan C," I whispered as the train finally arrived between me and Gareth in a shrieking clattering steel blur.

15

From the moment I woke up the next day, I had a splitting headache. But aching head or no aching head, I knew what I was going to do that day, what I had to do.

The first order of the day was a no-brainer so after I got out of the shower, I lifted my phone and sent a text to Aiken telling him I was too sick to head in.

This was a no-no on a new level. An intern sick call was akin to high crimes and misdemeanors at the ever hard-charging firm of Greene Brothers Hale, but I wasn't getting the job anyway, was I?

Aiken surprised me for the second time in our curiously hot-and-cold contentious relationship a moment later when he texted back.

I understand. Got you covered Faye. Feel better.

He really did feel crummy about helping GBH to slip the knife between my shoulder blades, didn't he? I thought, staring at the text.

"Big whoop, Aiken," I said as I tossed the phone onto my bed. "Your sympathy and a hundred bucks will just about get me a bus ticket back to the trailer park."

Instead of getting into my work stuff, I put on a pair of wine-colored lululemon leggings and a T-shirt and the Yankee cap Cavan had gotten me at the stadium back in June. After I tightened the laces of my FILA sneaker knockoffs, I quickly headed out and down Mott Street straight to the Six train.

I was on a mission. Since my insight on the way home the night before, I'd been thinking deep and hard on my new plan.

I had most of it worked out. Most. That "most" wasn't "all," I knew was quite dangerous. With something like what I was planning, I knew that I better damn well know all of it, every inch.

But not knowing everything didn't matter. At least for now. Since there was a major time crunch to consider, I had to get the ball rolling now or forget about the whole thing.

When I arrived with the rest of the late morning Midtown commuters at 60th Street and Lexington, I was the last one off the train. The uptown platform I had disembarked on was the same one where I had seen Gareth the night before, and I walked over to the now empty bench he'd been sitting on.

I sat on it myself and looked around. For what? I thought as I tapped a finger to my lips. To get some kind of scent maybe? I thought it was something like that, though I wasn't really sure.

After ten minutes and a couple more trainloads of stressed-out commuters spilling out beside me in the muggy, grimy underground station, I finally headed up the subway stairs onto the sidewalk across from Bloomingdale's.

It had been a little gloomy when I set out from Chinatown, but now it was sunny with a clear blue sky overhead as I crossed Lexington and came west through the stream of commuters. Even the ache in my temples seemed to let up a few iotas as I put my head on a swivel, scanning the sidewalks.

My idea might have been crazy, but at least it was something, I thought as I walked quickly along. It felt good to be doing something especially when the other option was nothing at all.

Gareth literally could have been anywhere, I knew, as I crossed the four lanes of Park Avenue continuing west. But people—even ne'er-do-well homeless drug addicts—were creatures of habit, weren't they? They hung around the same places, familiar places, places where they felt safe.

I went by Stella's next at 63rd and Madison where some tired-looking white-shirted prep cooks were rolling open the doors to the street, just opening up. Lingering to peer inside, I obviously didn't see Gareth in there among the lime-green booths or even Tommy who worked nights. Even though it was the morning, I actually could have used a lemongrass daiquiri.

"Make it a pitcher to go," I mumbled as I turned the corner through the midmorning heat continuing west.

I came out on the corner of Fifth across from Central Park. I thought I would head over to the bench near the Simon Bolivar statue where I had seen Gareth lying out the week before. But when the light changed and I crossed the street, I suddenly had another idea.

Instead of going left toward the statue, I went straight in under the leafy shade of the Central Park trees and then made a right onto a curving interior cobblestone walking path that led north for the zoo.

I actually knew the park a bit from being Cavan's unofficial co-jockey on the weekends. I always liked when we trotted past the Park Drive entrance around the zoo with its families and smiling excited little kids. I kept thinking about how if I were Gareth and grew up around here, there would be a connection there, good memories, safe memories.

The zoo didn't open until ten, but I saw there were hot dog vendors already setting up around where they sold the tickets.

As I sat down on a bench before the kiosk, a smiley Hispanic woman with a neon yellow tennis visor pushed a wagon-like Styrofoam cooler on wheels over the cobblestones toward me.

"Bottled water?" she said.

As I paid for one and she rolled off, about thirty feet behind her on the path I suddenly saw a thinnish man in a gray track suit jacket with the hood up heading east past the kiosks.

He had his back to me, but I instantly sat straight up, as I could have sworn I caught a flash of strawberry blond hair.

As he got on a path to an old castle-like building that was beside the zoo, I stood immediately and went after him. As I reached the path, he was already going up a set of stairs that led back onto Fifth Avenue and I started jogging to keep up.

I immediately halted as I reached the top.

It was him. There was a crosswalk to 64th Street directly opposite of where the stairs let out, and he was standing before it next to an ice cream truck waiting for the light to change.

It's hard to describe how strange it felt as I realized this. To throw myself out here flying blind and to have predicted where Gareth might be and be right.

It felt more than random.

More than just luck.

It felt like a sign.

16

When the light turned, I waited ten seconds before I crossed Fifth Avenue, shadowing him. I hung back even more as he headed east down 64th. Past Madison there was a lot of construction, and I stayed half a block back as he went in and out of the shadows of the sidewalk sheds.

When he arrived at Park Avenue, I crossed to the north side of the street and watched as he stopped and yawned and rubbed sleep out of his eyes. From his crazy hair and wrinkled track suit jacket, he looked even more homeless than the day before, I thought.

He was down and out all right. You could tell he'd been sleeping rough.

I thought he would turn up or down Park Avenue but when the light changed, he continued east toward Lexington.

He ended up going back to where I had started, into the subway for the Six train by Bloomingdale's. When I followed him down onto the southbound platform, I couldn't see him for about thirty seconds and I thought he might have been on a just departing train. But then I saw him way up near the front.

We both got on the next downtown train. He got onto the first car and I got onto the third, and when the train pulled out, I went into the second car and walked up to the front to watch him through the window. I thought he would take out his phone like everyone else, but he just sat there staring into space with a troubled look on his pale scruffy face, preoccupied with something.

The train filled up and I couldn't see him anymore, which is why I almost lost him about twenty minutes later when he got off at a stop I'd never been to before called Astor Place. I only noticed he'd disembarked when he walked past on the platform, and I had to jump out in a flash just in time to dodge the bing-bonging closing door.

I lost him in the crush of the crowd on the platform, and when I got topside, I couldn't see him anywhere. It was only when I crossed the street toward some cube statue thing in a plaza that I saw him in line at a coffee cart.

As I stood at the corner of the plaza, pretending to look at my phone, waiting for him, a sense of dread began to build up in me, a sense of doubt. I started to wonder what in the hell was I really doing, thinking maybe I was going a little crazy here.

I really might have ended it right then and there and headed back to my Box in Chinatown. To do what I didn't know. Cry? Bang my head against the cheap wall? Then maybe canvass the neighborhood and apply for a job as an arcade attendant or a fish restaurant waitress? Learning how to speak Chinese couldn't be that hard, could it? I thought.

But then I took a deep breath. Behind me somewhere, there must have been some kind of BBQ restaurant with an exhaust that smelled of woodsmoke and charcoal. The smell kept making me think of my old Kentucky home that I never wanted to head back to.

So, when Gareth finally scored his iced coffee, I was right on his tail again.

We headed east through a section of Manhattan that was beyond my experience. It seemed like kind of a happening section with bars and funky boutiques and stately old buildings along the leafy cross streets. We went two blocks then three, and then he made a right to the south for a few blocks and then made another left.

Gareth liked walking as well as running, didn't he? I thought as I tailed him. No wonder he stayed so thin.

I'd lost count of how many blocks east from the Astor Place subway station, but we were on a street called Riverton when I saw the housing project.

It was the Williamsburg Bridge housing projects, I quickly looked up on my phone, and instead of boutique T-shirt stores, on the next corner across from it, there was a bodega with tough-looking inner-city kids clustered in front.

As I saw Gareth cruise past the youths and across the street toward the gargantuan and rough-looking building complex, I balked a little and thought about heading back and waiting for him at the Astor Place subway.

But who was I kidding?

I jogged toward the corner.

I was in too deep.

Stopping now wasn't an option.

Thankfully, the kids left me alone as I passed them but some old guy clucked his tongue at me from a bus stop on the other side before I saw Gareth up ahead walking along the front of the projects on what was aptly called Pitt Street.

He didn't head into the building complex but went up a short block along its fence and entered a park on its other side. It was called the Hamilton Fish Park, I saw by the sign I passed as I followed him into it.

There were a bunch of basketball courts and a public swimming pool with about a thousand screaming kids in the water on the other side of a chain-link fence. When I arrived at the fence,

I saw Gareth next to a playground on its other side. He was sitting on a bench with three young thuggish-looking men. One of them stood up for a second and sort of hovered over Gareth like he was going to hit him. But instead, he just patted Gareth playfully on the back as the other two laughed.

I drank my bottled water as they continued to sit there. Beside the bench, there was a brick building, a public bathroom maybe, and as I watched, a very muscular dude who wasn't wearing a shirt came out of it, sipping from a little OJ carton with a straw.

He sat down next to Gareth and they shook hands.

And then Gareth was up like a shot and heading west out of the park.

17

I had thought he would take his fix, or whatever it was called, somewhere on our walk back to the subway but he didn't stop anywhere.

An uptown Six came almost straightaway when we came back down into the Astor Place station twenty minutes later. Gareth stayed in one of the middle cars this time with me in the one right behind him.

When we got off back at 60th, I thought he would head back to Central Park, but he surprised me by heading east instead of west. I followed him another two blocks to Second Avenue where he made a left. He surprised me again two blocks north by walking up the stairs of a very strange-looking concrete building in the middle of the block.

I didn't know what the heck it was until I saw the Roosevelt Island Tram sign. This was a new one for me, I thought as I read about it on a plaque beside its stairs. The tram was like a ski chalet cable car that went up from Second Avenue over the East River alongside the Queensboro Bridge to a place called Roosevelt Island.

When I saw the tram coming in, I panicked a little as it was only a one-train-car-like vehicle about the size of a living room. Where was I going to be able to hide from Gareth on that? I thought. But to my delight, it was very crowded on the platform up the stairs. When I squeezed in with about fifty other people and grabbed on to one of the hanging straps, I couldn't even see Gareth.

"Where to now?" I mumbled to myself as the door closed and we swung up.

It was almost like an amusement park ride as the car went up beside the bridge and over the East River. There were a lot of tourists in the car. French by the sound of them.

Was Gareth on a tour as well? I thought. What the hell was he doing? Day tripping?

I looked down through the smudged cable car window at the gray swirl of the East River.

From what he'd purchased down at Fish Park, he was soon going to be tripping on something, I knew.

Roosevelt Island as it turned out was a thin strip of land in the East River very close to Queens. It had some crummy-looking residential high-rise buildings on it, but there was some open space I saw as we lowered down toward it, strolling paths and grass and trees.

I had to get off first because I was near the door, and I followed the crowd down the stairs and stopped and made a play of doing something at the MetroCard machine. When Gareth passed me thirty seconds later, we were in walking mode again as he headed north for the high-rise buildings.

On the other side of the buildings, I watched as he walked steadily onto a car bridge that looked like it was heading into Queens.

"Come on," I said, my poor legs aching at this point. "Not Queens now? Give me a break."

The bridge did let out into Queens on a street along the river called Vernon Boulevard. On it, catty-corner from the bridge entrance, was a soul food restaurant and an auto repair shop and in between them was a thin four-story yellowish brick building.

On the stoop of this small run-down building sat a young woman, a pretty Asian woman with a baby stroller in front of her. I almost passed out as I watched her stand up and perform one of those running, jumping, wrap-your-legs-around-someone hugs on Gareth as he arrived.

"Shut the front door," I said as they did some heavy lip locking before she hopped down. Gareth was smiling ear to ear as he took the baby out of the stroller and tossed her up once and then again. I was still shaking my head as I watched them head inside.

"Now there's something you don't see every day," I muttered.

I was still standing there staring up at the windows of the crummy little building from the rusted bridge walk when my phone jingled.

Hey you. How's work, Cavan had texted.

When I called back, he didn't pick up until I was halfway back to the tram.

"Good news," I said. "They may be letting us out early today. Where are you now? At the statue?"

"Yes. Just me and old Simon Bolivar and Lily, all sad and alone. Are you coming for a visit?"

I stared back at the yellow brick building then out at the East River. South past the bridge the incredible Manhattan skyline looked hopeful again suddenly, fresh and new and shiny like something from a postcard.

Then I smiled.

"Yes, Cavan," I said as I turned. "I'll be right there. I'm on my way right now."

18

The next day was a Saturday, and at about ten o'clock, I was back uptown again standing outside on the second-story concrete balcony of the Second Avenue depot of the Roosevelt Island Tram.

It was really muggy that morning. The gray sky looked like it was going to rain, but it didn't. My legs were tight and cramped from all the walking I'd done the day before, and I was bored and hot and itchy and uncomfortable.

But it didn't matter. I needed to suck it up now. I was getting close to this thing. I knew I was.

"Here we go. This one. It has to be," I said as I turned to where the fifth cable car I'd seen since I'd arrived was slowly approaching from the east.

I watched the car track down on its cable along the 59th Street Bridge. It was the craziest thing, really. A European ski chalet in the middle of New York City, but there you had it.

As the Swiss-knife-red cable car finally arrived above Second Avenue, it paused for a second, allowing me to peer through its wide front window.

"Shit," I said as I finished sifting through the faces in the crowd.

Gareth wasn't on this one either.

As the people disembarked, I went to the corner railing and stared down at the avenue. The Upper East Side was known for its classy apartment houses, but this part of Second Avenue was all gray and brown ugly high-rise buildings. Even though it was Saturday, there was quite a bit of traffic in the street and on both sides of the bridge on-ramps, but I didn't see anyone on foot.

Come on, I thought as I drained the last of the iced coffee I was holding, making a slurping sound.

After I chucked the cup into the trash, I checked my phone and saw that Cavan had texted me again to see if I wanted to get some lunch before he had work.

What's up? What r u up to? he had texted.

"Dammit," I said, tapping my phone against my forehead as I closed my eyes.

What was I up to?

That was a damn good question.

I thought I was up to getting myself out of the destruction of my life. But maybe I'd just been imagining things. Just been letting my angry mind run away with a truly crazy solution.

Maybe Cavan was right, I thought, looking at my phone again. Maybe what I needed to do was to sit down with him and tell him everything. About how I wasn't getting the job. About how they were totally unfairly screwing me. Screwing us.

Yeah, I thought, suddenly feeling extremely depressed. That'll be a fun conversation. I couldn't wait to lay out in detail how our life together was going to end before it even began.

But I didn't relent.

"Siri," I said to my phone. "Set timer for thirty minutes."

I doubled down on sucking up the suck by dividing the next half hour between watching the stairs behind me and the cable cars coming in.

Then I heard the beep, beep, beep of the alarm.

Oh, well, I thought, lifting my phone and thumbing off the alarm. Time to call it a day.

I had just started texting Cavan back to meet him when someone called out.

"Excuse me. You there. Excuse me."

I ignored the voice for a second, distracted, thinking it was maybe a tourist looking for instructions on how to ride the cable car.

Then I looked up and my mouth dropped open.

Gareth was at the top of the stairs, staring me directly in the eyes. He hurried over and folded his arms as he stopped in front of me.

"I knew it," he said. "The look on your face. You're so busted. You've been following me. Why are you following me?"

I stared at him with my mouth open, trying to come up with something to say.

"Following you?" I finally sputtered out.

"Don't even try," he said. "I saw you yesterday. Down at Astor Place. Then on the train on the way back to Midtown. You're Priscilla's work friend from Stella's. I remember you. It took me a while but I finally figured it out. I never forget a face.

"What the hell is this? Why are you following me?"

I saw he was all cleaned up this morning. He had a hipster thing going on, skinny jeans and a gray long sleeve tee, and a slouchy navy knit hat over his unruly rusty hair.

"Stop stalling. Tell me now," he said.

I bit my lip. This part was going to be a hurdle, I knew. I needed to be careful not to scare him off. But as I stood staring at him, I realized there was no way to lay things out without it sounding completely crazy.

He would either do it or he wouldn't, I thought. I'd just have to lay Plan C on him and hope for the best.

"You're right, Gareth. I am following you," I said, putting

away my phone and suddenly offering him my hand. "I'm Priscilla's work friend. My name is Faye. Faye Walker. I was hoping I could talk to you."

"Talk to me?" he said, studying me as if I were totally nuts. "What do you want to talk to me about?"

"I need to ask you something," I said as I lowered my unshook hand. "Something important."

"About what? About Priscilla? Did she send you? What the hell?"

"I, um. No," I said. "Priscilla has nothing to do with this. I came completely on my own. It's... I have a proposal for you."

He looked at me funny again.

"A business proposal," I said quickly. "A very lucrative one for the both of us."

"A business proposal?" he said, cocking his head to the side. "What? Like you want me to make an investment or something?"

"In a way," I said. "We need like...a bar or something so I can explain. Can I buy you a drink? There's a bar up on the corner of Third."

He was still staring at me as if I were bonkers.

"If this is about my family's real estate company, you're talking to the wrong party, sweetie. I have zero to do with all that. Less than zero. You need to contact Smith & Haynes directly. You can find the website on the internet. Or don't. I don't care. Just sayonara and adios, okay? Stop following me."

"Gareth, this is something specific to you," I said as he was about to head onto the cable car. "Not your family. To you. Incredibly specific, in fact. I know this seems crazy, but I can explain if we sit and talk."

Several emotions suddenly crossed his face then. A flash of anger followed quickly by what looked like terrible fear. His gaze darted down the stairs behind us, and Gareth looked as if he thought he was boxed in, about to be trapped.

"Wait," he said, staring at me. "This isn't another of those freaking interventions, is it? They hired you or something through Priscilla and my sister. That must be it. I told my sister how many times? Okay. Listen. You tell them for me. Nice try but I'm not going back to that freaking facility. I'm not. Okay? Just screw off."

"No, no, no, Gareth," I said quickly. "It's nothing like that. I'm not here from your family. Honestly. I have an incredible business proposal for you. I know it's weird to drop this on you by following you, but it's... You'll see when I explain. I have an idea we can both make bank on. No joke. I just need five minutes to explain."

He went to the stairs and then came back and stood in front of me again. He shook his head and had refolded his arms, but I could see he had calmed down some.

"Five minutes, I swear, Gareth," I said, waving for him to follow me as I walked for the stairs. "C'mon. Let me buy you a drink."

19

The bar I'd already scoped out was some sports place a block east on Third Avenue and 60th called Third Down. There were big screen TVs everywhere, and the corner booth we brought our drinks to looked like box seats at a stadium. The best thing about it was that it was dark and, except for the bartender, completely empty.

"So, what's this um…big proposal," Gareth said, rolling his eyes as he sat across from me.

I took a deep breath as I stared down at my hard cider. This was it. My last chance to turn back.

I didn't take it.

I should have.

I suddenly rubbed my hands together.

"I'll just say it. How would you like $1.5 million in cash, Gareth? Tax free. No one gets hurt."

Gareth lifted up his bottle of IPA as he laughed.

"What is this? Like a kid's game or something?" he said after a sip. "A mind experiment?"

"No," I said, staring steadily at him. "I'm completely freaking serious."

He took another slug of his beer then wiped his mouth with the back of his hand.

"If it wasn't Scarlet, then my brother sent you, right?" he said, scratching at his scruff. "He'd do something like this. Because this is a joke, right? Am I being filmed? What the hell are you talking about?"

"Listen closely now, Gareth," I said. "Because this is where it gets good."

"Wow. The drama builds. As you can see, I'm holding my breath," he said with a sigh.

"Where do I work?" I said.

"With Priscilla?" he said, making a dismissive duh face as he shrugged.

Gareth was a piece of work, wasn't he? I thought, wondering if I should continue.

When he wasn't busy becoming emotionally unglued at the slightest provocation, he did a great job at acting like a true arrogant shit.

"Yes," I said patiently. "I work with Priscilla. Where?"

"How the hell should I know?" he said.

"I work at a bank, Gareth. Not just any bank but Greene Brothers Hale. You ever hear of it?"

"Vaguely," he said and took another sip of his beer.

"Good," I said. "That's just the way they like it at GBH. They like staying under the radar. GBH is a merchant bank that specializes in managing the money of very, very rich clients. Not just any clients either. Your father, Robert Haynes, is a client at our bank, Gareth. We manage his vast wealth. His account is, in fact, managed directly by my personal work group."

He peered at me as he put his beer down. Then he took off his slouchy hat and passed a hand through his hair.

"So, what the hell does that mean to me? He's got money stuffed everywhere, that mean greedy old miserable bastard."

"My bank is special, Gareth. Greene Brothers Hale is a private bank that offers special perks and services to its extremely wealthy clientele. One of those perks is called kidnapping insurance."

"Kidnapping insurance?" he said.

"Yes," I said. "Sitting not a hundred feet from my basement office on Madison Avenue is an old bank vault with lockboxes for clients' valuables. Inside of it are safety deposit boxes, and in the back of the vault behind a little gate are two rolling suitcases filled with ten million dollars in cash. This money stands ready at all times to be used for ransom in case a VIP client's family member is ever kidnapped."

He smiled suddenly. He opened his mouth to say something but then didn't say anything.

But that was okay.

I could read exactly what he was thinking in his eyes.

He sat up.

"Does it really?" he said.

"One of my duties," I said, "is to be in charge of this money. To make sure the transponder packs that are inserted in with the bills are in working order and to have all the paperwork with the bills' serial numbers on it ready to go for the FBI if it's ever needed."

He was blinking at me now. I'd finally gotten his full attention.

"You don't say. The FBI doesn't do all that?"

"No," I said.

I took a small sip of my cider and placed it down.

"I do."

"Wait, so you're like...you're like not kidding. You're saying what? We...we fake my kidnapping or something? To get the money?"

I stared at him. Then I winked as I raised my drink.

"Now you're finally picking it up, Gareth. You really are fast like Priscilla said. I'm impressed."

He continued to stare at me with his caramel-colored eyes. The arrogance in them had been replaced now by an almost childish curiosity.

"Does Priscilla know?" He shook his head. "No, she doesn't. Or you would have asked her for my number. No, wait. You probably wouldn't have wanted to call me, right? That's why you were following me."

I raised my drink again.

"This is a no texting, no calls, no records of any conversation, Gareth. A just me and you in real life sort of conversation."

He laughed, stared at me.

"Faye, is it? That accent. Where are you from, Faye?"

"Kentucky," I said.

"Where'd you go to school?"

"Tennessee," I said.

"How'd you start working at some fancy Wall Street bank from Tennessee?"

I sipped some cider.

"Because I'm really, really smart," I said.

"And humble, too," he said with a chuckle. "What are you smart at? Finance?"

"No, better. Math," I said. "I solve complicated equations, Gareth. My latest problem is that GBH is screwing me over by not offering me a job I truly deserve. Which is why I'm sitting here with you having this conversation. I want a severance package."

"But wait," he said, frowning. "How do we do it? What about the FBI? They'll interview me. Interview? They'll interrogate me. There'll be press, too, probably. I don't know about all that. That sounds risky. Too risky. I don't feel like going to jail. And how do we get the money? They'll be tracking it. How are we going to pull all that off? Me and you? Look at you. What do you weigh? A hundred twenty pounds? Some little coed?"

I smiled.

Because suddenly it was *we* now.

I had him. I knew it as I sat there. He was going to do it. I could read it in his eyes. He was sick of the street. Sick of sleeping rough. Sick of the way his family and his stupid decisions and his life had shoved him around.

Plus I saw the way he had lifted that baby.

That was his daughter.

If I had to guess, he even had some sort of normal life that he was half-heartedly putting together over there on Vernon Boulevard.

And now the thought of all that easy money was already working into his bloodstream like—

Like heroin, came a sick little voice in my head.

It didn't matter. I had him. I could safely let him in on my plan. At least the part he needed to know about. Though safely was probably strong. With what I had planned, safe had nothing to do with it.

But if Wall Street had taught me anything so far, it was no risk, no reward.

"But how are we going to do it?" he said again. "How are we going to outwit the freaking FBI?"

"Before I divulge the extremely clever details of my plan, Gareth, I need to know that you are in."

He gave me another roll of his eyes, but when he smiled, it was a genuine one.

When he did that, I suddenly saw the cute guy I had seen at Stella's again. The charming fun Gareth who could have taken a girl like Priscilla to the prom.

He even laughed again as he lifted his beer. He looked at me closely as if for the first time.

"Not just clever but extremely clever details, are they? Interesting. I thought you said there was ten million. Why do I only get a million and a half?"

"That's a detail, Gareth," I said, smiling myself.

I lifted my cider toward him.

"That you can only find out once you commit."

"Fine. You got me, Faye," he said. "I'm in."

He finally clicked his bottle to my glass.

"I can't believe I'm even thinking about doing this," he said.

I let my breath out. Then took a hit of the cider. A long one this time.

Me neither, I thought.

"Okay," I said. "So, here's how it will go down."

PART TWO

THE VAULT

20

That night I was supposed to go out on a dinner date with Cavan, but his relief buggy driver didn't show at the last minute so he had to cancel to work a double shift.

It actually worked out though. Now that I'd brought Gareth successfully on board and Plan C was officially rolling, I needed to pull my own double shift on the ten tons of research I now had to do.

The next morning, I woke up early and got dressed and headed back up to Midtown but over to the far West Side this time. I took the Six downtown to Cortland Street and then caught an A train all the way up to the Port Authority Bus Terminal.

After I followed the grimy steps on the other side of the turnstile up into the mall-like building, I looked around until I found one of its electronic boards.

Finding what I was looking for, I went up to its second floor and pushed through the door of one of the arrival gates.

It opened outside to the back of the beat-up building where

there were a bunch of greasy underpasses and exhaust-blackened concrete ramps that led down west toward the Lincoln Tunnel.

As I took out my phone, I wondered if Park Avenue Priscilla had ever spent some time here in the seedy underbelly of the glorious Port Authority. Or even if she could tell you where it was if you placed a gun to her head.

When I looked up from checking the time on my phone, a big gray-and-blue Greyhound was rolling up one of the ramps on final approach. The roaring rattle of it off the concrete as it pulled to a stop a foot in front of me wasn't enough to shake my molars loose but pretty close.

My sister, Caitlin, was the first one off, and we both gave out an immediate screech when we saw each other and made a spectacle of ourselves.

As we stood there hugging, I really couldn't have been more relieved or pleased. Because from the moment I realized I wasn't getting the job, perhaps the biggest dread of all was having to call her and tell her our plans were canceled.

As soon as I had been offered the internship, we'd been planning on her coming up to the city to start a brand-new, wipe-the-slate-clean, noninsane life. Like myself, Caitlin was a kind soul, but she'd had a bunch of crazy friends in high school that easily led her astray. When her best friend, who was half a meth head, had been crippled in a wreck the month before, I knew if I didn't get Caitlin the hell out of there and up here with me pronto, she might never make it out at all.

"Wow, is it good to see you!" I said, wiping at a tear as she peeled me off her.

"How do you think I feel?" she said, laughing as she wiped at her own eyes. "My goodness. I'm finally here."

"Let me look at you," I said, putting her at arm's length.

Caitlin looked like me but was a little shorter and a little curvier. She had dark chestnut brown hair to my blond and hazel-colored eyes while mine were blue.

I inspected her cheap leggings, her more than a little frazzled hair. Not ashamed or meanly, just assessing the amount of work we had to do.

Had I looked this hopeless when I had first arrived? I thought, wiping away another tear.

No way, I thought as I smiled at my little sister's half-dismayed, half-amazed, fun-loving face.

I had looked far, far worse.

With a little polish, I thought, she'd be radiant.

"How was the ride?" I said as I pulled her little rolling suitcase the driver had taken out from the side of the bus into the terminal.

"Oh, riding the dog?" Caitlin said. "It was just perfect, of course. The five-star cuisine at the Gas-N-Sips was especially fine. And they only had to throw that one guy off for smoking weed outside of Pittsburgh. Though there was that other guy a few seats up who kept tap, tap, tapping the night away to the speed metal beat on his headphones. Guy had real talent."

I elbowed her as we laughed.

"What did Gramma say when you lit out?" I said as we maneuvered around a homeless woman in a slip stumbling and mumbling out in front of a Jamba Juice.

My sister snorted.

"What do you think she said? I love you? Don't forget to write? No, that would have been normal. This is Gramma we're talkin' here. 'You'll be back,' is all she said."

I hooked Caitlin's arm in mine like we did when we were little kids.

"Well, we'll just have to see about that, won't we?" I said. "She send me any warm regards?"

"No, not directly but she did warn me about your boyfriend, Cavan."

"Warn you about him?" I said, laughing again. "What's there to warn about him?"

"She said that Cavan being Irish and all, that he was probably a Catholic and that Catholics, according to her, were idolaters. 'You watch him, Caitlin,' she said to me, 'and whatever you do, don't become a Catholic and be praying on those beads.'"

We almost rolled on the ground laughing at that one.

"Oh, my, if that don't take the cake," I said. "Gramma, the suddenly devout Baptist, trying to give advice on soul saving. Real nice of her."

"Especially since the last time she's seen the inside of a church was probably when she was baptized," Caitlin said.

The Uber waiting for us out on the glare of Eighth Avenue turned out to be a beautiful new silver Chevy Tahoe.

"Look at you. You really are an uptown girl now," Caitlin said as we climbed aboard.

"Oh, Caitlin, darling," I said, imitating Priscilla's smooth high-class Park Avenue accent as we were whisked crosstown. "After all, it's only money."

As if, I thought as she laughed.

For the last few months of intern scrimping, I'd been so broke, I couldn't even think about money.

But now that Gareth was on board and Plan C was underway, it was time for me to bust out some emergency assets I'd been keeping under wraps.

In a secret compartment in the back of my wallet was a white plastic credit card that I'd never used before. I'd gotten it right before graduation at Chattanooga. There had been a student credit card booth set up for applications, and I had applied for the low credit, high interest card only for the direst of emergencies in the hopes of never, ever using it.

But if being jobless, penniless, and forever alone without Cavan wasn't a dire emergency, I thought peeking in my wallet to make sure it was still there.

What was?

"Where to first?" Caitlin said.

"You hungry?" I said.

"Starving," she said.

"How about we get some lunch and then since we're uptown, we'll do a little sightseeing and I'll show you where I work?"

"Sounds good to me," Caitlin said. "But when do I get to meet Mr. Cutey Pants, Colin Farrell impersonator?"

"Are you sure you want to meet him now?" I laughed. "Gramma might be right. He may be praying on his Catholic beads, you know."

"Come on, when?" Caitlin said.

I leaned in and blew a raspberry on my little sister's cheek.

"I haven't decided yet, dummy," I said. "You'll just have to wait."

21

We ate at a really cool casual burger place in a hotel near Carnegie Hall that Cavan had taken me to, and then we grabbed another Uber to Grand Central Station.

"What's that? The Empire State Building?" Caitlin said, stopping to stare up at the MetLife Building hovering over the enormous and beautiful art deco train station.

"No, and close your mouth, hayseed, before you catch flies," I said, hustling her out of the hot midday glare on 42nd and in through its doors.

"How do you not get lost?" Caitlin said as we came down the slope of worn marble tile into the vastness of the grand Main Concourse hall. "This is making me dizzy."

Just past where it leveled off, a crowd had gathered near the west balcony. They were standing around where a little black girl of perhaps ten was playing classical music on a piano. We stopped and as we watched, an older black man, her grandfather perhaps, sat beside her. The classical turned into some funny bebop where he played some of the high notes while she continued the rhythm parts.

I smiled at the pure delight on my sister's face as the girl and her granddad ended a couple of minutes later in a grand finale flourish.

"This place is magical," Caitlin said as the crowd whistled and applauded. "Just magical."

"You ain't seen nothing yet, sis," I said, tugging her hand and leading her past the famous clock toward the corridor for Lexington Avenue.

Outside, I pointed out the Chrysler Building across the street and then led her north along Lex past the post office.

We were coming across East 45th where Mornin', Mami and his crew hung out when Caitlin called out a step behind me. I turned to see that one of her cheap rolling suitcase wheels had gotten caught in a grate that was in the middle of East 45th.

"It's stuck," she said, pulling at it.

A total jackass in a honking, slowly passing yellow cab practically grazed my butt as I knelt down to take a look.

"The wheel is really wedged in there," I said as I went into my bag. "Just make sure I don't get run over."

I opened the little penknife I kept on my key ring. I was finally able to dislodge the wheel a minute later when another horn, a surprising train one this time, suddenly honked out.

But it didn't come from the street.

It came from under the street through the grate below.

Peering down through the metal slats, I suddenly felt a kind of ground hum and then I saw it.

Down through the darkness below, the top of a rumbling silver commuter train appeared. I stared at it mesmerized as it snaked through the black of the tunnel.

The train seemed to be heading back under the post office into Grand Central, I realized, back from where we had just come.

"C'mon," Caitlin said. "What are you doing? C'mon."

But I didn't move. I knelt there as if rooted, staring down at the gliding silver roof of the train.

It *was* heading into Grand Central Station. I was sure of it. The track passed directly under this grate.

Was the platform there as well? I wondered. Did the platform extend even as far as here, a block away?

"What now?" Caitlin said as I finally stood and walked to the sidewalk on the other side of 45th and stopped again. I stood looking down at the grate and then up at the elevated car ramp that hovered over the cross street above it.

A memory gnawed at me.

Then I suddenly remembered it.

The bag the mailman had tossed off the ramp onto the sidewalk.

Hey, Papi, catch!

I smiled, staring at the overpass, at the grate, the gears in my head turning steadily.

No, could it actually happen like that? I thought. *Could it be that easy?*

It could, I realized. It damned well could. Or maybe at least.

"Earth to Faye," Caitlin said. "Come in, Faye. I've seen that zoned-out look before. That crease in your brow. What mischief are you up to? What are you thinking about?"

"Nothing," I said. "Just a work thing, sis. C'mon."

22

"What's this?" Marvin called out as we pushed through GBH's brass doors.

"And they bring me gifts," Marvin said as I handed him his Starbucks. "What did I do to deserve this?"

"Marvin, this is Caitlin, my little sister. Caitlin, this is Marvin, the nicest man in New York and maybe in fact, the world."

"Aw, Faye, you're turning my head," Marvin said. "Look, I'm practically blushing. But why are you here at this dusty old place on a Sunday?"

"Just showing Caitlin around," I said. "She just came into town. Thought I'd show her where I work. She's going to be staying with me now, Marvin."

"Wow, aren't you lucky to have such a nice big sister," Marvin said to Caitlin.

"Don't I know it," Caitlin said, smiling.

"My goodness, that's a wonderful southern accent just like your sister's," Marvin said, clutching his chest. "I haven't seen so many beautiful southern belles since *Gone with the Wind*."

"And aren't we lucky to bump into New York's version of

Rhett Butler, you charmer you," I said. "Why don't you show Caitlin what it is that you do here?"

"What do you think I do? I stand here. I get older and on Thursday they pay me a thousand bucks. Things could be worse," he joked.

"You're alone today?" I said. "I thought that younger guy—what's his name? Kevin? Doesn't Kevin work with you on the weekends?"

Marvin leaned in close.

"Well, you didn't hear it from me, but for the next two weekends, Kevin really is here though you can't see him."

My heart rate clicked up several notches.

"I see. You're unofficially covering for him," I said.

"Did somebody say something?" Marvin said, looking around at the marble. "I didn't hear a thing. And what's to cover? Look at this place. On the weekends in the summer, it's a crypt. There's no one here except me."

I thought about that. And stifled a smile.

"Well then, I'm glad we stopped by to keep you company, Marvin," I said. "Give us the tour. Show us the impenetrable security setup here at the storied offices of GBH."

"Ha, impenetrable! If the crooks only knew! They put in the camera system in the nineties. Half of them don't even work anymore. What would they even take in a boring old office building anyway? The filing cabinets? The printer paper?"

I looked over Marvin's shoulder at the door to the basement.

So, he didn't know about the vault downstairs in our office?

I looked over as Marvin turned and sat stiffly on his little stool behind his desk.

He must not know, I realized. Exactly. It made sense.

Why advertise to the building staff that there was that much money sitting under their feet. I mean, I hadn't known about it either until I had to cover for Aiken for an entire week and Aiken's boss, Paulina, had clued me in.

I wasn't even allowed to tell the other interns. She'd been adamant about it.

I swallowed.

Only Aiken was in charge of the old vault then.

And I knew where he kept the key!

"Why doesn't GBH update them? The cameras, I mean," I suddenly said.

"Update what?" Marvin said with a hand to his ear.

"The cameras," I said again.

"It's not GBH. It's the building owners," Marvin said with a shrug of his little child-size shoulders. "It's the landlords who are the cheapskates. That's why GBH couldn't get rid of me, see? I don't work for the bank. I work for the building owners. I'm in the union."

My smile needed even more tamping down.

Things were falling into place here, click by click.

"Only in New York, huh, Marvin?" I said. "But give us the tour anyway."

I stepped over beside Marvin behind the desk and tapped at the screen showing the security camera feed.

"Show us, Marvin," I said. "Walk us through it. Impress a couple of young southern ladies. Show us the whole thing."

23

"So, what do you think of the apartment the second time?" my favorite real estate broker, Sabrina, said.

Caitlin and I had left Marvin an hour before and now we were way uptown back at the charming prewar apartment I'd looked at near Columbia University at 121st Street and Morningside Drive.

Somebody else was supposed to look at it this afternoon, but Sabrina had texted me the night before to see if I was still interested.

"What do you think, Caitlin?" I said to my sister as she came down the spiral staircase from the loft.

"I think it's perfect," Caitlin said.

"Perfect. I like sound of that," Sabrina said. "Music to brokers' ears."

This time she was wearing a silky peach blouse with a gray skirt and her pearls.

This girl didn't quit even on the weekends, did she? I admired her inspiring stylish hard-driving hustling moxie. I took a breath. I was going to need a ton of it myself to see things through.

"Can't get better than perfect, can you?" Sabrina said, smiling at me with an eyebrow raised.

"No, you can't," I said. "Okay, Sabrina. No more messing around. We'll take it."

"That is great! I thought you might, which is why I brought the paperwork with me. On a clipboard in the kitchen. Shall we?"

"This is so exciting!" Caitlin said as we arrived by the kitchen island.

"So, you got the job?" Sabrina said as I lifted the clipboard off the walnut butcher block.

"Uh-huh," I lied as she handed me a pen.

"This is good. You must be very sharp. Finance is even tougher than real estate. We must have drink together soon. You introduce me to your very rich bosses, yes? Not for romance. To sell them even more expensive apartment," she said, laughing.

I scratched down my name on the contract.

"Oh, and what is this?" Sabrina said as we arrived outside of the building downstairs and saw what was coming along the curve of Morningside Drive.

"You! What! What are you doing here?" I said to Cavan as he pulled Lily up and hopped down.

"Ladies," he said to Caitlin and Sabrina with a dapper tip of his top hat before he walked over and gave me a kiss.

"Well, we're meeting for a picnic anyway, right?" he said. "And Lily needed a stretch so I thought I'd come pick you guys up."

I suddenly saw he had flowers in his hand.

"You must be Caitlin," he said, crossing past me over to where she was standing on the sidewalk and handed them over. "I'm Cavan. Heard so much about you. I got these for you. Welcome to New York."

"Thank you," Caitlin said, wide-eyed and smiling and near to faint.

"Here. Come sit down in the carriage," he said, offering his elbow. She laughed as he led her into the street and helped her in.

"You are too much," I said as he winked at me.

I saw that Sabrina, too, was pretty wide-eyed as she stood there watching this insane display.

"Not just job. You have very own Prince Charming, too! Not fair," Sabrina said to me.

"Can we offer you a lift as well?" Cavan said. "There's plenty of room."

"To the subway on Broadway?" she said.

"My very next stop," Cavan said, offering her his elbow and leading her into the carriage as well.

When he was done, he took something down from the jockey box.

"Wait, what's this?" he said as he expertly popped the bottle of prosecco he was holding.

I'd seen him at this routine before. There was a reason why he scored such huge tips sometimes. I shook my head. He really was Prince Charming. Or maybe Prince O'Charming.

"You've thought of everything, haven't you?" I said as he poured sparkling wine into little plastic Party City flutes he always had on board.

"A drink, too! This is like a movie!" Sabrina said as he doled them out.

"She's right. You're incredible, you know that?" I said as he helped me up onto the jockey box and then climbed up beside me and took the reins.

"I am. This is true," he said as he skillfully got Lily to make a broken U-turn on the two-lane street. "I figured if I was meeting Caitlin there for the first time, I should make an attempt to make a good impression. How'd I do? Okay, you think?"

"I'll say," I said as he trotted us around the curve. "You hit it out of the park. I don't think she's able to speak yet. Or breathe. But how did you find us?"

Cavan took out his iPhone.

"Your man, Steve Jobs, whispered in me ear, darlin'. I don't know much, but I always know how to find a friend."

I thought about that as I suddenly stared at him.

Cavan was my friend, wasn't he? Not just my boyfriend. Not just my future husband. I'd had plenty of girl friends in high school and college, but he was hands down the best friend I'd ever had. In the three months we'd been together, we had shared everything there was to share with one another until there were no more secrets left.

Maybe that's why a sudden sense of fear wafted through me then. Out of nowhere.

Because I did have a secret now.

One I couldn't tell Cavan. Or Caitlin. If things went bad, getting either one of them in trouble was a no-go zone.

One part of me had it all nailed down but…there was something. Something.

"Always find me, Cavan," I said, suddenly hugging his arm. "Promise me no matter what. Always find me."

"What?" he said, staring at me. "Look at you, Faye. Your face. What's wrong?"

"Always," I said.

"Always," he whispered back in my ear.

"Hey! We can see you. No kissing up there," Sabrina said, and we all laughed as Lily clopped us across Amsterdam Avenue west toward Broadway.

24

The beginning of the workweek was as calm and uneventful as any I had spent at GBH, but on Thursday something happened.

All the interns, not just the interns at the Madison Avenue office but even all the interns from the White Plains office, had to go down to a Global Technology Conference that GBH was sponsoring at the St. Regis hotel.

The breakfast speaker was some boring woman from one of the Silicon Valley firms who talked about integration in an elaborate slide show TED Talk–style extravaganza.

She explained vertical integration, horizontal integration, even reverse integration. It was so brutal that after the sit-down lunch, a lot of us unfortunate attendees had decided to integrate some alcohol into our workday at the bar.

I was there waiting for Priscilla to come back from the ladies' when I heard two interns from the White Plains office, a couple of real fraternity bro types, talking on the other side of a booth at my back.

"Hey, did you hear about Artie and his score this year?" one of them said.

My ears perked up.

"Dabertrand? His score?"

"Yeah, dude, you notice the difference between the chick interns at our office and the ones from the city?"

"You mean how all the city intern chicks are smoking hot nines and tens while we got like the fours and twos? Oh, I noticed. Have to be blind not to."

"It's by design, dude. That's Artie. He picks them out like baseball cards. He selects the ones he wants and brings them all down to his lair and works on them all summer. Artie's harem, everyone calls them. My boss said every year he tries to work his way through as many as possible. This year he's up to three he said."

"Dude, no way. Three?"

"Way. I even heard he was with that one who was just in here."

"No, that dude Artie's a geezer! He's like seventy. He should be like…dead."

"This is the rumor," the other guy said.

I couldn't believe it.

That Priscilla wasn't the only one. Or that Dabertrand was that basic, that deceptive and animalistic. Artie's harem! It was hard to believe.

Yet, I could believe it. I'd seen the sick videotape with my own eyes. In fact, I wished I could unsee it.

I sat, shaking my head.

What an evil son of a bitch. How could he be like that? How could anyone? Especially with all of the sexual harassment laws and measures that were always touted to stop things like this from happening.

Then I realized how.

When you were connected with unlimited amounts of money, you didn't need to be accountable, did you?

What were laws or hearts or bodies or reputations or futures to the untouchable Dabertrands of the world?

They were a spoiled kid's toys, I thought. They were just another toy to break.

I'd never actually gotten into a bar fight. But I almost did right then and there as both of the frat house jackasses suddenly went mute as Priscilla came back in past them.

"Did our drinks come?" she said.

"No," I said, handing over her Gucci clutch. "Let's skip it, Priscilla. Let's just head back inside."

25

On Friday, I had lunch at Alice's Café, a teeny tiny bakery that was on the other side of Park Avenue on 58th tucked into the corner of the plaza of a black glass office building.

What I loved about it was that it was hardly ever crowded even at lunchtime and had little garden tables outside that were shaded by the building.

I usually brown-bagged it, but every once in a while, I'd treat myself to its Wednesday grilled cheese special and sit in the shade of the plaza and people watch the lunch crowd marching up and down 58th and in and out of the buildings.

I was sitting there, sipping an iced tea at twenty minutes after noon, when someone detached themselves from the crowd in the plaza and pulled out the chair of the garden table beside me.

"Well, hello, partner," Gareth said, sitting with his back to me.

He was wearing a short sleeve T-shirt today, and I couldn't believe the number of tattoos on his thin arms. Not full sleeves but almost.

For anyone to go that overboard with the ink was pretty strange to me. But a child of privilege? It was almost scary.

Once he decided to be a ne'er-do-well, I thought, Gareth had not messed around.

"How's the world of high finance treating you?" he said.

"Fine," I said without looking back. "All systems are still go. How's the homework coming?"

I had left him at the bar with one major task to complete, finding a place to stay during the fake kidnapping.

It was harder than it sounded. We needed him out of sight for at least two days before he "escaped." The challenge was it had to be a place where no one would recognize him or think to look for him or accidentally come across him. Hotels were out, friends' apartments.

Years back, a business owner had been kept in a hole along the West Side Highway until his ransom was paid. We needed something like that.

Having him stay in the trunk of a car for two days would be good, too, but it seemed a tad dangerous.

"I found it, Faye," he said. "The perfect place. In the Bronx."

"The Bronx," I said. "It's not a friend's place, right?"

"No. It's sort of attached to an old friend of mine, but he's not there. No one's there. It's a building that's been shuttered. A strip club actually. The owner's in the middle of a lawsuit, and the property has all of these violations against it. It's been shuttered for three years but lucky me has the key. I can definitely crash there. I have before and told no one about it."

"A strip club?"

He laughed.

"You sound a little skeptical there, Faye. I don't blame you. I haven't actually been putting the old best foot forward these days, have I? But I used to be pretty together at one time, believe it or not. Not too long ago, I was in the real estate business as a broker with my dad, an up-and-comer as it were. Surprised your friend Priscilla didn't tell you my illustrious story."

"I don't have any friends, Gareth," I said. "Go on."

"When I was about seventeen, I started working for my father as a real estate broker."

"At seventeen?" I said.

"Why not?" he said. "Been around it all my life. Learned at the foot of the master, Robert Haynes himself. Anyway, I moved up quick. I was a natural. Started making real money competing against real brokers. The baby wonder, they called me. I was in *New York* magazine. Anyway, long story short, I got into a car accident and my knee got banged up real bad, got on painkillers and that was it. Bye-bye baby wonder, bye-bye everything."

"Where does the strip club key fit in?" I said.

"When I worked for my dad, I became friends with every lunatic on the East Coast who was trying to wheedle their way into the billion-dollar Manhattan real estate market. The former owner of the Bellaire—that's the boogie down strip club in question—was a crazy Cuban guy from Miami that I spent many nights partying with. To get into my good graces, he gifted me with a key to the crash apartment upstairs above the dance floor. The place closed down three years ago as they worked out all the illegalities in court, but the key still fits. I actually spent last winter there. Pretty much every night. Snug as a bug in a rug. It's perfect."

That did sound right. About perfect in fact, I thought.

What was even better, I thought, was learning more about Gareth's past. Selling real estate was no joke. You had to be a pretty competent and a pretty convincing bullshit artist. Gareth would be getting grilled by the FBI no doubt and to tell the truth, I was worried that he would crack.

But maybe not, I thought, glancing back at him. Maybe not.

"No one knows about it?"

"Not a soul. My little personal hole in the wall."

"Not even your girlfriend over on Vernon Boulevard," I said.

He laughed.

"You're good, Faye. You've met Sylvia?"

"No, I saw you with her the first day I followed you."
He laughed.
"No, Sylvia doesn't know anything. That's why I like her so much. I pay the rent on the rattletrap with what's left of my trust fund and that's good enough for her."

"Cute kid," I said.

He laughed again.

"Crazy, right? Junkie with a baby. I stop and start, trying to get things going for them, but keep falling off the wagon. But after you came into my life, Faye, I'm thinking maybe I take this score and get us out of here clean. Open up a real estate shop somewhere else. Somewhere where I can start over again. Southwest or I don't know, Idaho, maybe. Sell people potato farms or something. Whatever. I got a place to stay during the score, so what's next on my end?"

"It's on the folded paper I'm sitting on," I said, standing. "Don't get run over or arrested, okay, Gareth? See you in a bit."

26

Friday night, Cavan was dying to take me out, but I told him I felt sick.

Which wasn't even a fib. I was sick. With worry.

Then Saturday morning came, and at 8:00 a.m. I was standing on the southeast corner of Madison Avenue and 60th staring up at the offices of Greene Brothers Hale.

Madison Avenue on that early August morning was as empty as Yankee Stadium on Christmas Eve. There wasn't a person on either sidewalk in either direction and hardly even any car traffic.

That was good. That no one was around was perfect.

"This is going to be a piece of cake," I whispered, trying to psych myself up.

Yet, I paused at the corner, staring up at the merchant bank's C-suite windows trying to still my increasing panic. As I stood there trying to build up my nerve, across the street the door of the florist opened and a guy holding flowers came out and started almost comically running west up 60th as if he needed to pay tribute for some romantic transgression.

I looked up at my office building again with my wide-open eyes.

My own transgression was just about to get started, and there was nothing romantic about it at all.

Do it, I thought.

I crossed the street and knocked on the glass of GBH's locked lobby door.

As I waited, I smiled up at the camera.

Was that going to be my downfall? I wondered.

Not if you don't screw things up, said a voice in my head as the lock buzzed.

"You again on the weekend!" Marvin said, buzzing me in from his desk.

He had his security jacket off and was sitting with his sleeves rolled up and his tie loosened, eating a Danish with a cup of coffee. A little portable radio beside his coffee was softly playing some jazz music, a trumpet picking up the tempo.

Being Saturday, Marvin was taking it even easier than usual, I saw.

That was good. With what I needed to do, the more Marvin was maxed and relaxed the better.

"Oh, yeah. Me again, Marv. I'm heading out to the Hamptons with some school friends staying up here in Midtown, but wouldn't you know it, they just woke up. They told me they would be a few hours, so I figured I'd come in and catch up on a few things."

He bit into his Danish.

"I figured you were doing something fun," he said, swiping crumbs off his lap as he chewed. "You look different. So, um, summery."

He was referring to the very flowy, past the knee flowered dress I was wearing.

I restrained myself from smoothing it down.

There was a reason for that.

A three-million-dollar reason to be precise.

"Why, thank you," I said. "I am summery, aren't I, Marvin? I feel summery."

"You pack pretty heavy, huh?" he said, smiling down at the rolling suitcase I was hauling.

"You know us ladies," I said. "I actually have some of my sister's stuff, too. She's already out there."

"What's that book there?" he said, referring to the one sticking out of the rolling case on top.

I looked at his raised eyebrow, his mildly curious expression.

I knelt and unzipped the top of the rolling suitcase, making sure Marvin saw the clothes on the top before I stood and showed him the book.

"An LSAT prep book?" he said, turning it over. "That's for law school, right? Wow. You're thinking about heading to law school now?"

"Well, they haven't chosen the new hires yet so I have to keep my options open, you know."

"First, she's in finance now law. All work and no play. Don't you have a boyfriend, too, Faye?"

"You're my boyfriend, Marvin," I said, zipping up the bag and crossing the marble for the door to the basement.

"You know, Faye, on the weekend, I'm supposed to get people to sign into the book here."

I stopped.

"Really?" I said, turning. "Sure."

"Just kidding, kiddo," he said. "For pretty country bumpkins, I always make an exception."

27

The door to the basement was centered in the middle of the lobby's north wall ten paces past Marvin's desk. Behind it, the descending stairwell had a dozen steps and a landing where you turned and then another dozen steps that let you out into a corridor in the center of the building's basement foundation.

To the left down the basement hallway was the door to our office space. To the right was the area where the building maintenance crew had their shops and locker room, and in the wall directly across from the steps were three unmarked doors.

The first door starting from the left was the men's restroom and the second was for the ladies' restroom.

And behind door number three—the only door with a lock on it—was the door to the vault.

But I didn't head there.

Yet.

I made the left and headed down the musty-smelling basement hallway and went in through the pebbled glass door of my office. Inside, it was a pretty open setup with all of our desks starting on the left and going around the room in a kind of horseshoe with the door to Aiken's office on the right as you came in.

My desk was the one just opposite the door, and I went to it and sat. I opened the drawer of my desk and unzipped the top of the rolling suitcase and took the LSAT book out and put it in the desk. Then I removed the folded PJs and some underwear from the rolling case and stacked them on top of the book and closed the drawer.

And then I zipped the rolling case closed and just sat there staring into space.

As I sat, I remembered reading an ancient saying in some college class.

There's planning on riding the tiger. And then there's riding the tiger.

"Oh, boy, is that right," I said quietly as my right foot began tapping at the ground.

Getting the vault key wasn't the problem. I'd already had been in Aiken's office on Thursday after everyone had gone and found it exactly where he always kept it—in the right-hand desk drawer.

And being in the vault itself wasn't the problem, as you could keep the door shut and there were no cameras inside.

What *was* the problem was that there was a camera in the hallway by the stairs.

Marvin had told me that video feed was not recorded to his knowledge.

But he was about eighty years old so I couldn't really bank on it.

I had debated trying some *Mission: Impossible*–style trick to block the hall camera's view or something, but I soon realized that was way above my pay grade. That unless it came off flawlessly it wouldn't really matter. If there was an investigation, I was the only one down here. If the camera had an issue, who else could have tampered with it?

But in my favor from the angle of it, and my looking at the

feed with Marvin the week before, it didn't show the vault door just the bathroom ones. It would show me heading past the ladies' room toward the building maintenance staff lockers and shops, which was pretty suspicious, but at least it wouldn't show me directly opening the vault door.

I was actually more worried about Marvin seeing me and noticing I hadn't come back and coming down to see if I was okay or something while I was still in the vault.

But come on, I thought as I sat there still tippity-tapping my foot. That wasn't going to happen. Marvin was probably back asleep right now.

Stop stalling, I thought.

You need to do this now.

28

I stood and grabbed my case and rolled it to the door of Aiken's office. As I opened his door, I realized I was already sweating.

I went to his desk and knelt down.

And almost had a heart attack as the soft rolling sound of the drawer was suddenly interrupted by the shrill ringing of the phone on Aiken's desk.

I stood there frozen, staring at the blinking red dot on the interoffice phone, as the still-opening drawer painfully hit my knee.

I thought after its third ring I would hear Aiken call out from its loudspeaker in his slightly catty voice.

"What are you doing in my office, Faye?"

But the ringing stopped and the red light went off and there was no creepy message. Just me standing there in the silence.

Get moving, I told myself through gritted teeth.

I quickly reached down and grabbed the vault key and closed the desk drawer and then Aiken's door as I left.

I grabbed my rolling case and went out into the hall with it. I could almost feel the eye of the camera on the back of my head as I passed under it, and I went and stopped in front of the vault door.

The lock on the door was just a regular one, and I smoothly unlocked it and hit the lights just inside on a right-hand switch. After I rolled the case in and closed the door shut behind me, I just stood there for a moment staring.

Inside of the hall door was a little broom-closet-size alcove and beyond that about five feet in was the vault.

The vault was something.

It was one of those big old thick steel ones that was there from the time when the ground floor of the GBH building was a real bank back in the 1930s. It was something to look at all right. It was made of all steel and the vintage circular door was two-feet-thick.

The door was laid wide open back against the wall of the vault itself, and it had a little steering wheel in the door's center that looked like the wheel of a pirate ship.

In the initial tour I got from Aiken's boss, Paulina, she told me the door couldn't close. Something had happened with one of its hinges, which was why they had just made a regular door around it during a renovation.

If the door of the vault was vintage, inside was anything but. Past the two-feet-thick steel opening, there was a shiny gray marble floor and floor-to-ceiling shiny stainless-steel lockboxes on both sides that gleamed under the fluorescent light like the showroom of a jewelry store.

I could feel a change in the pressure of the air almost like I was under water as I finally stepped through the vault's hobbit hole doorway, dragging my rolling case. As I stopped in its center, I could see the other two rolling suitcases straight away. They were at the back of the vault in a stainless-steel cage that almost looked like an old-fashioned jail cell.

When I unlocked this gate with the second key on Aiken's ring, it opened smoothly and silently on its well-oiled hinges, and I brought out the first of the two rolling suitcases and laid it down on the gray marble floor beside the case I'd brought.

Then I took off my flowy dress right there under the fluorescent light between the lockboxes.

There was a good reason why it was so flowy. Underneath it almost to my knee, I was wearing XL bicycle shorts over XL slimming shapewear that went up just underneath my sports bra.

And inside of these oversize underthings, bulging out almost like I was wearing a fat suit, were stacks of blank paper wrapped in rubber bands.

I had eighty of these blank paper stacks attached to my person. And another two hundred twenty of them in my case.

Each stack had a hundred paper blanks, which meant I'd cut out a full thirty thousand of them in all from an almost full ten ream box of printer paper. I'd been at it all week with a paper cutter back in the bedroom at my new apartment rental in Morningside Heights, and with the remaining trimmings of the cuts on the floor I could have held a ticker tape parade.

The first thing I did was open the money case all the way and turn it over and shake the five million in cash out onto the bank vault floor. Then I flipped the case back over and started to fill it with the first layer of blanks. When I was done, I cut the paper wrapper on one of the real stacks of hundreds and placed real Benjamins at the top of the blanks in under the rubber bands, one for each blank paper stack.

Then I smiled.

Because when I was done it looked even better than I thought it would.

What I referred to in my head as the great switcheroo was probably the most essential part of my whole plan.

As I had explained to Gareth at the bar, since I knew where the vault key was and the security was a joke, robbing GBH was actually the easy part.

The problem was getting away with it.

When they inventoried the kidnapping insurance money in the vault the next quarter, if a red cent was missing, there would be people who would get a visit from the folks upstairs and then the FBI.

As one of the few holders of knowledge about the kidnapping insurance money location, it was a pretty safe bet that I would be the first or maybe second on that list.

But with our fake kidnapping scheme, that inventory would never happen, would it?

Because every red cent of the three million bucks I was about to steal was going to be accounted for as a loss in the kidnapping.

The genius at the heart of my fake kidnapping plan was that it wasn't even a fake kidnapping to get a ransom.

It was a fake kidnapping used to cover up an embezzlement.

As I told Gareth, I would steal the kidnapping money first and replace it with paper. Then once we set up the fake kidnapping not only would the FBI be kind enough to take the evidence of our theft out the door of the bank for us, they would then efficiently deliver it back to us at the drop site for disposal. Wasn't that nice?

Then at the ransom drop site, we wouldn't have to care about getting away with the money. We had already done that.

All we would have to care about is destroying the paper blanks.

This plan was so genius because it would be the world's first kidnapping where the kidnappers didn't care about getting away with the ransom money.

They would only care about destroying it.

The FBI would retrieve seven million back for the bank, and once Gareth, quote, unquote, escaped, it would all be okay. It would all blow over. In fact, it would probably look like a big win to all the powers that be.

At least that's what I kept telling myself.

"Yeah, Einstein," I muttered as I began to stack the second row of blanks in the case.

"Now let's see you pull it off."

29

It was almost an hour later when I zipped the case shut and returned it to the barred section at the rear of the vault. I could have done it more quickly, but I couldn't miss a trick. The case had to look perfect. And with the real two million stacked back in on top of the fake three million, it did look perfect.

Even so when I finally locked the vault door behind me in the basement hallway, I felt kind of funny.

When I had come in, I had been hauling money-shaped paper. Now I had eight hundred thousand dollars in real money strapped to my thighs and torso under my dress, and another cool $2.2 million in my jam-packed rolling case.

I knew in my head the real money was the same weight as the paper, but it didn't feel that way. For some crazy reason as I walked for Aiken's office to put back the key, the real money felt a lot heavier.

A minute later, after I got the case very carefully up the twenty-four basement steps, I took a deep breath before I opened the door to the lobby upstairs.

To the left of it, I heard Marvin's radio playing classical music now. And then as I stepped out, I saw Marvin still keeping it casual in his shirtsleeves, sitting on his little stool beside his concierge desk. As I watched, I saw him turn the page of a *People* magazine that he was reading.

Still, as I crossed toward him, I was terrified he would ask me why I was walking kind of stiffly.

But my fear of my lumbering bulky gait dissipated considerably as my little friend looked up with a warm, relaxed smile. If he was suspicious, he was hiding it incredibly well.

"That didn't take long," he said as he turned down the radio.

I almost laughed as I walked the three million dollars right past him.

"Yeah, my friends just texted. Time to go. Thanks, Marvin," I said as I arrived at the side door and he buzzed it.

"Faye, wait. Stop right there," Marvin said at my back just as I was one foot out the door.

"Yes, Marvin," I said, swallowing before I turned.

Marvin folded the *People* magazine as he crossed the distance.

"Look," he said, showing me the folded magazine.

It was a full-page picture of Reese Witherspoon wearing a cowboy hat.

"This is who you remind me of," he said, smiling.

"Reese Witherspoon?" I said.

"Yep," Marvin said. "Another sweet southern belle. You could be sisters."

I smiled.

"Thanks, Marvin," I said, stepping out fully into the street. "She's a little bit older, but you always know how to compliment a la—"

"Well, hello there. What's this?" said a voice at my back.

No, I thought without looking. *Just no.*

"Walker, right?" said Master of the Universe Arthur Dabertrand as I turned.

Instead of Savile Row, he was in white shorts, and a chambray shirt the same blue color of his billionaire eyes. No caramel briefcase today or billionaire umbrella, though I noticed he was smoking an obnoxiously large and smelly cigar. He gave it a hearty puff as he smiled down at me.

"What are we doing here on the weekend, Walker?" he said.

I stared up at him, my mind racing for a response, racing fruitlessly.

Because with my worst nightmare suddenly come true, Dabertrand himself suddenly staring at me, I wasn't just shocked.

I was mind out of body sensation level discombobulated.

"She's going out to the Hamptons, Mr. Dabertrand," Marvin said quickly. "She's meeting friends, and she just stopped by to say hello to me a second ago. Didn't you, Faye?"

It was Marvin's logbook, I realized. He hadn't signed me in on it. He didn't want to get into trouble.

I could have kissed him for that.

"That's right," I said, smiling euphorically at Marvin for the incredible save. "I was just saying hi to my favorite coworker. I'm actually in a rush. I have to go. I—"

"Wait, wait, Walker. The Hamptons, is it? Today's your lucky day," Dabertrand said, shoving something in my hand before I knew what was happening.

I looked down.

It was a set of car keys.

"See the car there?" he said. "That's my car."

I looked to where he was pointing with the cigar. Some kind of red convertible, a Ferrari or something, was parked at the fire hydrant near 61st with a white Labrador retriever sitting in it.

Of course it was, I thought as my discombobulation started to instantly return.

"I'm heading out to the Hamptons myself, Walker. I'll give you a ride. Just throw your suitcase in the back and keep Henry company, and I'll be down in a minute."

Before I could respond, Dabertrand had already gone into

the building with Marvin trailing him and the door clicked shut in my face.

"You have got to be out of your freaking mind," I said to myself as I rolled the money-packed suitcase toward his convertible. It was actually a Mercedes, I saw. Some kind of supercar thing.

As freaking if, I thought as I stopped beside it.

"As freaking if," I repeated out loud as I looked up at the GBH executive suites.

"Here, Henry," I said, dropping the keys between the dog's paws.

Then I jogged quickly around the corner, waving wildly at a passing taxi, a Nissan Quest minivan.

The driver was some glitter-eyed West Indian guy listening to Bob Marley.

"Where to?" he said.

"One hundred and twenty-first and Amsterdam," I said to my getaway driver as I pulled my cash-filled rolling suitcase and my cash-wrapped butt quickly off the street and slid the door shut.

30

Back at the apartment I spent the rest of the afternoon doing some reno and cleanup.

The ticker tape parade of paper shreds actually filled two Hefty bags, and I brought them out onto the sidewalk and walked over two blocks to a construction site on 119th Street where there was Columbia University student housing nearby, and I tossed them in a dumpster.

When I came back, I cut out a section of the Sheetrock wall in the back of the bedroom closet with a box cutter and proceeded to stack the three million dollars in cash between the studs. After I Sheetrocked it back up and smoothed the spackle over it, I knew it needed some sanding and paint. But since I wanted to let Caitlin move in as soon as possible, I thought it would be fine for now.

Cavan had to work all day Sunday, so Caitlin and I spent the day moving us out of the Box up into the Morningside Heights apartment and doing some shopping. We bought some kitchen and cleaning stuff and ordered those bed-in-a-bag things and picked up some groceries.

When Sunday night came and we settled down into our sleeping bags, Caitlin said it reminded her of old times being kids and going to Gramma's for the first time.

It reminded me of that as well, I thought as I stared at the ceiling unable to sleep, a heady combination of anxiousness, fear, and terror.

I did eventually manage to get a little sleep, but when I woke, I was no calmer than when I'd gone to bed. After the no-net tightrope walk of Saturday, if anything the butterflies in my stomach were swirling even harder that Monday morning.

But they all died an instant death as I came into the basement office a little late to see the members of GBH Team Basement freaking out at a minor catastrophe underway.

Everyone was clustered around McPhee's desk. Some major wires he'd uploaded on Friday hadn't settled into their receiving accounts.

"Thank God you're here," McPhee said when he spotted me. "The mess up looks like it's on my end, Faye, but I don't know what the hell I did wrong."

I glanced at his screen.

"Relax, McPhee," I said. "You did nothing wrong. Try the treasury escalation department. I hear they just added another couple of layers of review. They're always adding stuff without notifying anyone about it."

"Thank God you're here," McPhee repeated as he quickly lifted his phone.

I'd just sat and put my bag down when my phone beeped.

"Faye, could you come in here," Aiken said in my ear.

What the? I thought as I stood. *Faye again? He always calls me Walker.*

"Sure," I said, thinking, was this it? Had I missed a camera? Had I been busted? Or was it about not watching Dabertrand's Merc for him? Had it gotten towed?

I forgot to breathe as I crossed the twenty feet to his office door but quickly forced myself to as I turned the knob.

"Faye, please have a seat," Aiken said.

I followed orders and sat in the chair in front of his desk. The one I'd been rifling through about forty-eight hours earlier. I tried to read the expression on his face, but as usual, there was none.

"Okay. I don't do this. In fact, I've never done this," Aiken said.

Do what? I thought, fighting the urge to start biting my nails.

"I'm not even sure if I should be doing this," he continued. "But here it is. I heard about a job offer on the other side of the phone. I think you'd be a great fit."

As he said this, it felt immediately like I was stuck to the chair. As if I'd been suddenly crazy glued to it.

What on earth?

"The buy side?" I said.

He nodded.

Our bank, which processed orders for the hedge funds, was known as the sell side. The other side of the phone meant the buy side.

He was talking about helping me to get a job at a hedge fund.

Basically, the greatest thing that could possibly happen.

Getting a job at a hedge was the holy grail. It wasn't as good as getting picked as a trader at GBH.

It was actually better.

He was hooking me up, I realized. My consolation prize wasn't a set of steak knives after all. Aiken was hooking me up big time.

"Walker? Yoo-hoo? Are you still with me?"

"Really?" I managed to get out. "You're not kidding."

"Do I kid, Walker?"

"Where is the job?" I said, wide-eyed.

"Broadhead Mountain Capital," he said as he handed me a business card.

Gerald Dorsey, it said along with a double-digit address on Broad Street.

I glared at him.

Broadhead Mountain was as big as its name. It was a whale. Like GBH, Broadhead Mountain was all about hard-core big global flows of money, currency exchanges, exotic multinational financial constructions.

Only with much smaller staffs that divided up the unfathomable profits.

"But," I said, still shell-shocked.

"No buts. Go now. I mean right now. Gerry is waiting to interview you right this very minute. He needs someone forthwith so I said you were on your way. The iron is hot. Strike, Walker. Strike."

Aiken didn't have to tell me a third time.

I ran out and went to my desk and grabbed my bag.

31

There have been times in my life where I've had mixed feelings, but as I settled into the back of a taxi a block away from GBH up on Fifth Avenue, my mind was literally split in two about what to think.

With three million dollars in stolen cash sitting in the closet of my new rental up on 121st Street, my nerves were already at the breaking point.

And yet as the taxi carried me south past the Plaza and I looked out at the sun sparkling off Trump Tower and the glitzy high-end storefronts, I felt the first tingles of a building elation.

Was this it? I kept thinking. *Was this my moment? My last mile to the finish line tape after how many years of scraping by?*

I knew it was not wise to think this, to get my expectations pumping again. I had rightfully expected to win a job with GBH, hadn't I? And boy, had they pulled the rug out from underneath me with that.

But I couldn't help myself. I didn't just *want* to believe that I had accomplished a goal I'd been slaving half a decade for.

At that point in the emotional roller coaster ride that was that crazy summer, I existentially *needed* to believe it.

We seemed to speed quickly downtown through Midtown but at 14th Street, we hit traffic and went east past Union Square Park over to Broadway.

In the Financial District we hit some traffic again, and we stop and go-ed for a while. Outside of Trinity Church, I couldn't take it anymore so I decided to get out and walk.

I crossed Broadway and walked down Wall Street and about a block-and-a-half down, I halted beside the statue of George Washington on the steps of Federal Hall.

Looking with George across the famous intersection at Wall and Broad with the New York Stock Exchange in the background, I sighed as I took a moment to take it all in.

What most don't realize about Manhattan is that its skyscrapers are actually relegated to two separate sections of the island separated by several miles. Midtown—where Central Park and Rockefeller Center and Times Square and the Empire State Building were located—was the most famous, most populated part.

But down here in southern Manhattan, the oldest part of the city, the vintage stone office buildings had an ancient temple thing going on with statuary and elaborate stonework in the deep-set windows on both sides of the winding narrow cobblestoned streets.

Like Grand Central there was something Old World timeless about it, I thought, as I stared at the crisply snapping American flags strung along the Greek columns of the Stock Exchange.

I'd never been to Rome, but there was something very Ancient Rome about it as if a horse-drawn chariot might appear at any moment around the bomb barriers.

"Now to face the lions," I said as I stepped down Broad, following the directions on my phone.

I went down another block and right across from Stone Street, there it was on my left. My new potential office. The dark forty-story black glass tower of 83 Broad.

"Can I help you?" said a stocky black middle-aged security guy standing behind the concierge desk inside. His stony, drill sergeant's face scanned and rescanned the lobby over my shoulder as he said this.

Former military, I thought. Probably armed. This was the big leagues, I thought. No loveable pensioners need apply here.

"I have a job interview with Broadhead Mountain Capital," I said.

He assessed me for the first time rather skeptically.

"Name?" he said, lifting a phone.

"Faye Walker."

He spoke quietly into his phone and then as he hung it up his hard-edged face suddenly broke into a friendly smile.

"Broadhead is up on thirty-eight, Miss Walker," he said, pointing to my left. "The elevators are right over there."

"Thanks," I said, suddenly smiling myself.

If I had thought the view down Broad Street was something, as I got out onto the glass-windowed corridor of thirty-eight, I realized I apparently hadn't seen anything yet. Not only could I see the One World Trade Center freedom tower hovering on my right, I could also see New York Harbor with dozens of ships going back and forth in front of the Statue of Liberty.

At the end of the corridor, in front of the slickest zinc glass-walled office I'd ever seen, sat a very pretty blonde woman in her forties with her hair in a bun. She was smiling as if waiting for me.

"Faye, right?" she said as I stepped up.

"That's me," I said.

"Mr. Dorsey is waiting for you," she said as I heard a demure buzzing at the glass door to her back. "Make a right as you go in, and his office is straight in front of you at the end of the hall."

I was thinking Mr. Dorsey would be a silver-haired CEO

type like Dabertrand, but as I came in through the open door of his office and spotted him standing behind the horseshoe of computer monitors that edged his desks, I saw he was a neat midsize brown-haired guy in his late thirties.

He smiled as he turned from his window, which had an even better view of the harbor.

"Faye, please have a seat," he said, gesturing to a pair of leather club chairs in the room's corner.

As we sat, what stood out most to me besides his age was the ordinariness of Mr. Dorsey. Not handsome, not ugly, of average height and with slightly hooded brown eyes, on the surface he didn't look like very much at all.

He might even be a nice guy, I thought. He looked normal enough.

"So, you work for Alex, huh?" he said, smoothing down his white business shirt and blue-and-coral pink tie as we sat.

"I do. He's a great boss," I lied.

"Yeah, great guy," Mr. Dorsey said, suddenly yawning.

"I'm so sorry," he said when he was done.

He took a deep breath, puffing out his cheeks as he exhaled it.

"Late night last night," he said. "Which brings me to why I asked you to come down here. Alex tells me you're very sharp, and I'm looking for somebody sharp. You were a math major, right?"

"That's right."

He tented his fingers together.

"All right. Now for a crazy question. How are you with kids?"

32

"Kids?" I said.

"Yes, kids. Or more specifically, babies."

"Um, I don't have any, but I'm all right with them, I guess. What—"

"Faye, here's the job. I need a nanny. My wife and I do. But not just any nanny. I need a nanny who can help me keep track of things here at the office when I'm home or on vacation."

I peered at him.

"I don't think I understand. You don't need me to work here at Broadhead?"

"Well, kind of. I mean, sometimes. See, I have a town house on 67th Street off Madison with a maid's room. You would have to come live there to take care of the baby and my older son, Benjamin, who just turned two. But at the same time, I would need you to keep in constant contact here at the office. I need someone to help me sort things out, capture stuff and break it down for me when I'm at home. Which means you would also have to travel with us. I have a place in Connecticut I go to almost every other weekend, and in the winter I go to Palm Beach. You'd be wearing two hats, admin and nanny but I promise..."

He handed me a slip of folded paper.

"You'll be compensated very, very well."

What an idiot, I thought as I sat there staring at the folded paper. What a stupid idiot.

A nanny?

And a secretary?

A damned nanny-tary? A live-in one? That was the big consolation prize? To be basically enslaved by this jerk. What other needs would he eventually require? I wondered, as we would all be sleeping under the same roof.

Even if I were to consider the job—and I wasn't—I would never see Cavan again.

Had GBH done what it was supposed to do and hire me, I thought as I looked back at the folded paper again, would Aiken have sent Priscilla down here for this interview?

He would not have. Not in a million years. The Priscillas of the world *had* nanny-tarys. Only little people like me became them.

"I know this is sudden. But what do you say?" Mr. Dorsey said.

He rubbed at the bridge of his nose and rocked back in his chair as he stared at me, waiting for my reply.

That's when it happened.

I started laughing.

"Did I say something funny?" Mr. Dorsey said, genuinely confused.

I laughed harder. Then I puffed out my own breath as I stood and stepped to the window.

Oh, I should have known, I thought as I took in the hundred-million-dollar view. I laughed some more as I watched a ferry pull into the island where the Statue of Liberty was.

What did the inscription say? Give Me Your Tired, Your Poor.

Well, screw that, I thought.

"Is that a no?" Mr. Dorsey said.

I nodded as I stared out at his sunlit Elysian fields some more.

"A big fat one," I said.

"But you didn't even look at the offer."

"No. No, I didn't," I said.

"I thought Alex said you were looking for a foot in the door," Mr. Dorsey said.

I stood there looking down at him.

A foot in? I had three million dollars in cash buried in my closet up on Amsterdam Avenue. I had everything I needed, I realized. Everything.

I didn't need a foot in. I needed two feet out and I was almost there.

"I'm not interested, Mr. Dorsey. But thanks," I said, handing him back his folded piece of paper.

33

To celebrate my nanny-tary career being over before it began, I decided to take the rest of the day off without asking, and the next morning, I was up very early.

Because Plan C was on again.

Oh, was it on.

I headed north this time to St. Nicholas Avenue in Washington Heights.

The street name made me think of Christmas and the North Pole until I came up out of the 181st Street subway station for the One train and saw that it was strewn with check-cashing places and dentist billboards and mom-and-pop stores that sold baby clothes and furniture.

Just like in Midtown, many of the buildings up in this grungier section of the city were also under construction. Though I noticed most of the sidewalk sheds up here were covered in graffiti.

As I passed through one and came past a place called Tropical Seafood, I heard salsa music coming from the open window in an apartment above it. This was drowned out a moment later by the choppy electronic screech of a siren-roaring ambulance that appeared at the next corner and went flying north up St. Nicholas.

Maybe one of the elves had just OD'd, I thought. Or had Rudolph taken one to the chest in a drive-by?

The place was pretty lively all right, I thought, as I tucked my Yankee cap down lower over my eyes. Especially considering it was about 5:30 in the morning.

I'd gotten on the subway down in Chinatown a little before five and hadn't seen five people on the ride up Broadway. Off-hours subway rides could be dicey, I knew, actually dangerous if you ran into the wrong person or people, but I'd lucked out so far.

I stopped and looked across the street a block ahead and finally spotted the SMOKE SHOP 24 OPEN DELI sign that I'd headed all the way up here for.

Bingo.

SMOKE SHOP 24 OPEN DELI was the establishment's actual name from Google Maps, and what was pertinent to me about it was that it possessed something I needed for the next part of Plan C.

A bitcoin ATM.

Now that it was full speed ahead, all cylinders go with Plan C, I needed to make a series of purchases. To do that, I needed to get some of the cash I'd stolen back into a legitimate account. And Bitcoin was my first step.

That was why I was now carrying fifty thousand dollars in hundreds in my bag. It was a dangerous thing to do anywhere, let alone in a notoriously crime- and drug-dealing-infested area like Washington Heights, but I couldn't help that, could I? I needed to make a deposit, and it needed to be discreet.

"No risk, no reward," I whispered to myself as I took a deep breath.

As if in reply to this, suddenly very nearby a voice called out.

"Yo, buy me a juice?"

To my left, a homeless man stood from where he'd been sitting in a doorway. He was older, maybe sixty or so. A black guy, tall and very thin. He was shirtless and in a pair of pale blue Nike sweatpants. He was also shoeless.

Startled motionless, I watched him wipe sleep out of his eyes. He looked like he had just woken up.

"Yo, buy me a juice, man. C'mon, I just need a cranberry juice."

The sound of the homeless bum's voice seemed to break the spell of my frozenness, and pretending I was deaf, I made an instant wide berth as I jogged out into the street and crossed the avenue.

An electronic bell went off as I came into the bodega. It had stacks of beer cases on the right like a moat in front of a counter with a Plexiglas shield.

Within this plastic deli security booth sat a heavyset maybe Middle Eastern man with dark curly hair and a bright yellow-and-white-striped polo shirt stretched tight across his impressive gut. There was a Band-Aid above his right eye that was edged dark with what looked like dried blood.

"Bitcoin?" he said in a surprisingly nonaccented normal voice.

When I nodded, he smiled and gave me a wink.

"Who needs a bank, eh?" he said as he pointed his pudgy chin toward the back of the untidy store.

34

I went down the aisle and between a case of vape pens and lighters and a rack of chips, I stopped before the bitcoin ATM's yellow metal box.

I'd already checked out how to do it online. You had to create a bitcoin wallet first, which I had already done with an app I'd downloaded onto a Tracfone burner phone I had purchased yesterday afternoon.

Buy bitcoin? it said on the touch screen.

I pressed it.

Please scan your bitcoin wallet address.

I did, holding the QR code on my app to the scanner.

A second later, my address appeared on the screen along with the words:

Insert money.

I took a breath and then I took a long look around beside and behind me. I couldn't see the counterman or better yet a security camera. No one but me and the chips.

What the hell? I thought, turning the bag around in front of me and taking out the first loose hundred.

"In for a penny in for a freaking pound," I mumbled as the machine gave off a wee cha-cha-cha whir as it ate the first bill.

There was actually a five-thousand-dollar limit, so I had to do ten different wee cha-cha-cha-ing transactions.

After I was done and I pressed a button to confirm that I was finished it said: *Send bitcoins?*

I held my burner phone QR code bitcoin wallet back up until there was a ding from my phone.

I looked at it.

Received $50,000 in bitcoins, it said.

I smiled.

Alrighty then, I thought as I turned on my heel and headed for the door.

There was a strange sound outside as I hit the sidewalk, and I turned to see it was the shirtless, homeless black man standing ten feet away, slapping a palm against his forehead.

Of course, it was.

He turned sharply toward me.

"Where's my juice?" he cried.

"I, uh, forgot," I said, immediately turning and going back inside.

I came in and looked at the counterman. I wondered if I should call the cops or something. But that would take time, and then there would be a report or something.

"What is it?" the counterman said.

I went to the drink case and grabbed an Ocean Spray and put it on the counter.

"Is this for you?" he said, squinting at me. "It's not, is it? This is for that Rodney. Is he out there? Is he bothering you?"

He went to the window behind him and peered through.

"That son of a bitch. I knew it. He's at it again. I told him a hundred times. They arrest his ass, but then they let him out and he comes right back. I'm sick of his strong-arm robbery shit. That's it. I'm done."

"No, it's okay. It's fine," I said.

But apparently it wasn't fine.

Out from behind the counter and to the door with a speed that was remarkable for his size went the Middle Eastern counterman.

What happened next was stunning. Rodney's back was turned as we both headed out, and the heavyset man did a kind of crow hop and, without preamble, smacked a fist into the back of Rodney's head. He must have known how to box or something because Rodney, who was not a small man, teetered for a second and then fell face forward into the garbage bags, instantly knocked out. Or who knew? Dead maybe.

"There's your cranberry juice, Rodney," the counterman cried down at him. "How you like them cranapples? You want some more? I got plenty more."

"Thank you," I called back without turning as I ran for my life in the opposite direction down St. Nicholas for the subway.

35

The bike path was at the Hudson River and 30th Street on the far West Side, and when I got to it after work that Tuesday night at about seven in the evening, the setting yellow-orange sun was making impressionist patterns on the silver water.

Finding a seat on a free bench, I noticed that the sun was also shining off the obelisk of One World Trade Center down at Wall Street near where I'd rearranged Mr. Dorsey's world view.

As I thought about him and about how the counterman up in Washington Heights had knocked Rodney into the garbage bags, I laughed to myself. I was really becoming a New Yorker now, wasn't I? I was a hard-boiled criminal among criminals from high to low. And maybe I was punch-drunk with all the stress and craziness by that point, but I was oddly cool with it.

When in Rome, I thought, as I watched a woman in a bikini with a parrot on her shoulder skate by on Rollerblades.

I sat waiting, watching the bicyclists and the West Side Highway traffic on my left. Across the lanes of traffic, there was some kind of huge warehouse with water towers on the top like something out of an old noir movie.

Staring at them, I thought about my mom who had loved all those black-and-white movies. Older and wiser now, I wondered how she and my dad had hauled themselves out of the hellhole holler of poverty they started out in. By hook or by crook, no doubt.

And they had really made something of themselves. With my mom to support and to inspire my father, he had been one hell of great provider, a man who worked overtime every chance he got and whose biggest vice was drinking a few beers when he went fishing. Had my mom not died of cancer, there's no way he would have backtracked and ended up in jail.

Momma had given out, but she never gave in. I remembered her grip on my arm from the hospital bed, the hoarse cry in my ear for me to take care of my little sister, to not forget.

No, she had never quit. Not once.

"Me neither, Momma," I said as I watched a sailboat glide upriver. *Me neither.*

When Gareth showed at eight, he surprised me. He'd shaved and had even gotten his hair cut. Scrubbed up with the tattoos hidden in the long sleeves of a nice white dress shirt, he looked normal. Better than normal. Almost preppy. Like a Wall Street guy coming out of work.

"The up-and-comer returns," I said as he sat beside me.

"High time for a makeover," he said back with a smile. "Past high time. I'm not late, am I?"

"Nope. Right on time," I said.

"So, how's things?" he said with a wink.

"Things are 100 percent go," I said back with my own wink.

I took a couple of sheets of paper out of my bag. I handed them to him along with my burner phone.

"The script is right there, what time to call, and everything."

I watched Gareth read the script. He started smiling. Then he laughed. He punched at his thigh.

"Holy shit! This is such genius. I can't believe it. It's so funny. You really are brilliant, Faye."

"I told you," I said, smiling. "At 12:10 now. Don't forget. It could be a little later. But no sooner. Any questions?"

"Not a one. I can't wait," he said.

"All right. Then talk to you tomorrow," I said, standing.

"Faye?" Gareth said.

He was looking down at the phone in his hand.

"Yes, Gareth?"

"You know," he said. "I could just take off with this bitcoin money. This 50K. It would be a good score for me."

I looked at him.

"I do know that, Gareth," I said carefully. "I'm trusting you here, partner."

"Why would you trust a junkie?" he said, finally looking at me. "You shouldn't do that."

Staring at him in the evening light, in his eyes I saw an amount of pain I was not expecting.

Not fair, I thought. This was business. He couldn't go and make me care about him. I had too many other damn people on my list.

"That's on my end," I said, looking at him.

"What is?"

"Who I decide to trust," I said.

He took a deep breath.

"Thank you," he said.

"For what?"

"I've been feeling pretty sorry for myself lately, Faye. I've made a lot of mistakes in my life. I threw away a ton of gifts, burned friends—good friends—just torched 'em, just burned through them. And well, I guess this, um, this thing we're about to do, it's made me realize a lot of things."

He wiped a tear from the corner of his eye.

"I basically thought I was in a box, but you showed me maybe I got one last exit door left out of this mess I made after all."

He laughed.

"I'm going to get my shit together," he said. "Get away from this city. Going to take my family. Go have a life, you know, Faye? I have a daughter. She's...she's..."

He tilted his head toward the rippled water. The swaying sailboat was at the point where the yellow-orange sunset was making patterns on the water now.

"So small," he finally said.

"I know, Gareth," I said, holding back my own tear as I gave him a fist bump now. "Buck up, camper. We've still got some things to do here. Let's stop talking about it and get it done."

36

By midmorning, Aiken and half the team had left for the rest of the day on some company walkathon thing for a Harlem church food bank. The rest of us got pretty slammed until lunch, and at noon after the rest of the stragglers bolted for air and food, I was sitting at my desk, leaning back in my chair staring at the inside of my cubicle.

I stared at my pens sitting in a Fourth of July Starbucks mug I'd bought, the little stuffed Yankee beanie baby Cavan had gotten me, the beige fabric on the cubicle wall.

At 12:05 I sat up and positioned my work phone in front of me just at the edge of the desk.

Gareth really could burn me, I realized as I had a staring contest with it.

Guess I was about to find out.

I smiled as it rang at 12:10 on the dot.

Maybe not, I thought.

I waited for it to trill twice before I lifted it the receiver.

"Greene Brothers Hale. This is Faye."

"Hello, I have a family sovereign account with you guys, and

I'd like to open a new account," Gareth said as per the instructions I'd handed him the night before.

"Absolutely," I said, casually playing with a rubber band as I leaned back. "Is there someone you normally work with here?"

"Yes. Mr. West."

"If you would hold for a second, I'll see if I can contact him," I said.

I sat up and pressed the hold button. I counted to a hundred silently as I pretended to try to link up with Mr. West, whoever he was. I knew our fake conversation was being recorded, but I wondered if they actually had keystroke data on the internal phones. I didn't think so.

"I'm sorry, sir," I said as I pressed hold again. "He seems to be away from his desk. Perhaps I could help you. You said you need to open a new account?"

"Yes, I do. An offshore one like the one I already have."

"Absolutely. Let's get you started. Your name, please."

"Robert Haynes," Gareth said, giving me his father's name.

I typed it into my account database.

"Yes, excellent. I have your information right in front of me," I said. "Address, please."

"Three East 78th Street, New York, New York."

"Phone password," I said.

"Yankeefan99," Gareth said, reading off the information I had already gotten out of the database for him.

"Very good, and mother's maiden name."

"Jennings."

"Perfect. Thank you so much, Mr. Haynes. So, you would like to open a new account. What kind of new account?" I said.

"A checking account just like my Cayman account. I just need a new separate one."

"A new account at Grand Cayman Trust?" I said.

"That's the one."

"Absolutely. What would you like to designate this second one as? Should we call it checking account number two or...?"

"Call it Lemongrass Holdings," Gareth said, reading off my script.

There were several reasons for the ruse we were pulling here. The most important was that we were at a point in Plan C where we would have to make some larger purchases and rentals to complete the fake kidnapping.

We obviously needed to shield ourselves from these purchases so we were now in the process of doing something I often did for GBH clients, opening up a cutout offshore account out of the Cayman Islands. An account for Gareth's father that he did not know about.

Into this account would go the stolen fifty thousand I had converted into bitcoin that was now in a UK bitcoin banking exchange account I'd also falsely set up in the name of Robert Haynes using the private info I had on him.

This way, if the shit hit the fan and the Feds traced anything, they would find a Cayman Islands account behind everything and hit the brick wall of the Cayman's notorious banking privacy laws.

That was just fire wall one.

Further looking into it, if they even could, they would find that Robert Haynes—*the* Robert Haynes, billionaire real estate mogul—was the owner of the account and therefore was somehow behind the kidnapping.

Of his own son!

If it did get that far, GBH would be in a quite a quandary. For decades, Robert Haynes had paid over a million dollars every year in fees to the bank. There was no reason to think that this wouldn't be the case into the future.

Would GBH push the matter and sic the Feds on him for a measly loss of three?

I didn't think they would. What was justice and integrity when a million plus in yearly fees was on the line?

Gareth, who possessed a great deal of animosity for his father, especially liked this little backup insurance aspect of our plan.

The possibility that if our hoax did go south and the Feds found his father's fingerprints all over it, and might even arrest him for it, was one that Gareth found almost too delicious to bear.

Through tears of laughter after I suggested it, Gareth had said that if it came down to it he himself would testify in open court that it was his father's plan the whole time.

"It would be the sweetest revenge of all time, Faye," Gareth had said. "I'd put the old buzzard inside, and he wouldn't have the foggiest idea what was going on!"

"Excuse me, are you still there?" Gareth said.

"Lemongrass Holdings it is," I said into the phone. "Now, would you be funding this account today, Mr. Haynes?"

"Yes. From another account, a UK account. Is that a problem?"

"Not at all," I said.

"Ready for the routing number?" Gareth said cheerily.

I could practically hear his smile.

"Let's see. One second. Okay, shoot," I said with a smile of my own.

37

At five on the dot, I got up from my desk and left the GBH office building and crossed Madison and went east on foot a block down 60th Street to Park Avenue.

I crossed over to the east side of the avenue and made a right and walked south. Below 59th, the apartment houses soon became office buildings with a growing pedestrian crush of just freed office workers exiting from them. Most of them, like myself, were also headed south and we marched together, an army of business-casual uniformed soldiers heading toward where the glass slab of the MetLife Building hovered above Grand Central Station like a shiny black headstone.

At the base of the MetLife Building and a block north of it at 46th Street, there was another older, smaller and much more ornate prewar structure called the Helmsley Building that had been built in the 1920s.

Researching the entirety of the area for the past weeks, I knew that its claim to fame was that the uptown and downtown lanes of Park Avenue went through this building under elaborate coffered arches that were described as car portals.

Beside these car portals were smaller pedestrian tunnels that went through to 45th Street, but as I crossed 46th Street with the rest of the commuting crowd, instead of heading into the east pedestrian tunnel, I did something quite unusual.

I headed to my right and walked into the east car portal instead.

It was like heading into a highway tunnel, and the horns of taxis coming straight at me blared loudly in the covered space as I hugged the left-hand wall and headed up its car-exhaust-scented asphalt slope.

This strange elevated roadway I climbed up onto was known as the Park Avenue Viaduct, I knew, and it had been built at the turn of the twentieth century as a way to have Park Avenue get around the newly built Grand Central Station.

As I came out the back of the Helmsley Building car portal and arrived at the viaduct's East 45th Street overpass, I saw that it, too, looked like something from the Gilded Age. Beneath the old steel girder guardrail of it were green-painted metal panels inlaid with a shell design like something out of a prominent gentleman's library.

I stopped along the row of them. As I glanced down and saw the windows of the post office on 45th, I realized I was at the spot on the overpass where I'd seen the postman drop the mailbag onto the 45th Street sidewalk that morning that seemed like a thousand years ago.

"Don't jump, baby!" yelled some passing jackass in a work van as I hoisted myself up onto the Gilded Age overpass's top guardrail. I ignored him. I looked over.

And there it was.

The grate on the surface of 45th Street where my sister had gotten her bag stuck was right there beneath the overpass.

It was a straight shot. It could be done, I thought, staring at it.

I smiled as I hopped down and hugged the wall again back down toward 46th Street.

Not only could it be done, I thought.

It was about to be.

38

When I arrived back at 46th, I took the pedestrian walkway this time and stepped out at 45th and stopped and stood on the sidewalk before the street grate, staring at it.

In my research I'd also looked up how utility workers opened manholes in Manhattan. I thought at first that they maybe had locks on them or something, but what I had learned is that they were just heavy metal covers levered open with pry bars or manhole hooks.

The grate I was staring at, I realized, was actually three grates sitting in a rectilinear metal frame recessed into the street. By placing a pry bar in through the bars of a grate, could it somehow be wedged open? I wasn't sure.

Then I suddenly saw it. Between the first and second grates, there were two thin strips of metal connecting them. They were hinges, I realized.

Hinges!

Hinges meant something was meant to open, right?

I quickly walked over the grate to the other side of 45th Street and made a left and walked east down to Lexington Avenue counting my steps. I was at 104 when I got to the corner, and then I made a right and counted out 311 more steps from the corner to the Grand Central entrance at 43rd Street.

I hooked another right and entered the station at what was known on the Grand Central map as the Graybar Passage. Now with the shoulder-to-shoulder packed rush hour crowd in the corridor, I started counting my paces again only this time backward from 104.

When I got to zero, I stopped and turned to my right.

13 Track 13, it said on the marble above an opening.

I smiled.

But I didn't head down onto the track platform. Not yet. I headed farther into the Main Concourse and stood by the wall of the east balcony just observing.

How many people were there? I wondered. Several thousand easily, all moving and crisscrossing in a nonstop flow. I closed my eyes. The muffled reverberation of the countless steps was almost soothing in the vastness of the soaring vaulted interior like the calming rush of a mountain stream.

When I opened them, I oriented myself using the compass app on my phone. North was to my right, south was to my left, east was to my back, and west was through the famous cathedral-like windows in front of me.

That was another advantage of using Grand Central Terminal for this. As it was basically the size of a town square, only inside a building, it really was very disorienting every time you went inside it. Just figuring out which direction you were headed was hard enough. Trying to track one person in the moving human jigsaw puzzle out on the concourse at the same time would truly take some doing.

I headed back to Track 13 and passed under the sign and paused for a second. Not surprisingly just on the other side of it, there was a video camera trained right on the stairs and two others trained on the two tracks that the platform bisected.

They would be a bit of a problem, I figured. Have to work on that.

Down the steps, I began to walk north up the platform under the bright overhead fluorescent lights. I noticed how the ceilings here were low, which didn't make sense. When I had seen the train through the grate from the street, it was at some distance. Did the ceiling open up at some point? It must.

The platform I was on was actually between two tracks, Track 13 on the left and Track 11 on the right. There was already a waiting train in Track 11, and as I continued to walk, a train loudly clattered into Track 13.

The train stopped and the doors whooshed open and passengers began to disembark around me. Trying to keep my count on my paces, I almost bumped into a blonde tourist mom holding two blonde tourist sons by the hand and then a bald old man lugging a North Face backpack as I continued in a dead straight line like a fish swimming upstream.

As I neared the ends of the two parked trains, I noticed that though the overhead fluorescents ended, the platform kept on going north into a spooky unlit area past them.

I was still about thirty paces off my count when I reached the edge of the lit part of the platform past the trains so I walked into the darkness another ten feet, stopped, and stood looking.

All of Grand Central had the smoky sweet burnt-wood scent of train tracks, but here it was weapons grade. As my eyes adjusted, I could see that the tunnel opened up into a wider subterranean complex with other tracks out there, a confusing maze of them with pillars here and there along with constellations of track lights. In the distance, the dark concrete walls that the lights illuminated looked like the shafts of a mine, or who knew, maybe the tunnel passageways to hell itself.

I was still staring at the hot, smelly underground highway to hell five minutes later when about twenty feet farther into the dark of the tunnel from where I was standing, I noticed there was a column in the center of the platform ahead.

I stared at it. My pace count was about right where it was located. Did it have something to do with the grate?

As I walked over to it, I first thought it was just a solid concrete column but when I came around the front of it, I saw there was a doorway-size opening in it that looked like the firebox of a large fireplace.

Then I flicked the flashlight on my cell phone and saw the ladder rungs embedded in the opening's back wall.

"OMG!" I said as I stuck my head in and looked up and saw the bars of daylight from the street grate thirty feet above.

It was the 45th Street grate! I'd found it!

The column on the platform wasn't just a column. It was some kind of an emergency fire exit out of the tunnels with the grate opening up onto 45th as some kind of escape hatch.

I stared up at the grate. Bars of light from the street were actually streaming through it the way you see light sometimes coming through a stained-glass window.

We would definitely be able to open it, I thought.

I stuck my head out of the opening and looked out of the shadows back toward the light of the platform.

And I couldn't even be seen here, I realized.

It was perfect. Perfect!

This would work, I thought, rushing back toward the trains and light before someone spotted me.

Holy shit, this would really work, I thought. This was set up on a tee.

39

Two days later at lunch, I was back in Grand Central Station at the end of the platform between Tracks 41 and 42 this time. Beyond the end of the platforms north in the tunnel, all the upper-level tracks went alongside each other. So, if I picked up the money in the shadows of the 11/13 platform, instead of coming straight back up that platform, I could head north and then cross over the tracks and come back on *another* platform.

As trains came in and out constantly, I figured I could even time it so that I came back into the Main Concourse with a fresh load of passengers.

All the extra running around was necessary to avoid the cameras at the platform stairs. They would definitely see me going up platform 11/13. But they wouldn't see me come back out. If I came back into the Main Concourse on another platform with a crowd, especially dressed differently, it would be a nightmare to find me.

They wouldn't even know *if* I had come out. They might even figure I just headed north up the tracks into the maze of the train tunnels. They'd be completely stumped.

That's why I was here now.

It was time for a test run.

My phone was in my hand, and I lifted it to my ear when it finally rang.

"Yes?" I said.

"I'm in the lobby now," said a woman's voice. "Are you here yet?"

"I'm close by. Just give me a minute," I said.

After I hung up, I flicked open the stopwatch app on my phone.

"And they're off," I said as I pressed it and headed up the platform.

I went at a slow, steady pace down the platform, slowing even more at the stairs as if I were carrying something. I came up the stairs and out into the corridor and made a left.

Thirty feet up, I entered into the dull roar of the Main Concourse with its mingling crowd teeming with crisscrossing people. I wove my way through them as I passed by the entrances of several other tracks. Midway in the concourse between the track entrances were stairs and an escalator.

To MetLife Building and 45th Street, it said on the marble above.

I headed under the sign and onto the escalator and went up.

At the top was the MetLife Building corridor that let commuters out onto 45th Street, but right in front of where you opened the door was another escalator that I got on.

This escalator was for workers in the MetLife Building itself, and when I arrived at the top of it and saw a security guard by the turnstile before the elevators, I stopped and clicked off my timer and smiled.

Just under three minutes.

It would take me just under three short minutes to get from the money drop to here.

And then I'd be gone, I thought.

A sixtysomething fireplug of a woman with owl-like glasses was standing behind the security guard, playing with her phone.

I slipped on a pair of the biggest most obnoxious fake Chanel glasses that I could find on Canal Street and then popped a piece of gum in my mouth as I approached her. The glasses and gum went with the too-tight skirt and too-flashy silk blouse and extra makeup I was wearing to complete my bridge and tunnel look.

"Ms. Bernardi," I said, chewing. I didn't know how to do a Jersey accent, but I did know how to make myself sound less southern.

"That's me," she said, glancing quickly up from her phone. "Ms. Miller, right? You ready?"

"Ready," I said.

The turnstile arm dropped as she placed an electronic badge atop the reader. We walked over to a waiting elevator and stepped in, and she hit 54.

"Did you get the cashier's check? I messengered it over," I said as we quickly ascended.

It was a fourteen-thousand-dollar check. Seven thousand a month plus a one-month deposit for a thousand square feet. Manhattan office space was not cheap, but for my purposes, worth every penny.

"Yes, thank you," Ms. Bernardi said as she looked up from her phone. "You guys are in quite the hurry, aren't you?"

"Well, my bosses saw the property online and liked it so much and didn't want to lose it."

"What does this Lemongrass Holdings do again?" she said.

"It's a Caribbean Investment Fund that's trying to get a footprint in Manhattan. That's what my cousin told me."

"What does it invest in, if I might ask?"

"I'm not sure," I said. "Probably stocks and bonds? I'm like, you know, just assisting on a freelance basis for now with a chance of being hired on permanent. They just wanted me to facilitate a few things for them. Get the ball rolling on an office. That sort of thing. I got the job from my cousin. She works with them at Goldman. They're a client of hers."

"Goldman Sachs?"

"Yeah, that's right. I think that's the name of it."

"Great firm. Where do you work now?"

"Me? I work at a tire store in Parsippany."

"Gotcha," Ms. Bernardi said, going back to her phone.

"But I'm hoping to get on permanent like I said."

"Uh-huh," she said.

On the other side of the elevator door on fifty-four was a rather drab-looking corridor with beige doors on both sides. Ms. Bernardi led me down the right-hand end of the hallway and around a corner.

"And here's suite 5412," she said, keying open a door.

Now I understood why it was so expensive. It had floor-to-ceiling windows and the view straight up Park Avenue was spectacular, like you were in an airplane.

I walked to the window and looked north at the trees of Central Park. From this height, the buildings of the East Side and Midtown before it looked like the tops of giant chess pieces in a tightly clinched match. One where all the pawns had already been removed from the board.

I took a deep breath.

Well, not all of them, I thought.

It was crazy, but instead of feeling nervous right there and then, I didn't.

And with impersonating people and cobbling together fake companies and stashing several million dollars in stolen cash in a closet uptown, I definitely had some reasons to be.

But I didn't feel nervous at all.

I felt proud of myself.

I was so close now, I thought. So close now, it wasn't even funny.

"Wow, I'm dizzy," I said. "No wonder it's so expensive."

"Well, you get what you pay for, honey," Ms. Bernardi said.

I imagined her on a witness stand swearing that it was me that she rented this office to.

Then I imagined myself with my hair not blown out, not dressed like a tramp, and wearing no makeup simply denying it.

One of the main reasons why I had decided to actually go through with this was the audacity of it. I was wised up enough to know that even with all my cutouts and blinds, there was a chance someone might figure it out and come after me and I might be sitting in a courtroom.

That's why my cover didn't need to be airtight, I knew. It just needed to be jam-packed with lots and lots of that reasonable doubt that juries are instructed to consider. In the end, I had to create a situation that, if it came down to it, a jury might have a little evidence but not enough. Put on the stand in my own defense, I would play the saddest most confused little Kentucky coal miner's daughter they ever saw.

But it wasn't even going to come to that.

At least I hoped not.

No risk, no reward, I thought.

"Here's the electronic badge and the key to the suite. Anything else I can do for you, sweetie?" Ms. Bernardi said, laying them on the low windowsill.

"Not a thing," I said. "Thanks so much."

"Will you come back down with me?" she asked at the door.

"No, thank you," I said, checking my watch. "I'm waiting on a delivery."

It came ten minutes later.

"This Lemongrass Holdings?" said a voice from the still-open suite door.

A white guy in Dickies wearing glasses came in. There was a large machine on a dolly behind him.

"Yes, that's right. In here, please," I said.

"This is some printer," said the delivery guy, rolling it in.

I smiled as I looked at the industrial shredder I'd rented that afternoon.

"Over there in the corner is fine," I said as I popped some more gum.

40

One team was wearing red and white and the other was in green and gold and as we watched, everybody went nuts as a green-and-gold guy booted the ball through the uprights above the goal.

It was after work and we were up in Cavan's neighborhood, way up in the north Bronx, at a field that was beside another terminal, for the Number One subway line.

After I got home from work, I found Cavan and another buddy of his, named Jockey, waiting in Jockey's car in front of my Chinatown apartment to take Caitlin and me to see Jockey's brother play a game of Irish football at a place called Gaelic Park.

"So, that's one point, right?" my sister said as we sat in the stands.

We were eating french fries, or chips as Cavan called them, from a cart outside and washing them down with plastic cups of ice-cold tap beer from a bar that was attached to the field.

I didn't know which was more delicious or refreshing, the salty fries or the lager.

I smiled, watching Cavan watch the game.

I'd been hitting things so hard lately I had almost forgotten what unwinding felt like.

"So now we're ahead by one, right?" Caitlin said.

"Right. Good, lass," Cavan said. "Our team, representing the great county of Meath, is still holding on by the skin of its teeth."

"Well said," added Jockey, who was on the other side of Caitlin. "You're a right poet, Cavan. A gentleman and a scholar."

Jockey was a short cute straw-haired Irishman who was very sarcastic and lively. A colorful character, Cavan called him.

"Six to five?" Caitlin said.

"That's right. You're paying attention," Cavan said, elbowing me. "Much better than your elder sister here. It took me weeks to teach her the rules."

"And I still don't know them," I said, smiling as I elbowed him back.

"So, you're saying they don't have Gaelic football down there in Kentucky?" Jockey said to Caitlin with a wink. "Is that right? It can't be."

If truth be told, the whole purpose of the afternoon was a bit of a double date setup between Caitlin and Cavan's younger buddy and roommate.

"No," Caitlin said. "We just have the regular kind of football in Kentucky."

"Regular?" Jockey said.

"You know, the Friday night kind with helmets."

"Impossible," Jockey said. "How about hurling? You must have hurling."

Jockey winked again. He was referring to the other even crazier Gaelic sport that was like a mix between lacrosse and golf, only the clubs were swung near people's heads.

"Hurling? Oh, sure," Caitlin said, winking herself. "There's lots of hurling. That usually takes place after the parties when people drink too much."

We were laughing at that when the ball suddenly came sailing down out of the sky straight at us.

"I got this," Cavan cried as he leapt to his feet and hopped off the stands. But Jockey was there a step quicker.

Jockey went to kick it, but Cavan blocked the kick and we all laughed as he kicked the ball back himself.

"Now that's how it's done, son," Cavan said, slipping his hand into mine as he sat back down.

"It's nice to see you laughing," he said in my ear. "Nice to see you at all with the way you've been going with that damn job."

I'd told him there had been a special project at work that was making me stay late and on weekends. I wasn't even lying.

"It'll be over soon. I promise, Cavan. All part of the Plan like I said. I just need to nail this down."

"You and your plan," he said. "You're maybe not the only one with a plan, you know? Others can have secret special plans for people."

I felt my heart swell in my chest as he said this.

A secret plan of his own? What did he mean? Could it be?

I had never even brought up the M word with Cavan or even the E word.

But Cavan knew. Of course, he did. He saw right through me. He could read my thoughts.

No, it was even better than that, I knew.

He could read my heart.

"What sort of plan?" I said, looking at the mischief in his eyes.

"It wouldn't be secret plan if I revealed it, now, would it?" he said, rubbing his palms together. "It's just between me and Lily for now."

We went inside into the field bar after the game where they were playing Irish music. One side of the bar was open to the field, and it was such a wonderful feeling to drink in its shadows and to hear the beautiful fiddling while we looked out at the sunset light glowing gold on the grass and stands.

Caitlin, sitting beside me, suddenly squeezed my hand.

"Thank you, Faye," she said in my ear.

"For what?"

"For this," she said, gesturing at the gold-lit field, at the smiling and laughing people around us.

"This is really nice. So sweet and fun and exciting. It's just wonderful."

"Then why are you crying?" I said, looking at her.

"Because it's all so beautiful," she said.

"That's the Guinness talking," I said. "How many have you had?"

"No," she said, wiping at a tear as she kissed me on the cheek. "You're the greatest big sister...ever. You got out, away from Gramma, and came up here and made this...this wonderful life for yourself and you didn't forget me. You didn't forget me. I was worried that you would forget me."

"Never," I said, crying myself now.

Don't you worry, little sister, I felt like telling her as I thought of the week coming up.

Crying time is about to be over for the both of us forever and ever amen.

41

Four very busy days passed like I was operating on autopilot and then it was time.

Thursday night at two o'clock in the morning in a white Tyvek suit and gloves with my hair up under a white plastic hard hat and wearing sunglasses, I was behind the wheel of a van rolling north on Avenue B beside Tompkins Square Park downtown.

The van was a 2000 Ford E350 Super Duty bought on Ebay from a private seller in Allentown, Pennsylvania, and delivered by uShip to a street parking spot on Riverside Drive. Like the equipment now stored in the back of it—a traffic barrel, a huge foldable work tent, traffic cones and stanchions, orange traffic tape, pry bars and other tools—it had been purchased online by the fictitious Lemongrass Holdings of 28 Walkers Road, Georgetown, Cayman Islands.

The van and all of the rest of it was squeaky clean with no electronic trace to me or Gareth. We hadn't even used our own addresses to get the equipment or the van keys by utilizing the in-store pickup service at various UPS stores around the city.

As I came up on the next block, I saw Gareth where he said he'd be, sitting on the steps of a brownstone church by East 8th Street, pretending to be zonked out.

At least, I hoped he was pretending.

I took a breath as I slowed down.

The moment had come.

My first fake kidnapping was underway.

I actually jumped the van up on the curb a little as I brought it to a screeching stop in front of Gareth. Then I put it in Park and hurried back into the cargo area and threw open the side doors.

Gareth, now standing on the other side of them, winked at me as I rushed back for the driver's seat.

"Hey, yo! What is this? Get off me!" he yelled.

He slapped at the inside of the van's door loudly as if he was struggling with someone as I slid back behind the wheel and gave him a thumbs-up that I was ready.

"No! Get off me! Help! Help!" he yelled as he kicked the door a few times more loudly and then threw himself into the van. He slammed the two swing doors loudly behind himself as I peeled out around the corner onto 8th Street, racing east.

I made the left at Avenue C and waited until we were on the FDR Drive heading north before I turned around.

"How do you think we did?" I said to Gareth who was putting on his own Tyvek suit over his clothes.

"I was about to ask you," he said.

I laughed.

"I loved the 'help' yell," I said. "That was pretty authentic."

"Too much gusto?" he said.

"No, perfect. Question is, did someone hear it?"

"That's no question at all," Gareth said. "There's a village of junkies living in the park right along the fence across from St. Brigid's. Half of them are paid snitches for the precinct cops. When this drops, they'll race each other to tattle about it."

"I hope you're right," I said.

He laughed as he looked at all the equipment around him.

"I can't believe you put all this together. Bought all this stuff online and even the van. You are one diabolical young lady!"

"I'm just getting started, Gareth. Midtown exit coming up. Put your sunglasses and hard hat on and keep your head down."

42

We got off the FDR at 42nd Street just before the United Nations and came up and made a right onto 3rd Avenue and drove up three blocks to East 45th and made the left.

And then two minutes later, we were there.

I slowed and pulled the van over the grate underneath the Park Avenue viaduct pass and stopped.

"How we looking?" I said to Gareth, who was peering out the tinted rear windows.

"Give it another foot."

I inched forward.

"There you go," he said, and I put it in Park.

This next part was a little tricky but like everything else in Plan C, I'd managed to come up with a solution.

The area around Grand Central Terminal being pretty much dead center of the biggest city in the world, there were obviously a lot of cameras around capable of viewing the spot where we were now stopped.

I'd already taken care of the van plates by removing the Pennsylvania ones and replacing them with fake temporary New York

State in-transit vehicle permits that I'd printed out. They were faker than a three-dollar bill, but if we got pulled over then the whole thing would be over anyway so it was worth the risk.

What was more of an issue was not being spotted during the setup. How could we possibly open a street grate that was most likely under surveillance?

That was where the collapsible giant work tent came in.

Gareth opened the back doors and we walked the tent out in front of us, and it popped fully open like an automatic umbrella. We quickly tied its sides to the bumper and van door hinges with its guy ropes.

Standing on the street inside the tent, I smiled when we were done. Now no one on the street outside—and more importantly no cameras—could see us or what we were doing.

"Now for the moment we've all been waiting for," I whispered as I started pulling out the huge pry bars. I handed Gareth one and knelt down and looked at the hinges.

"This side," I said, pointing.

The pry end of each bar just barely fit into the gap, and we placed them at the top and bottom of the edges of the grate.

"On three, okay?" I said as we each stood holding the upright bars.

"One, two, three."

We hauled back and the pry bars slipped out of our hands with a tremendous clang as the grate swung up immediately with almost no resistance at all.

"Yes!" Gareth whispered, pumping his fist.

We stood at the edge of the now-open grate, staring down into the street. I grabbed a flashlight and showed Gareth the rusted escape hatch ladder rungs embedded in the concrete wall beneath us. As we stood staring, a train pulled out of Track 11 thirty feet below. Gareth looked at it, shaking his head.

"Unbelievable," he said.

"Now for the finishing touch," I said, pulling out the orange-and-white-striped traffic barrel.

I'd already cut the lid off it, and it fit almost perfectly over the open hole.

When we had it weighted down with sandbags, we both looked up at the roof of the tent above it.

"Just drop it right off the viaduct into the hole," he said. "Swish."

"Uh-huh. Two points, no net," I said. "And I'll be down there to catch it."

"So easy even an FBI agent could do it," Gareth said with a laugh as we broke out the rest of the cones to finish setting up the area.

43

It took us another ten minutes to secure the area around where the cylinder of the traffic barrel now lay atop the open grate like a chimney on top of the escape hatch.

Around its perimeter, we laid out a wall of orange traffic cones and stanchions and wrapped it all in orange tape. After we were done, we untied the tent and got into the back of the van. Slowly and carefully, we collapsed the tent so as not to disturb the cones, and pulled it in after us and closed the van doors.

"How does the work area look?" I said back to Gareth by the rear window as I got behind the wheel.

"Like it belongs there," Gareth said, punching his thigh. "Like it's been there for a year."

We headed straight as an arrow west to the West Side Highway. We went north then until we reached the Cross Bronx Expressway east. We got off at the Major Deegan Expressway south and two exits past Yankees Stadium, I got off into the south Bronx.

I drove around for a bit listening to Gareth's directions. The neighborhood was an industrial section of the south Bronx near the Harlem River known as Mott Haven. We drove past a FedEx facility, a block of warehouses, a barbed-wire-wrapped parking lot filled with moving vans and taxis.

Past an overpass on East 138th Street, Gareth told me to make a right onto a narrow run-down street called Cornell Avenue.

We passed several abandoned-looking tenement buildings with Spanish cerveza billboards attached to them.

Beyond the tenements was a lumberyard and just after that, where the road dead-ended near the Major Deegan, was a windowless stucco building about the size of a car wash with a parking lot next to it with an unlit neon sign above it.

The Bellaire Club.

The structure had a green awning on the street side but as we rolled up, I saw that underneath it instead of a door was a graffiti-covered steel shutter with a padlock.

"Kill the lights and drive around the side," Gareth said, pointing.

"You're sure nobody knows about this place?" I said as we pulled in front of a side steel door. "Your father won't think to look for you here?"

He laughed.

"Um, no," he said. "This one is my little secret. Pull up by the side door there."

I pulled the van in tight. Gareth hopped out and slipped the key in.

"See? Still fits," he said, coming back for the flashlight and the two bags of groceries I'd gotten for him.

"What time you got?" I said.

Gareth checked the burner phone I had given him.

"Coming on three."

"Okay. I'll call around eight. Get some sleep but don't forget to wake up for this next part."

He laughed again.

"Forget? I wouldn't miss this next part for the world."

44

I retraced the streets back onto the Major Deegan north and got onto the Cross Bronx Expressway and headed north until it became I-95 and I took it through the Bronx into Connecticut.

When I pulled into the first rest stop over the border, it was three thirty in the morning. I drove to a darkened corner of the massive lot and got out and ripped off the fake temporary tags and screwed the original Pennsylvania ones back on. Since the van was paid for and not reported stolen and had been sold privately, it could sit there in the rest stop for months or maybe forever before somebody noticed it, I knew.

Instead of an Uber, I called an Arecibo Car Service because it took cash. After I buried the van in the more frequented part of the lot closer to the pumps, it was waiting for me by the rest stop entrance itself.

I told the driver, a sixtysomething Indian gentleman, to take me to the White Plains train station, but after I paid him, instead of getting on the next train back into the city, I called another car service that drove me back instead.

It was all about covering my tracks now. Making it as hard

as possible for them to pick up a scent. And even if they did, they would lose it.

I had the car drop me off a block from my Morningside Heights apartment, and I went inside and upstairs and took a shower and came out and laid out my clothes and set the alarm for seven.

45

I thought I would have trouble sleeping, but I had gone right out and when the alarm woke me up, I actually felt refreshed and ready to go.

I put on workout stuff so that my Yankee hat and sunglasses made more sense, and I walked out to Amsterdam Avenue and hailed a cab. I had the taxi dump me out at Broadway and Wall Street, and I jogged south to the end of Broadway and went across Bowling Green into Battery Park.

I caught the next Staten Island Ferry and sat on the right-hand side of it, watching the morning sun lighting up the Statue of Liberty.

I was starving by the time the boat arrived at the St. George Ferry Station on Staten Island, and I went into its very nice mall-like concourse and got a bacon, egg, and cheese on a roll and a cup of coffee from a gourmet deli.

It was almost eight when I was done, and I went into the ladies' room and put on my office attire and came out and lifted my burner phone and called Gareth.

"You ready for this?" I said as I followed the concourse into a stairwell that led to the parking lot.

No one parked at the top level, so I had the covered part at the top of the stairwell all to myself. I had scoped out the secluded little spot two weeks before. I was going to need some privacy now without any cameras on me.

"Let's do it," Gareth said.

I took a deep breath as I arrived near the top landing of the stairwell and sat on the concrete steps.

I flicked on the voice changer app before I called the number for Gareth's father's personal cell phone. The voice changer app was already on a setting called Bad Alien that made me sound at the same time menacing and genderless. It was impossible to tell who I was.

"Hello?" said Robert Haynes in a somewhat sleepy voice.

"Is this Mr. Haynes. Mr. Robert Haynes?" I said.

My disguised voice came out even weirder and lower and more intimidating than I thought.

"What in the world?" Robert Haynes said.

"Listen very closely. This is not a prank. Do not hang up your phone. We have your son, Gareth. We have kidnapped your son, Gareth. Do you understand?"

"What?"

"Wake up, Mr. Haynes," I said. "We have your son, Gareth. Listen!"

I placed the phone to my burner phone.

"Dad! Oh no! Oh, Dad!" Gareth said on cue. "Dad, these guys! These guys! Please! You have to help me!"

"Gareth? Is that you? What is this? What are you up to now?" Robert Haynes said.

"Dad! Please listen! These men grabbed me, Dad!" he whimpered. "This isn't a joke, Dad. I'm naked, Dad. They took my clothes."

"What!" Robert Haynes cried, finally awake now.

"They have guns, Dad. They're going to shoot me. You have

to help me, Dad. They kidnapped me. Please give them whatever they want. I don't want to die."

"What is this? A joke?" Robert Haynes asked.

But his voice rose higher as he said this. He sounded afraid. Crazed. He seemed to be in shock.

"A joke, you stupid old man?" I cut in. "Listen carefully to the punch line."

I placed the phone back to Gareth's.

"NOOOOO! AHHHHHGH!" Gareth screamed with unholy fury.

Then I hung up, cutting off the call.

"How does he sound to you?" I said to Gareth.

He laughed.

"Like he doesn't know whether to shit or go blind, the rat bastard. How am I doing? Convincing?"

"Extremely," I said.

"You should hear yourself," Gareth said.

Gareth did not like his father. No one did, he had said. Robert Haynes was a very vicious and ruthless person who had, in his rise to the top of Manhattan real estate, gleefully fired people for the least offenses and had destroyed several business partners by not paying them what they had agreed on, thereby driving them into bankruptcy. Gareth figured that our caper and deception against him would only be giving his father a tiny dose of a bitter medicine that he had lovingly administered to others.

But for the first time in the whole plan as I sat there in the parking lot stairwell, I was suddenly unsure.

It was how Robert Haynes sounded. Like a frightened old man. We really had terrified him. He had to be scared out of his mind.

We were tormenting him, I realized. Despite his faults and supposedly bad character, he was a real person, and I was tormenting him for money.

Toughen up, said another voice inside of me. *Feel bad about it later when you're rich*.

We waited a minute before I called Robert Haynes back on a second burner.

"Do I have your attention?" I said in the alien voice. "Did you listen to your son or should we hurt him again?"

"No, no, please," Robert Haynes said. "What is it? What do you...what do you want?"

"What do you think we want? Money. This is a kidnapping. We are professionals. We receive the money, your kid goes free. We don't, he dies. It is very simple."

"I don't... I don't understand."

"We do not expect you to understand, Mr. Haynes. You are a very wealthy man. To deal with such matters, there are specialists in these situations. Lawyers. We have dealt with such people many times."

This hogwash and the kind of affectation I was putting on came from a documentary I'd seen on YouTube about cartel kidnappings of rich people in Mexico. Why couldn't they move up to New York and do it? Seemed plausible to me.

"You have to find one who has negotiated matters such as these. Do you understand?"

"Yes."

"We will call in thirty minutes. Have such a lawyer standing by."

46

Thirty minutes passed. Thirty long minutes. This part was a little dicey as I wasn't sure if they could set up with a trace in so short a time. Whether they could or not, I would have to be quick.

I was still sitting in the stairwell of the parking garage when I dialed Robert Haynes's number with my third burner phone.

"This is Attorney Albert Maxwell," a voice told me. "I'm representing Robert Haynes. What do I call you?"

"I don't give a shit what you call me, counselor," I said in my bad alien Mexican cartel voice. "I only give a shit that you pay me. Ten million dollars in cash. Today. I repeat, today. Or Gareth Haynes will be killed. Very, very painfully."

"Ten million dollars is outrageous!" Maxwell cried. "How can such a large amount of cash be acquired?"

"Mr. Maxwell, do you think we are fools? Like you, I, too, am a professional. This sum can indeed be acquired within an hour for a family like the Hayneses. I know this from personal experience. No police. No FBI. You have until noon today to acquire this money. At that time, you will be given instructions where to deliver it. Or not."

"Or not?"

"Or not and we'll kill Haynes's son and move on to someone else. There are many wealthy families in this town. Do you think we care which one pays us? Now get cracking. Time is money, counselor."

"But that's too much money and too little time."

"Fine. Then Gareth Haynes will die."

I clicked off the line and then stood and ran out into the parking lot.

It fronted the harbor itself, and I ran over and tossed the burner phone into the water.

"Trace that," I said.

"Hahaha!" Gareth cried from the other phone as I started down the stairs for my car that was waiting by the terminal entrance. "You were awesome!"

"You think?"

"Hello? That crazy menacing voice? You sounded like Pablo Escobar's go-to hit man."

I laughed myself a little then. The voice changer really did sound terrifying.

"I was in the zone, wasn't I?" I said. "How are you doing?"

"Me? I'm fine. I'm chillin' like Bob Dylan. Catching up on my reading. I haven't even opened the Pringles yet. Don't worry about me. You're the one who has to do the heavy lifting now. Your day has only just begun."

"You're telling me," I said. "Barring any disasters, this is it until Halloween, Gareth."

We had already decided to let things cool a few months before we met to split up the money.

"Halloween it is. Now get in there to work and kill it, partner," Gareth said.

47

I walked into my GBH basement office at a little after nine.

I'd done my research on how the FBI handled kidnappings.

A lot of the effort in the beginning on their end would be verifying the complaint, talking to witnesses, confirming everything. They'd be all over Gareth's social media which was virtually nonexistent in the last couple of years. Next, they would interview Gareth's family to see if there was anything specific going on in Gareth's life that might have prompted the kidnapping and to make sure the family themselves didn't have anything to do with it.

Gareth had said his sister, Scarlet, knew that he sometimes stayed in Tompkins Square Park so the Feds would likely contact the local precinct and hopefully pick up on the tip about Gareth and the van from the local snitches. After that, they would do a neighborhood canvass and probably try to get a surveillance camera recording to confirm that the kidnapping was legit.

Once all that was done, they would establish a command center at the Haynes residence and put a trap-and-trace on their phones to record incoming calls. It was only then that they would talk about the family's options.

Options such as whether to use the kidnapping insurance ransom money from Greene Brothers Hale.

For a regular family with a kidnapped child, all this work by the FBI would probably take at least a few days. But for a family as connected as the Haynes, I was thinking five or six hours.

But I was wrong.

It took less than two hours for all hell to bust loose.

My desk phone rang at 10:41 on the dot.

"Walker?" said a voice.

It was Aiken. I thought he would be here, but he was up at a meeting at the GBH offices in White Plains all morning.

"Yes?" I said.

"Walker, drop everything. Something incredibly gigantic has come up."

"Should I put on the speakerphone for the rest of the team?"

"No, no. Don't do that. In fact, hang up the desk phone and go into my office and call me back on your cell. Do it now."

My eyes went big as I stood and crossed the room.

"What's up?" McPhee said, glancing at me as I passed.

"Beats me," I lied, shrugging.

Here we go, I thought as I went into Aiken's office. I sat at his desk and took out my phone and dialed.

"Okay, Walker. Real quick now. When I was away, they gave you the vault tour, right? The vault down the hall?"

"The vault with the lockboxes? Yes. Paulina showed me."

"Okay. Here's the story. And you cannot—and I mean not, not—breathe a word of this to anyone. Do you understand? No other team members, no one."

"Of course. What is it?"

"There's been a kidnapping."

"What!?"

"I know. Calm down. Just listen, Walker. One of our clients' kids has been kidnapped and the kidnappers are demanding ransom, and long story short, the FBI is on their way right now to you to pick up the kidnapping insurance money out of the vault."

I stifled a smile. Holy shit. It was working. Wow.

"Oh, my goodness!" I said. "The money in the suitcases. Of course. I remember. This is horrific. Who's the client? Who got kidnapped?"

"It's...that doesn't matter," Aiken said. "What really matters is I'm an hour away and even Paulina is with me and the Feds will be there in ten minutes and you are going to have to open the vault for them."

My initial delight at my plan falling into place exactly the way I wanted dissipated as I let out a very real nervous breath.

I had been counting on Aiken to deal with the Feds. Now I had to do it. I didn't know if that was good. I didn't think so. The farther away from this I was, the better. But now I was going to be center stage.

"Um, okay. Open the vault. Got it. What about the key? Do you have the key?"

"It's in my desk drawer, left-hand side."

Right-hand side, you mean, dummy, I thought as I faked looking for it.

"I don't see it!" I said, pretending to panic.

"Oh, shit. No, sorry. Right-hand side."

"Okay," I said, letting out an audible breath. "Now I see it," I said, pulling the drawer.

"It's in your hand?"

"Yes. Now what do I do? Should I go up to the lobby and tell security?"

"No! Listen, Faye. No building security. No Marvin. He is to have nothing to do with this. The FBI is going to come down the back elevator through the service entrance, okay? The staff doesn't even know they are FBI. We need to keep this as low-key as possible. Go out into the hallway and wait by the vault door. They are going to be there in about five minutes."

"I'm going."

"Don't hang up."

I left Aiken's office and opened the door into the hall and walked over and stood next to the vault door.

"Okay. I'm here next to the vault door."

"Good. I'm just getting the text. They are there. Look lively, Faye. We're on our way back to the city. We'll be there as soon as possible."

"Wait. Boss?" I said.

"What?"

"Do they have to like sign something or do I give them a receipt? Is there some kind of protocol?"

"No, no. Just open the vault and give both suitcases to them."

"But it's a lot of money, right? Shouldn't we—"

"It's ten million dollars, Walker. This is big league stuff, okay? Take a deep breath. This is no-bullshit, life-and-death stuff we're dealing with so don't screw this up."

48

The FBI agents actually took another ten minutes before entering the hall from the service workers side of the corridor.

They were two tall men in surprisingly nice dark blue suits. One was older fifties and outdoorsy with executive hair, and the other one was about thirty-five and very slim and had nicely cut short hair and was surprisingly athletic and handsome. They were both neater and more stylish than what I was expecting.

Watching them approach, I wondered if the FBI had some sort of special team for dealing with the superrich. Because these guys were almost as intimidatingly polished as Dabertrand. They could have worked on Wall Street themselves.

"Hi. Faye Walker? I'm Agent White and this is Agent Conrad," the older outdoorsy one said, casually flashing his credentials.

"Hi," I said, swallowing as I turned the lock. "Here's the, uh, vault."

I flicked on the lights inside and led them in through the hobbit door of the vault itself.

"Okay, uh, let's see. You need, um, the, uh…"

"The money, yes," the intimidating country-club-golf-pro-looking Agent White said, snapping at me. "The ten million dollars. That's what we're here for. We're not here to open an account."

"This way," I said, heading over to the little jail cell bars at the back.

As I was about to slip the key into the lock, I suddenly dropped the key ring with a loud jangle.

Because there was a single dollar-bill-sized piece of blank printer paper sticking out from underneath one of the cases.

"New hands?" said the older agent, rolling his eyes. "We don't have all day, honey. I don't know if you've ever heard of kidnapping, but it's sort of a life-and-death thing. There's kind of a time element here."

The younger handsome one, Agent Conrad, rushed forward and helpfully lifted up the key ring for me just before I could get it.

"Don't listen to him, Faye," he whispered with a wink as he handed the keys back. "We're all a little hyped up here. You're doing great. Just slow down and take all the time you need."

"Okay," I said, unlocking the cell door.

I was just about to step on the paper as I handed out the first case when I suddenly saw that it was okay. It wasn't one of my counterfeit paper blanks. It was just one of the deposit box receipts that had fallen from a shelf above.

I was being ultra paranoid, I realized.

I wonder why? I thought as I swept it into the corner of the little cell with the sole of my shoe as I handed out the second case.

"Okay, um, gentleman. Let's see. There's something else," I said as I took a little duffel bag off the shelf. There was a folder and what looked like two walkie-talkie units in it.

"In each rolling suitcase, there's five million dollars in one-hundred-dollar-bill denominations, and these two GPS units here," I said, blooping them on and pointing to the map on the screens that showed Madison Avenue, "are linked up with transponder units embedded in the bottom of each case."

This actually wasn't true. When I'd stolen the money two weeks ago, I'd moved all of the transponders into the case without the fake money in it. The case with the fake money blanks in it was gloriously transponder- and trace-free.

"Money Garmin, I like it," the younger Agent Conrad said, smiling, as I handed him the GPS devices.

Agent White glared at him.

"Yeah, uh-huh, thanks," he said. "And we were told the money is already marked? There's a list of the bills?"

"Yes. In the folder here in the bag," I said, handing over the sheet of random serial numbers I had replaced the real list with.

Doing the old switcheroo on the serial numbers had actually been easier than taking out the money itself.

I had full access to the bank's internal security programs through Aiken's password, and it was just a matter of deleting the entries in the Excel spreadsheet marked VAULT MONEY SERIAL NUMBERS.

Replacing the two hundred random serial numbers of the hundred-dollar bills in the cases with ones I had made up out of thin air had been my pleasure. It was the very least I could do.

"Okay then. We're out of here," Agent White said, grabbing the first case and rolling it out of the vault.

"Great job, Faye," Agent Conrad said as he grabbed the handle of the second rolling case. He suddenly offered me something. It was his card.

"If you have any questions," he said.

"Let's go, Conrad," Agent White called from the corridor.

"Duty calls," Conrad said.

But he lingered for a second, smiling at me.

"That accent. You're from the south, Faye, right? Where?"

"Kentucky," I said.

"I knew it. I'm from Texas. We southerners need to stick together in this crazy town. Maybe after all this, we could grab a drink or something," he said.

I looked at his stark chiseled Lance Armstrong smile. He seemed like a sweet talker all right. I'd met those.

Playing the stupid southern intern, I stared back as if starstruck.

"Oh, definitely. I'd like that," I said, pouring on the Kentucky moonshine as I hugged the card to my chest.

49

Without telling a soul, I left the office a minute after the FBI and went out and got a taxi on Madison.

I had the driver drop me off right out in front of the Morningside Heights apartment, and I ran upstairs and threw off my blouse and skirt.

I'd already laid out the little black dress I needed to wear now, and I quickly pulled it on and slipped on the gray raincoat that was next to it. I checked the coat pockets for the black wig and sunglasses before I pulled on my sneakers. Then I ran into the kitchen where I'd set out the last and most crucial item on my list.

I strapped the empty glossy black cello case to my back like a backpack and quickly headed out the door.

My wig and sunglasses were on by the time I left the building, and the first free cab I found was on the downtown side of Amsterdam.

"Grand Central," I said after I barely managed to get the bulky case into the back seat beside me.

Twenty-five minutes later, I got out and paid the driver and restrapped the cello case to my back and came into the terminal from the 42nd Street side.

I'd come down the slope into the Main Concourse when I spotted the first one. She was standing under the west balcony where my sister, Caitlin, and I had seen the little black girl playing the piano. Like me, she was wearing a gray raincoat and a black wig and sunglasses and had a cello case beside her.

Then when I passed the information booth, I saw the second one—same raincoat, same black wig, same sunglasses—wheeling her cello case to my left.

I'd hired them.

Those two along with ten others. They were all female, all cello players. They were to wait by the west balcony from eleven to two and when I party texted them, they were to toss off their raincoats to show their little black dresses and perform "With or Without You," the old classic U2 song.

Pretending to be a marketing firm, I'd told them the flash mob stunt was being filmed for a new music school app and was sure to go viral. They didn't seem to ask too many questions when I immediately Venmo'd each of them five hundred dollars up front.

It was for a stunt all right, but a music school had nothing to do with it.

Once that ten million dropped down through the escape hatch onto the 11/13 platform, who knew what the hell was going to happen? Not me.

That's why I was going to need a head fake. I needed to have all eyes looking at the west balcony while I was exiting stage left with the ransom.

I closed the distance to the Graybar Passage and then I was there.

I entered under the 13 Track 13 opening.

Hurrying down the stairs, the warm breeze of a train incoming onto Track 13 swept a newspaper up off the trestles and into the air in front of me close enough to make me duck.

I went to my right away from it as well as the gushing flood of passengers from the train's opening doors. Walking steadily with my head down, it took me two minutes to walk into the unlit shadows at the end of the platform.

And then a minute later, I was in the escape hatch staring up not at a grate this time, but at a square of wide-open blue sky edged just barely with the Park Avenue overpass.

I pulled on a pair of rubber gloves before I took out the first burner phone. I swallowed as I looked at it. This was going to be traced 100 percent. They were going to get a bead on me.

But just not a close enough one.

At least that was the theory.

No more time, I thought as I hit the button. Ball was in their court.

"Hello," said the lawyer, Maxwell. "We have the money."

"I know," I said in my bad alien kidnapper voice. "Listen to my instructions. Head straight to Washington Square Park. Take Fifth Avenue from Midtown and head south. Do not deviate. You have twenty minutes."

I hung up and turned off the first burner phone and dropped it into the large signal blocking Faraday bag I'd brought along. The copper-lined bag, one of the most expensive on Amazon, said it made cell signals impossible to track.

"Please be true," I mumbled, glancing up at the street.

As I waited, I saw that another train was heading in from the tunnels onto Track 11 on my right.

So that the driver wouldn't see me, I walked around the column of the escape hatch to the back of it and once the train passed, I walked back around into the opening again.

The Track 13 train had just begun to pull out beside me on my left when the timer was up.

I waited until the train was gone before I called on the second burner.

"Where are they?" I said in greeting.

"They are just pulling up before the monument."

"What is the money being carried in?"

"Suitcases. Rolling suitcases. There are two of them."

"What color are they?"

"Black."

"Tell them to roll down the passenger-side window and hold the cases up beside it."

"Do you want to see the cash itself?"

"No," I said. "I trust that Mr. Haynes is not dumb enough to play games as the result will be his son's death."

"Do you see them?"

"Excellent. Now tell them to go left on Waverly and back around to 8th Street and take 8th Street east to 4th Avenue and 4th Avenue to Park Avenue South. I will call back."

I bagged burner two and waited five minutes and hit the redial on burner three.

"Okay, they are there," the lawyer said.

"Tell them to drive north back to Midtown."

"Okay, they're doing it. What now?"

"Tell them to keep driving and pull over when they get to 38th."

I hung up and replaced burner three with burner four.

The train in Track 11 began to pull out. I waited until I saw its rear red running lights before I dialed.

"Are they there?" I said.

"Yes."

"Tell them to proceed north, calling out the cross streets as they pass them."

"Thirty-ninth," he said.

"Fortieth."

I waited.

"Forty-first," he said. "They say they are coming toward the overpass around Grand Central. Shall they stay on?"

"Yes," I said. "Tell them to go up on it. And go slowly. I don't care if they get honked at, they are to go slowly."

"Are we are getting close to the drop-off?"

Shit! What the hell was that supposed to mean? Had they triangulated me?

Ignore it, I told myself.

"No questions," I said. "Just tell them to go slow."

"They are on the ramp leading up going slowly."

"There are two turns on the overpass. Tell them to announce when they are at the second turn," I said.

"They're there."

"Do they see Grand Central on their left?"

"Yes."

"Tell them to pass it and go even slower now. In front of them, there is an old green painted metal overpass right before the third turn. They are to stop their car beside it on the right-hand side."

I waited.

I suddenly heard honking from directly above. I looked up at the blue square of sky.

Holy shit! It was happening now. They were right above me. It was really happening.

"Okay, they are stopped. I see them," I said. "Tell them to take the cases of money out of the car now."

"They are out with them."

I stepped out through the opening and stood to the side of the escape hatch in the shadows.

"Tell them to look over the overpass toward the north side of the street. In the street, there is a construction work area. Do they see it?"

"Yes."

"In the center of the work area is a garbage-can-like orange traffic cylinder that is directly beneath the overpass. They are to drop both suitcases of money from the overpass into the cylinder. Now, this is critical. So, listen carefully.

"They are not to miss! Each case must go directly into the cylinder. If they do not—if the cases land on the street or do not make their way into the cylinder—I will hang up this phone and Gareth Haynes will be killed and you will never find his body. No games. Got it?"

That's when I heard it.

A whistling whiff and then a very loud thump sounded from the escape hatch beside me.

And the first suitcase full of money tumbled out onto the platform.

With another whiff and a thump, the second one appeared and I hung up and peeled off the cello case and ran straight for them.

50

I dropped the cello case down onto the muck-coated concrete beside the cases and then knelt and pawed at the bottom of the first one.

Since the two cases were identical Maxlite Travel Pro Fives, in order to distinguish them, I had placed two simple strips of clear tape in an X-marks-the-spot on the bottom of the trick one with the three million in paper inside of it.

"Yes," I said as I found the tape on the first one and peeled it off.

Now for the tricky part, I thought as I unzipped the case and flipped it over and dumped the stacks of money and blanks onto the ground.

I opened the cello case and as quick as I could began tossing the packets of paper blanks into the case. It took less than a minute to toss in the three hundred fake money packets, but then I took another terribly precious minute knocking the rest of the real money around and across the concrete to make sure I didn't miss one blank.

Missing just one would be the end of it.

I hadn't.

I closed the cello case and zipped it. Leaving the two million splayed across the platform behind me, I grabbed the second unopened case with the five million and the two transponders and raced down the platform back toward the terminal.

I slowed a little as I came out into the lit part of the platform and I entered the first car of the train in Track 13. The car was completely empty, and I went to the first triple seats near the front and stuffed the suitcase with the five million in cash underneath the seats as far as it would go.

Quickly leaving the car, I hurried back into the shadows down to the escape hatch and lifted the cello case with the now sixty-six pounds of blank paper in it onto my back.

Then I walked past the two million in cash still sitting there, down the platform deeper into the tunnel.

Another fifty feet ahead, I stepped over a little chain at the end of the platform. On the other side was a small set of stairs leading down to the tracks themselves, and I headed down and looked to my left.

And groaned as I looked out at the dark sea of tracks before me.

Because now came a tricky part.

I had to get from Track 13 to Track 41 where I would come back into the Main Concourse.

Bad enough that the weight on my back was already making my knees a little wobbly, but I now had twenty-seven tracks to cross.

With twenty-seven third rails.

Like the subway, I knew that the Metro North trains also had third rails that were basically big fat live high-voltage electrical wires running alongside the tracks to power the trains.

Exposed on the side facing the tracks, if I tripped and made contact with one of them, it would be all over. When Cavan had pointed them out to me in the subway on one of our first dates, he'd said several people died every year in NYC by falling off the platform and accidentally coming into contact with them.

I was now going to hop twenty-seven third rails with almost seventy pounds on my back while dodging any incoming or outgoing trains!

I thought of a classic video game in the haunted arcade back in Chinatown called Frogger where a frog has to cross a busy highway.

Even that game didn't have a third rail that would fry you if you slipped. And in reality, you only got one life.

"Love Ms. Pacman, kids?" I mumbled crazily into the darkness of the tunnel.

"Now introducing, Ms. Frogger!"

But I couldn't get bogged down, I thought as I took an LED headlamp out of my pocket and pulled it over my wig.

The first of the seemingly endless line of tracks lit up as I clicked it on.

I didn't have the time.

But I did take my time. I was smart enough to do that. I wouldn't be able to enjoy my generous self-administered severance package if I was electrocuted to death now, would I?

At each of the raised third rails I looked both ways for any trains before I carefully stepped over them.

And I lucked out on the train traffic. As I passed the midway mark, I hadn't seen any coming in and out, and only when I was coming on Track 39 did I hear one clatter by in the far distance behind me. Then I was there at Track 41, and I crossed over it and started walking back for the platform.

There was a train in the Track 42 slot, I saw, as I climbed the stairs onto the platform. I hurried forward and I entered its first empty car, and I stood just inside its front door and threw down the heavy cello case trying to catch my breath.

"Shit, pay attention," I mumbled as I took off the headlamp and peeled off my gloves.

As I tucked them into the cello case's pocket, I felt for the wipes and napkins I had put there to clean myself up a little, and I scrubbed at the sweat on my face. Then I took off the raincoat itself and folded it and tucked it into the cello case compartment along with the wig. Out from another of its compartments came a NY Mets cap that I pulled on along with another slimmer pair of shades.

I looked at myself in the camera mirror of my burner phone like I was taking a selfie. In my little black dress now with my hair in a bun, I looked far different from the raincoated, black-wigged figure who had a few minutes before walked onto platform 11/13.

Just as I did this, I smiled as a train rolled into Track 42.

Anything else? I thought as its doors whooshed open.

Duh, I thought, flicking my burner to the text app with the flash mob numbers on it.

Begin now I typed and I hit send and stepped out onto the platform and headed for the stairs with the arriving crowd.

It took a minute to cross the platform and arrive at the stairs where I kept my head way down for the cameras.

But up top and walking along the right-hand side of the passage trying to act as calm and normal as possible, I suddenly panicked as there was some hubbub ahead.

I could feel my pulse in my neck as I noticed that people were packed together too closely.

Shit! Had the FBI gotten here already? Were they locking the place down?

No, of course not, it was just a regular pedestrian traffic jam, I saw with a smile.

A second later, the ocean of people parted, and I was in the hectic rush of the gloriously open Main Concourse under the slants of streaming cathedral window light.

I cut to my left straight along the fronts of the other tracks toward the MetLife escalator, and as I walked, I scanned right toward the west balcony.

The dozen girls I had hired were now at their places on the other side of the space before the balcony. They had their coats off and people were stopping to look at them.

"C'mon, c'mon," I said.

A crowd had gathered around them and as the first strains of "With or Without You" started, it seemed like everybody in the whole terminal paused for a split second to turn and watch.

It actually wasn't everybody, I suddenly noticed. Cops—antiterror cops—atop the west balcony and another team by the ticket counter in the slot that went out to 42nd were sweeping their binoculars over the crowd.

I'd never seen them do that before. Binoculars? Really?

But by then I had reached the escalator.

The MetLife Building 45th Street it said on the pale creamy marble arch I walked under, and I stepped onto the escalator and began to ascend.

51

After I left the dramatic soaring Main Concourse space, the rest of it was so routine it was practically boring.

I came out into the MetLife Building's lobby and continued up on the second escalator.

At the top, there wasn't even a security guard near the turnstile before the elevators this time, and I had the next elevator car all to myself all the way up to fifty-four.

In the office suite with the industrial shredder, I made short work of the fake paper bills and the three hundred real ones. It had a crosscutting feature that literally turned everything into a fine dust. My wig went next and even my raincoat and Mets cap and the two pairs of sunglasses.

Beside the suite's big picture window, there was a much smaller window that I opened a crack, and when I tossed all the evidence out in handfuls, it instantly dissipated in the wind above Park Avenue as if it had never existed at all.

Then it was over.

I slapped my hands clean of the dust and washed them in the suite's executive washroom. Then I put on a copy of the outfit

I had worn into work that morning, and twenty minutes after the fake money had hit the platform, I was out the front doors of the MetLife Building walking back up Madison looking for a taxi, free as a bird.

"Hey, there you are," Aiken said as I came down the stairs from the lobby of GBH minutes later. "Where were you?"

"Lunch," I said, checking my watch. "Am I a little late? I'm sorry. You said be discreet so I was just acting like everything was normal."

"Oh, right," Aiken said, nodding. "Good thinking. I'm sorry. This is all so crazy. Come into my office and tell me what happened."

"Well, I gave the FBI guys the suitcases like you said," I said as I sat down. "And that was pretty much it. I locked up and put the key back. Has there been any word?"

"No, nothing."

"Who was kidnapped?"

"The client is Robert Haynes and it was his son who was kidnapped. Gareth is his name."

"Wow. That's terrifying. How old is the child?"

"He's actually in his twenties."

"Oh. Who do they think took him?"

"Well, one special agent at a meeting said there have been a number of South American and Mexican groups doing kidnappings of late. But mostly only in Texas."

"Like drug cartels?" I said.

"That's what I heard. The cartels apparently have groups that specialize in kidnapping the children of the rich. Clients are freaking. They think this might be the first one in New York."

This was so awesome, I thought. My ruse was doing its thing. They didn't have the foggiest clue.

"Does everyone know? Will it be in the papers?"

"I'm not sure. I just hope they will return the young man."

"Of course," I said, faking my concern.

I thought about the vault down the hall. The gloriously empty vault.

I actually felt weird about it now that it was over. I knew I shouldn't get ahead of myself, but it had gone off without a hitch. It was almost too easy.

I was going to be the first intern in the history of interns to leave with a $1.5 million severance package.

Tax free.

PART THREE

THE GETAWAY

52

The next day was Saturday, and as the "kidnapping" turned twenty-four hours old, Cavan and Jockey and Caitlin and I had a blast of a day giving Caitlin a whirlwind NYC grand tour.

We took the subway all the way out to Coney Island and rode the Cyclone roller coaster and had a hot dog at the famous Nathan's where they hold the contest every year.

After that we headed back into Manhattan directly to Central Park's Delacorte Theater where I had gotten us all tickets for one of the famous Shakespeare in the Park plays they put on every summer.

This year it was *Macbeth* but instead of the classic castle-and-dagger-style play, they had updated it to World War I, and it was surprisingly boring. By unanimous decision, we left at the intermission to get some pizza down in the village at John's, and then we headed over to Grand Central to catch a train to Cavan and Jockey's Irish neck of the woods up in Woodlawn.

Coming into the terminal, I didn't see any crime scene tape or FBI agents with notebooks. Even the dozen cello players I had hired were nowhere to be seen.

I thought I might be a little nervous but coming across the Main Concourse, I felt fine. In fact, when we were heading down the stairs for our train in Track 21, I looked into the darkness north of the platform and actually laughed at what I had managed to pull off.

We sat on the left-hand side of the car backward to the motion of the train, and as we came out of the tunnel up into Harlem, I stared amazed and happy out at the sunny buildings.

This would be our life now, I thought, looking out. Our happy New York life. It was starting now. What I had always wanted.

"Well, aren't you feeling merry?" Cavan said as the conductor clipped our tickets.

"I told you once that work thing was over, I'd be back," I said.

"You weren't kidding," he said.

Cavan and Jockey's tiny place was in the basement of a big house on a leafy street three blocks from the Woodlawn station. There, we freshened up a little and Cavan grabbed his acoustic guitar, and we walked up a few more blocks to a little bar called the Fireside Pub where Cavan was playing a no-pressure classical Irish music gig with a couple of friends.

At the table near the front, Jockey and Caitlin were almost head-to-head they were sitting so close. They were hitting it off even better than Cavan and I had hoped.

It really was an almost perfect day, but as I sat and watched Cavan tuning his guitar, I started to feel funny.

Maybe guilt has a time lapse to it or something because it was only then that I started to feel some.

It wasn't for taking the money or fooling the FBI. I had no problem with that.

It was because of what I had done to Gareth's father. The surprise and shock and fear I had put him through was real. I tried to tell myself that it was just a prank call or something, but it wasn't.

I'd emotionally tortured a dying old man for money.

And it wasn't even over yet, I realized. As I sat here, he was by the phone wondering whether or not he was ever going to see his son alive again.

I remembered being a kid waiting at the hospital near the end with my mother, and I put a hand over my mouth as the lights suddenly dimmed and Cavan began to play.

53

Cavan wrapped up his gig around eleven, and the fellas walked us back for the train.

"You look tired, Faye. Get some sleep now," Cavan said as the train doors closed.

We got off the Metro North at 125th Street, and when the Uber dropped us at the apartment in Morningside Heights, it was half past midnight.

"Shower, PJs, bed," Caitlin chanted as we stumbled into the elevator.

Even though Caitlin and I had just our sleeping bags down on the hardwood of the apartment living room, she went out like a light. I, on the other hand, had trouble sleeping.

A lot of trouble.

And it had nothing to do with the hardwood floor. I kept thinking about Gareth's father. He probably wasn't sleeping either, was he?

That's when I remembered it. The last piece of evidence. In the bedroom on the shelf above the Sheetrocked money was the last burner phone I had used to communicate with Gareth.

I hadn't looked at the news once to see if the kidnapping was being covered.

I didn't even want to know until tomorrow when Gareth "escaped."

Tomorrow when it got dark, the plan was for Gareth to leave the Bellaire and head over to the Major Deegan and flag down a car. When the police arrived, he was going to claim that a group of masked Spanish-speaking men had grabbed him downtown near Tompkins Square Park and thrown him into a van.

In the van, they put a bag over his head and ziptied his hands. Then with a gun to his head, they made him call his father.

He was going to say the van had stopped somewhere and he had been put into the trunk of a constantly moving car. They had driven around for two days—where he had no idea—but that he had been let out to eat and have water and to use the bathroom a few times near what sounded like a highway.

Then he had just been let go alongside the Deegan (near the strip club) and that's all he knew. And if they kept pressing him, he said he was just going to say he was too tired and freaked out and to leave him alone already or they could talk to his lawyer.

It was a foolproof plan and explanation. There was no crime scene for them to look for evidence to corroborate what he was saying. He barely saw the van and didn't even see the car. The only thing they could do to him was grill him and try to make him crack. But his being a child of the rich made even that not too likely as the rich can and often do sue the police department for bad treatment.

I listened in the dark to my sister sleeping. Then I stood and went back into the bedroom and opened the door of the closet.

When I saw that a message light was shining from the burner phone screen, my lungs stopped working immediately.

But how could that be possible? We were to have no contact unless there was some kind of emergency.

I looked at it. I didn't want to, but I did.

There was a one-word message on it.

help

54

"Where the hell are you going?" Caitlin said as I laced up my sneakers.

"Work thing," I said.

"In the middle of the night on a Saturday?" she said.

"No rest for the weary in the city that never sleeps," I said. "The foreign markets are open. I just need to check something at the office. I'll be back soon. Just go back to sleep."

The first taxi I hailed down a block from my apartment was driven by a very sober-looking white guy, an ex-cop dad type. I let him go and the next guy who stopped was a young African gentleman listening to gospel music, and I went for it.

There was actually a run-down motel a block or so away from the Bellaire on the other side of East 138th Street, I saw from the burner phone, so I told the guy to take me there.

"Are you sure you wish to go there, miss?" he said in his musical accent after I told him the destination.

"Yes. Why?" I said. "What's it to you?"

He stared at me fearfully in the rearview.

"I've been to this 138th Street motel many times. There is much…dangerous nocturnal activity."

He meant prostitution, I realized.

"Just take me anyway," I said, pulling my hat down tighter. "It's okay."

"God bless you, my child," I heard him whisper.

When we got there ten minutes later, I got out and waited until the driver left, and instead of going in, I walked west toward Cornell Avenue where the Bellaire was, but as I got closer to the corner, I saw something.

Something very, very suspicious.

There was an SUV, a black one with its engine running, parked near the corner on the other side of the street.

As if the people in it were staring at the mouth of dead-ended Cornell Avenue, wanting to see who would head inside.

There was a driveway of what turned out to be a recycling center beside me, and I went to its shadowed recess and stood watching the dark SUV. It was a Range Rover. As I watched, it shut off its engine but no one got out.

I was still pondering the meaning of this two minutes later when there was a loud shriek of some kind of truck coming along on East 138th Street.

A second later, up at the corner came a garbage truck that stopped just before the corner, its headlights lighting up the cabin of the Range Rover.

In its bright beam, I clearly saw the back of the figure sitting in the front seat. It was a white guy, a big one with stocky bodybuilder shoulders, wearing a baseball cap.

When I saw that he was wearing a suit jacket, I freaked out. I thought of Agent Conrad and Agent White in their suit jackets.

"Shit, shit, shit," I said.

But as I watched, I saw the guy check his watch. It was no FBI agent's watch. It was gold and clunky. Even from where I stood across the street, I could tell it was a Rolex, one with a dark blue or maybe black face on it.

Whoever the hell the guy was, I didn't like it and I was retreating back toward the run-down motel when I heard the engine of the SUV suddenly roar to life. As I stopped and watched, it pulled out and made a right under the East 138th Street underpass at speed.

I stood there wondering about that. So maybe it had nothing to do with Gareth? A coincidence? Some nicely dressed guy out partying or maybe just coming out of the red light motel?

I decided that must have been it because if they were FBI and had found Gareth, there would have been a million cop cars already, right?

I hurried to the corner and across East 138th Street and onto dead-end Cornell Avenue. I started jogging as I passed the abandoned-looking tenements, and by the time I was at the lumberyard, I was full-out running.

It was only when I went to the side door of the Bellaire itself where Gareth had entered that I suddenly came to a complete stop.

Because the side door was slightly ajar.

55

I swallowed.

What the hell did that mean? Had he left? Where the hell was Gareth? Maybe he had to split to somewhere else?

I remembered the text.

help

He would not have contacted me unless it was something extremely important.

I had come this far. I decided I had to check.

I turned on the flashlight of my burner phone and nudged the door open wider with the back of my hand.

The inside of the Bellaire was surprisingly upscale. There was elaborate flowered casino carpeting and purple silk ribbons hanging from the ceiling and Tiffany Blue leather booths.

I passed a sign near the sealed-off front door that said No Hats, No Hoodies, No Baggy Jeans. Then I was in the room where all the action happened. On a circular platform rimmed with a brass rail was not one, not two, but three poles coming straight down in front of a wall of smoked mirrors.

I had pictured lots of things in my head when I came to Manhattan for my Wall Street internship, I thought, as I stood staring at them, but robbing banks and exploring abandoned Bronx strip clubs after midnight hadn't been part of it.

Maybe he had just left, I thought as I looked at the long empty bar on my left. That was it. Maybe we just got our signals crossed.

I should just leave, too, I thought. What was I doing? I was overthinking things.

But I hadn't, I thought, as I saw there was a swinging kitchen door with a porthole window in it at the end of the bar.

I'd thought of everything.

help, I thought again.

I continued in deeper.

Beyond the swinging door was a narrow all stainless galley kitchen.

And lying on the rubber mat in between the steel ovens and steel prep tables was Gareth.

He was naked, lying on his side, and on his wrists behind his back and on his ankles and around his mouth like a gag were layers of gray duct tape. Above the tape, his face was splattered with dried blood, and a great deal of it like a black river had spilled down from the back of his head behind his ear and along his neck.

As I took another step forward, the scent of blood and fecal rot that hung in the air suddenly hit my nostrils like a slap. Yet I took another step forward and moved my phone closer as I crouched down to see his face.

In the beam of my phone flashlight, I saw his eyes.

They were wide open.

He was dead.

Long dead. By the dried blood splatter at the back of his head, it looked like he'd been shot, maybe more than once. He'd also been beaten badly. You could see that clearly from the bruises. On his tatted arms and chest and even on his bare hip were purplish welts. The hands below the tape on his wrist were bloated and almost black as if his hands and fingers had been broken.

He'd been beaten and killed right here, I thought, idly raising the phone's flashlight beam over the dark splatter on the oven and fridge and wall.

Probably struck repeatedly and brutally with a blunt object.

I stood there like an idiot, playing CSI detective for another minute. And then for another two more minutes like a fool, I just stood there staring at him.

I was unable to move. It seemed like my shock-laced mind was trying to gain purchase, to find some reason and order in the chaos lying before me, but my mind was failing badly.

That's when I heard it. From far off, there was a sound.

Very faintly came the strain of a high-pitched sound, like a cry.

It was a siren.

An approaching siren.

56

What I did next surprised even me.

As I stood there staring down at the carnage—this shockingly unexpected brutal bloody carnage that I knew I was solely and wholly responsible for—and heard the approaching sirens, my initial reaction was to just wait for them. To hand over my guilt, to pass over my crime and shame to the first responding officer.

But then as if on their own, my feet slowly began to back me away from the body and I hit the swinging door behind me with my butt and I was back out by the bar.

Something seemed to flip within my head as I watched the door swing forward with a click, and the shock was gone, and I was rushing through the strip club, running for my life.

When I hit the side door and made it outside, I heard the siren blaring now coming closer from the mouth of the dead-end Cornell Avenue. As I stood with my back against the side wall of the Bellaire, wondering what in the hell I was going to do now, I suddenly saw its lights, its blue-and-red police lights, flicker along the stone wall of the overpass on Cornell Avenue's opposite side.

I heard the now deafening cop car arrive not ten feet away by the front door. The siren suddenly cut as the doors swung open.

"Yo, Sarge. Check it out. We're the first ones here," I heard a cop say.

I felt it in my heart when I heard someone kick the steel shutter of the club's closed front door.

"Door's frickin locked," another voice said. "C'mon, let's check the parking lot. There's got to be another way in."

When I peeked out a split second later, I just saw the cop car with its doors open so I instantly ran across for the weeds and shadows on the opposite side of Cornell Avenue by the overpass.

As I arrived and crouched down, I saw two more cop cars come around from beneath the East 138th Street underpass and swing onto Cornell. At the same time, the two first responders who had their guns out now came around from the parking lot side of the building and walked over by the open door where I had just been standing.

"Yo, yo, yo!" one of the first responding cops called out, waving to the other two teams of cops as they exited beside the first car.

"We got an open door. We're going in. Come on, come on!" he said.

As they all went in, I crouched there in the weeds, tapping at my head, as if trying to make it operate.

"Think, dammit."

I knew I couldn't head back up Cornell toward East 138th. I would be spotted in two seconds.

I turned the other way deeper into Cornell Avenue's dead end. I could see the lights on the Deegan behind a chain-link fence. I could probably get over it, but then what? Run along the highway shoulder? Be seen by how many people before someone called a cop?

With no other choice, I was jogging for it when I saw something else.

THE VAULT

Up ahead against the wall of the overpass I was hurrying along, I suddenly noticed a huge box, some kind of metal industrial street furniture. It had electrical conduits heading up the stone wall above it, and where the conduits connected to the wall were brackets that were almost like the rungs of a ladder.

The overpass, I thought, staring at the brackets. Could I get up on top of it?

Time to see, I thought as I ran up and leaped and pulled myself up on top of the cabinet-like box.

When I stood and jumped, I was just able to grab the conduit bracket, and by walking up the wall a little I was able to painfully get my knee on it. By pushing off the conduit itself for leverage, I was able to get a sneaker on top of the bracket and I finally stood up on it.

Then I was able to reach up and grab the next brace, and I repeated the process until I was at the top of the wall.

57

The shockers of my night just wouldn't stop, would they? I thought as I flipped myself over onto the overpass wall's other side.

I landed in gravel and stood and looked around at the four sets of train tracks.

I didn't know what the overpass was for, I hadn't thought that far ahead, but it was for a train apparently. Was it for the subway?

I looked and saw the logo on another electrical cabinet.

No, of course not, I thought, shaking my head. It was for the Metro North train.

"All roads lead to Grand Central," I said, feeling crazed.

But that was a good thing though, I suddenly thought as I turned to the west and saw the towers of a railroad bridge that led back over the Harlem River into Manhattan.

I peeked out over the train overpass wall at the strip club to see two more squad cars arriving in front of it.

That I hadn't already been caught was a miracle, I knew.

I needed to get the hell out of here and quick.

I took off down the overpass wall, looking up at the train

bridge as I headed for it. Some bridges are works of art, but this one was an ugly-looking rusted thing with a pair of huge menacing light-bluish metal towers bookending it.

To add more stress to my impromptu flight out of the Bronx was the raised rail three feet to my right that was running along the railroad tracks.

My old friend, the third rail. How do you like that? Just when I thought my days of playing life-and-death train Frogger were behind me.

"Oh, goodie," I mumbled as I ran.

As I got closer, I spotted the water of the Harlem River. In the sodium lights of the bridge, it had a metallic sheen to it, a dark almost green putty color. Arriving closer to the riverbank, I noted there was probably about a forty-foot drop between the bridge and the water.

The news just kept on getting better, didn't it, I thought, grimacing as I stared down at its shimmering surface. If the third rail didn't get me, the fall from the bridge into the filthy water would break my neck before I drowned.

That's when I felt it, a kind of shiver in the metal. A kind of twitch.

I stopped and looked back into the dark of the Bronx behind me as a long faint blat of horn sounded out. Then far in the distance, a tiny light came around a bend.

No, I thought.

But the answer was yes.

A train was coming.

A train was coming now.

This was not good as I was in an open area before the bridge tower. Even though the coming train was on the other side of the Manhattan-bound tracks, its headlight would expose me.

My only shot was to get to the center of the huge bridge tower to hide behind it, I realized. It was about a hundred feet ahead, and I would need to clear two third rails and the two sets of tracks on my right to get to it, and I needed to do it now.

I got up out of my crouch and began to run. I stopped and hopped the first electrified rail and began running between the tracks, then stopped and jumped over the second electrified rail.

As I ran between the second track, the train sounded its horn behind me again, much closer now.

As I kept running toward the shadow of the bridge tower, I was in a place beyond emotions, in pure fight or flight mode. Flight, in this case.

Oh, it was run-for-my-life time all right. Or at least for my freedom.

Because if I got spotted by the train driver, I was cooked.

Then I was there. I made it to a little concrete pad in front of the bridge tower and lay back against the old rusted metal of it just as the tracks all around became bathed in light.

As I waited, the shudder of the rusted steel at my back became a rocking and a second later, the blur of metal and lit windows of the speeding train beside me was close enough to kiss.

58

Blue-white sparks from the third rail jumped as the rusted hunk-of-junk bridge tower shook and beat against my back like it was trying to dislodge me.

Even when the train was past and out of sight, I just stayed there for a second, hugging myself as the metal rocking at my back slowly became gentler and gentler like a mother trying to comfort a crying baby.

When it finally stopped and I was finally convinced I was still alive, I knew I had one priority now.

Getting the hell off this bridge before another train came.

Thankfully, I saw in front of me there was an access walkway between the tracks that didn't seem to have any high voltage lines nearby. After I crossed the bridge onto the Manhattan side, I came out beyond the other tower and crossed the Grand Central–bound tracks and began walking along the shadow of the overpass wall.

As I walked, I spotted another highway, the one that ran along the Harlem River on the Manhattan side. Was it the FDR, the Harlem River Drive? I wasn't sure.

Whichever this highway was, I noticed one of its northbound off-ramps actually rose to just underneath the train overpass. As I got closer to the off-ramp, I saw that there was a high fence that ran alongside it.

I stopped right above the fence and looked down. I thought by going over the lip of the overpass, I could just reach the top of it.

But if I fell, it was a twelve-foot drop.

I had no choice, I thought as I carefully climbed up on the stone lip of the overpass and swung my legs over. I had to get off the bridge.

Just under the stone part of the overpass on the outside was a metal girder that I was able to grip the edge of as I dangled a foot down toward the chain-link fence. I had just gotten a foot in one of its diamonds and was carefully crouching down, holding the girder, when a car suddenly shot out from underneath the off-ramp tunnel right beside me, startling the hell out of me.

I slipped then and I free-fell for a split second but then flailed out with my hands. By sliding a hand into the fence diamonds, I wasn't able to stop myself completely, but the friction of the fence wire on the burning palms of my hands slowed me considerably as I sort of rode the fence down.

I even managed to stay on my feet when I hit the off-ramp asphalt. But before congratulating myself, I quickly realized I had a new problem. Not getting run over or even spotted by the next car.

The quickest place to hide was in the shadow of the tunnel under the overpass in front of me, so I darted in there. As my eyes adjusted to the darkness, I saw there was a jersey barrier on my left with just enough room to walk on the other side, so I quickly hopped over it.

I hurried down this lucky lane for the other end of the arched tunnel and had just allowed myself a tiny dose of relief when I saw the tent.

It was a dark dome-like camping tent with orange piping on

it. It had an overstuffed shopping cart beside it, and the whole thing almost completely filled the path between the jersey barrier and the tunnel wall.

I had just noticed that the edges of the tent seemed to be weighed down with cinder blocks when I heard its zipper open and a flashlight blinded me.

"Who the hell are you? What the hell are you doing and where in the hell are you coming from?" said a voice as I shied away from the light, pulling my hoodie over my head.

It was a man's voice, and as a car suddenly zoomed by in the tunnel, I saw it was an old man. A short stocky guy in a red plaid lumberjack shirt who was bald and had a long gray beard.

I almost started laughing then when I saw him.

Out of all the bridges and tunnels in Manhattan, I had to find one with an actual troll under it! Or was it Gollum, I wondered. Would we have a riddle contest now? For what I couldn't tell you. But at that moment, I would have paid a couple of hundred grand for an invisibility ring.

"Who are you?" he said again.

But I just tied my hoodie tighter over my face and hopped over the jersey barrier and ran past him and his tent down the off-ramp as fast as my feet would go.

I ran for about half a mile down to the four-lane highway and then ran across it when there was a break. My burner phone told me there was a BP gas station three blocks away at 125th and 2nd, and the car from Arecibo I ordered was there when I arrived.

Instead of Gandalf, the driver was a smiley middle-aged black lady with an old cabbie's hat over her dreads.

"Long night?" she said.

"It's all good," I lied, hiding my scratched-up hands.

59

If there was a bright side to my stress and adrenaline-mainlining nighttime escape from the Bronx, it was that when I came into the Morningside Heights apartment and threw off my ripped filthy clothes and took a shower and climbed into my sleeping bag, I was too exhausted to think about the implications of everything and so went right to sleep.

But when I woke up, the implications were right there, waiting patiently to bear down on me as I lay in my sleeping bag with the weight of a city bus.

That Gareth was dead seemed impossible. Impossible. Yet I knew it was true.

The duct tape. I couldn't stop thinking about it. Gareth had some with him. It was in the gear and groceries I had bought him. The plan was that he would wear some on his wrists and around his mouth the morning before his escape before he ripped it off himself.

No worrying about that now, I thought as I lay there with my eyes shot wide.

What the hell had happened? I remembered the guy in the

Range Rover. The big pale dude with the gold Rolex. Had that been his old friend, the Cuban, back to tune Gareth up for trespassing or some other old dispute? Or was it someone else?

And if they wanted to kill him, what was up with the duct tape? And how had he texted me? And—

I didn't think my eyes could go wider but they did.

It was a setup. I'd been set up. Gareth and I both.

Someone had known about our fake kidnapping plan.

And they'd turned it into a real kidnapping plan with a real live dead kidnapping victim.

help, I thought, remembering the text message.

And then they'd lured me in to take the blame for it. Someone had called the cops so *I* would get busted red-handed.

But who the hell would do this? Who could have known about it? There was someone out there who knew what I had done? Who? I couldn't think of a soul. It was so crazy.

The reality of Gareth's death and my total complicity in it began to really hit home then.

I did this to Gareth, I realized. *I* had thought all this up and lured him into it. He wouldn't have been there but for me. I'd used him. I knew he was a drug addict, that he was very vulnerable, and I didn't care. In fact, I had used that against him and roped him into this thing and had gotten him killed.

Brutally, I thought as I remembered his bruised and broken body. He looked like he'd been tortured or something.

That's when I heard the apartment door open. What the heck? Had I forgotten to lock it? What now?

"Hello in there?" Cavan called out from the doorway. "Good morning! Are ya decent, ladies?"

What on earth? I thought as I instantly stood.

"Cavan?" I said.

"Hurry out to the kitchen, sleepyheads," he said. "I've brought bagels. Bagels and great tidings."

I helped Caitlin up, and we walked into the kitchen together.

Cavan spilled a bunch of bagels out of a bag onto the island and laid out a package of cream cheese. Then the sudden pop came.

"You're out of milk so," he said, pouring champagne into one of his signature plastic flutes, "I've brought a little something else."

"Are you still drunk from last night?" I said as he handed me a flute.

"No," he said, smiling. "I'm drunk with happiness from when I opened the mail this morning."

He tossed a card out onto the kitchen island beside the bagels. A green card.

"What?" I said, staring down at it in shock. "It came!"

"Yes," he said. "It came. It finally came."

"When?"

"On Friday. But I only checked the mail this morning," he said.

"Oh, my goodness! Finally, finally, finally!" I said, hugging Cavan with everything I had.

"Wait, what does that mean?" Caitlin said.

"It means he doesn't have to leave!" I said.

"That it does," he said, holding his green card up with pride. "I already talked to my hook in the department. I'll be going right into the next NYPD class forthwith."

"Congratulations!" Caitlin said. "That's just great. Good for you."

But it wasn't great, I thought as the dark and terrible reality of what I had done stomped down on my euphoria like a bug.

Because as it turned out, Plan C had been completely unnecessary after all.

I pictured Gareth's broken body.

Gareth had died for nothing, and everything was very, very bad.

60

All Sunday long, I acted like everything was fine as Cavan helped us put a new coat of paint on the walls of the apartment. But when he left at six, I ran into the bathroom and locked the door and checked the news on my phone.

It was worse than I thought. Gareth's murder wasn't just the lead on the local news. It was the third story on the national networks.

HEIR TO REAL ESTATE FORTUNE MURDERED IN KIDNAP PLOT was the catchy tag line.

That night I didn't sleep a wink, waiting for the knock on the door. If I had been set up, whoever set me up could just make a phone call, right? If the cops came in, they would find the money without too much trouble and frog-march me out.

I was Ms. Frogger after all.

But as the morning light glowed in the window and I still hadn't been arrested, I thought that maybe it wasn't as bad as I thought.

Maybe whoever tried to set me up with the text didn't know exactly who I was. Maybe they knew that Gareth was involved in some crazy scheme, but not exactly who his partners were, and had sent the text to lure in whoever they were.

As I considered this, I was seriously contemplating a sudden road trip to someplace like Alaska. I had the running money that was for sure.

But in the end, I decided going into work was the best move.

If there was even a hint of a chance of weathering this, I thought as I got into the shower, I needed to find out as much about what was going on as possible.

Aside from the fact that I couldn't have been more scared or freaked out, I had a surprisingly calm and pleasant taxi ride into work. But my calm ended abruptly after I got me and Marvin our coffees and pushed in through GBH's doors.

Something was going on in the lobby and it wasn't good. There was a new security guard. A hard-edged, hard-ass-looking white guy with a cop mustache in a gray tactical uniform and ball cap. There was a line of some of the GBH traders in front of him by his security desk, and he looked like he was checking their IDs.

What was this about? I thought. *Where was Marvin? Was he in a room being interrogated? Was I going to be next?*

I thought about my Alaska plans again, about maybe just turning and leaving but then it was my turn.

"ID please," the hard-ass said.

"Hi," I said, handing over my GBH ID. "Is Marvin sick or something?"

He looked at me then flipped a page on his clipboard.

"Is Marvin the guy who usually works here?" he finally said.

"Yes," I said.

"I'm not sure," he said, handing me back my card. "They just sent me to fill in."

Aiken was coming out of the men's room as I arrived at the bottom of the basement stairs.

"Walker," he said. "There you are. I take it you've heard everything."

He seemed cranky. That was good. Situation normal there. I would have been much more surprised if he was cheerful.

"Yes, I heard. Coffee?" I said, offering him Marvin's.

"Oh, sure. Thanks," he said. "Come into my office for a sec."

"This is unbelievable," he said after he closed the door.

"I know. It's all over the news. How is it going? How is the family?"

"Devastated," Aiken said. "The son was only twenty-seven years old. He had actually been a minor celebrity only a few years ago. Real estate boy wonder. His father's protégé, they said."

I shook my head, trying not to think about Gareth.

"You see the *Post* cover?" Aiken said.

"No."

"Just brutal," he said as he lifted the paper off his desk.

THEY KILLED HIM ANYWAY said the headline with a photo of a young handsome Gareth. I could hardly even look at it. Yet, I couldn't look away.

"Did the FBI screw it up or something?" I said. "The bad guys got away? They got the ten million dollars and then they still killed him?"

He looked at me.

"Well, actually, don't believe everything you read in the papers."

"No?" I said.

"Listen, Walker. Just keep your mouth shut about this, but I just came back from a meeting upstairs. I got called in at 3:00 a.m., this thing is so crazy. The papers don't know, but we actually got most of the money back."

"What? For real?"

"Yes. The FBI recovered seven million of it."

"Wow! Must have been a screwup or something. Is that why they killed him then? They didn't get the entire ransom?"

Aiken shrugged.

"Maybe. That's what some people are thinking. I don't know all the details. It's a complete shit show."

Yeah, I thought, written, directed, and starring yours truly.

"At least that's positive for GBH," I said. "Getting the seven million back, right?"

"From our point of view, yes. The bigwigs, especially Dabertrand, are quite happy. And the insurance company is on the hook for the other three."

"What does the security guy upstairs have to do with it?" I said. "Where's Marvin?"

"We got Marvin to go on vacation for a few weeks. Clients are flipping over this. Straight up freaking. The whole Upper West and Upper East Side are beside themselves, thinking that their kids are next. The big cheeses thought a stronger show of security is the way to go right now. At least until all this dies down."

"What a crazy thing," I said, shaking my head in wonder.

"It is a crazy thing," Aiken agreed. "You didn't think you'd be in the middle of something like this when you took the internship did you? Never a dull moment at GBH New York."

"I'll say," I said.

"Well, that's about it," Aiken said, lifting his phone. "Just try to do your work today and again, just keep quiet. Especially with any press."

"You got it, boss," I said, making a zip-my-lip gesture as I stood.

"Wait, Faye. There was something I wanted to ask you about the hand-off in the vault," he said.

I turned, doing everything in my power not to swallow.

"Did you hand over the serial numbers of the money to the Feds when you gave them the cases? They were in a folder."

"Yes, of course. The folder was in the bag with the GPS things. I gave them the bag."

"Okay. Well, I guess they misplaced the folder or something.

They're asking about the numbers. They just asked me to messenger it down to them. I said I'd email it, but they want to have the notarized paper with the company logo if they ever have to present it in court."

"Well, I definitely handed it over," I said as I tried to leave.

"I have another notarized copy right here," he said, tapping at some papers. "You know what? I'd like you to handle this. Run it down for me to the FBI building downtown. It'll look good. Show the Feds GBH is eager to cooperate with them on this."

Me? I thought feeling a vein pulse in my forehead. Go down to the FBI building!

He put the notarized sheets into a glossy GBH folder and handed it to me before he lifted his phone.

"Head up to the lobby now. I'll get a town car for you," he said.

61

The FBI building at Worth Street and Broadway was a truly intimidating dark structure made of metal and headstone-gray blocks with weird little windows that made it seem more like a prison or maybe a mental asylum than an office building.

Made sense, I thought, staring at it. I was about due for a visit to a funny farm with all the sheer unadulterated insanity I'd brought upon myself.

The building, like every other one in Manhattan, seemed to be under construction as did the streets around it.

"This traffic is a nightmare," said the driver, a nice Hispanic guy in a suit named Mark. "You're getting the good gigs today, huh, Faye?"

"You're telling me," I said as we stopped and I pulled open the door.

As I got out of the town car on Broadway, there wasn't just one jackhammer going off but at least two. There was also a line of people on the sidewalk on the other side of Broadway waiting at the FBI building visitors' entrance so I got behind them.

What the hell was going on that there was even a line of visitors going in to see the Feds like it was a rock concert? But it turned out, visitors were only allowed in at ten.

Coming into the low-ceilinged, grim-looking lobby, I saw that there was an agent with what I guessed was a bomb-sniffing dog, a black Lab, by the metal detectors. As I dropped my bag into the scanner, the dog seemed to raise an eyebrow at me as it sniffed at my feet.

I thought about Gareth then and the smell of the blood.

Could it smell Gareth? I wondered suddenly. That's all I needed. A bomb dog that doubled as a cadaver one.

I got past the dog and showed the card Agent Conrad had given me to a squat bespectacled white lady at the visitors' desk. She gave me a pass for the sixth floor, and as I got off the elevator, another clerk, a male twin of the lobby one, glanced up from his desk.

"Yes?" he said.

"I have something to drop off for Agent White or Agent Conrad," I said.

He looked at me.

"Do you now?" he said.

"I'm from Greene Brothers Hale," I said snootily. "I have some very important, time-sensitive documents they requested."

That seemed to get his attention. His office chair actually squeaked as he sat up.

Down in my Kentucky holler, if you had said that, people would shrug at you. But name-dropping investment banks in NYC turned heads.

"Of course," he said, suddenly all business. "I believe Agent White is in an interview but let me buzz Agent Conrad."

I tapped a shoe as I waited.

"He's not picking up. I guess it would be okay if you waited by Agent White's desk. Head straight back to the cubicle in this corridor behind me and make a left. White's will be the third one on your right. There's a break room across from it. Have a seat in there and please have a cup of coffee while you wait. I'll tell him you're here."

I walked down the corridor and turned and found the break room and sat. A female agent in a cubicle just to the left of White's was eating something out of a takeout box. Eating loudly. I began to cringe at the amount of slurping.

When I stood to get a cup of coffee, I saw that the break room had a little window with a view over the cubicle walls back toward the reception desk and the elevators. I was looking out this window when I saw Agent White come out of the elevator.

And immediately stopped pouring the coffee.

It wasn't Agent White who made me slowly lower the coffeepot back down.

It was the little man who was with him.

The little bald man in the red lumberjack shirt and the long gray beard.

It was the troll, the homeless guy. The guy I'd seen when I'd hopped down off the train bridge.

No, I thought. This couldn't be happening.

He must have ratted me out to the precinct cops, and they'd sent him to Agent White.

It didn't matter why he was here. He was here and he had seen me. And if he saw me now and recognized me, I was toast.

I wasn't going to allow it to happen. No way. I couldn't.

I quickly looked around and then walked out to White's desk and tossed the GBH folder on it. Then I walked farther down the cubicle row away from the elevators and made a left-hand turn at the end of it into another row. I passed some doors on my right that looked like they were for offices before I came upon one in the corner that had an exit sign above it, and I pushed it open and started down stairwell for the lobby.

And almost went ass over tea kettle as I tripped on someone sitting there on the second step.

62

I called out as I stumbled forward, but then suddenly a pair of strong hands caught me around my waist.

"What the? Hey," a man said.

It was a tall athletic nice-looking man who smiled as he set me upright.

"It's you!" Agent Conrad said.

Of course it was Agent Conrad. Of all the agents in the building, I would have to run into the one who I had handed off the money to.

"Busted," he said, stamping out the dropped cigarette he'd been smoking.

"Smoking in the boys' room are we, Agent Conrad?" I said, quickly recovering.

He laughed.

"Yeah, nasty vice, I know, but there you have it. Not supposed to smoke at all in the building, but I come in here every blue moon. Our little secret, okay?"

I nodded, not knowing what the hell was going to happen next.

"But why are you here?" he said with a baffled look.

"Oh, I, um, was sent by work to bring you guys the serial number sheet from the money. I dropped it off at Agent White's desk, and I guess I got turned around."

"Yeah, I don't blame you," Agent Conrad said, leading me back toward the office. "This place is a real maze all right. C'mon, I'll bring you back to the elevators."

"Actually, to tell you the truth, I get kind of claustrophobic in elevators and this one here is a doozy. Could we take the stairs instead?" I said, starting down.

"Sure thing. It's Faye, right?" he said, following.

"That's right," I said, smiling back at him as widely and brainlessly as possible. "You remembered."

"Smile like yours, Faye, is hard to forget," he said as we headed down the stairs.

"I heard the news," I said as we turned a landing. "That's so terrible about the young man."

"Yeah," Agent Conrad said. "It was brutal. They killed him anyway, the bastards."

I thought about maybe asking about the ransom drop but stopped myself.

"Must be a real circus with the media and stuff," I said as we kept heading down.

"You wouldn't believe it," he admitted.

"Any idea who might have done it? The buzz at the bank is that it's the Mexican cartels."

"You didn't hear it from me but we have a few leads."

"You do?" I said, suddenly stopping on the next landing and batting my eyes at him as if I were standing in the presence of Elvis himself.

"A few," he said.

"I won't tell, I promise. Who do you think did it?"

"Well, a portion of the money was put on a Hudson line train bound for Cold Springs. We followed the transponder unit in the money and when the train pulled in at the last station, we watched the conductor come out with the bag and put it in his brother-in-law's car. We have them both in custody. They're both Hispanic. The brother-in-law is actually from Mexico so that cartel thing you're talking about, good chance might be a connect there."

That I did not burst out laughing as he said this was immensely difficult. Because they had nothing. Zero. Nada. Zilch. They hadn't even thought about the flash mob.

I'd thought the hound dogs were at my heels? They were three states over chasing a rabbit.

What had Gareth said?

So easy an FBI agent could do it.

J. Edgar Hoover was rolling over in his grave.

The conductor of the train! Whoever he was, I owed him a beer for his sticky-fingered attempt at a payday. Maybe a case. Or even a bar maybe.

"Now about that drink, Faye," Agent Conrad said as we reached the lobby.

"I'll call you," I lied as I speed walked for the door under the EXIT sign.

63

As I found my waiting town car on Broadway, the hits just kept on coming.

After I closed the door, I got a text from Aiken telling me to head up to Paulina's office for a meeting when I got back.

Paulina's office? I thought as I put down the phone. *Me?*

Paulina was a nice enough though quite snooty Brit. She was also Dabertrand's right-hand woman. Interns did not merely *go* to meetings in Paulina's office. This had to be a first. What now?

Paulina's office was on five, and when I walked into it, I actually shook my head.

How the heck was it an office? I thought, walking into what seemed like the living room of a Malibu beach house. There were white couches, a driftwood and glass coffee table, and a billboard-sized modern art splatter painting that looked like what was left of the paint section of a Home Depot after a twister came through.

"Faye, there you are, we're in here in the conference room," Paulina said, hooking my arm from my blind side and pointing me toward an open door.

And if her swag office didn't make you check your gut, there was Paulina herself, I thought looking at her.

She was almost as intimidatingly perfect as Dabertrand. Though forty-five now, she still had the pixie looks of the former model she'd once been. Not to mention the go-straight-to-hell Brit confidence.

And the clothes. Her clothes! Silk everything. Perfectly ironed scissor-sharp creases. Where did one get such clothes and how did one never wrinkle them?

Or was it her hair? The perfect cut and color of it seemed to shift by day like the movement of the sun against the horizon. Did she have a live-in colorist in addition to a nanny-tary? She must have. Bet money on it. Paulina's level of style required staff.

Then it got worse. As we came into the room, there was Dabertrand, sitting at the head of a small conference table beside Aiken. I'd just been air-dropped on Mount Olympus. The question was why.

"Faye, have a seat right here," Paulina said. "I took the liberty of already pouring you a coffee. Milk, one sugar okay? You'll need a coffee for this little meetup, I assure you."

I sat down and stared at everyone as Paulina poured her own coffee and sat on the other side of me beside Aiken.

"The reason we called you up here, Faye," she said as she lifted her cup, "is that we here—the four of us—are the only ones in the firm who are in this little... What shall we call it? Situation."

"*Unfortunate* situation," Dabertrand said.

"It was unfortunate," I said, staring down into my coffee. "The family must be going through sheer hell."

"Yes, precisely," Paulina said. "But what is also unfortunate, as it turns out, is the situation on our side of it."

"Our side of it," I said, sitting up.

"The ransom," Paulina continued. "I believe Alexander has told you that we retrieved a portion of it."

"Yes," I said. "Seven million I think he said."

"Yes, but three million is still missing," she said. "Which brings us to the reason why you are here, Faye."

I stared at her in near terror.

"Paulina, may I?" Aiken said.

"Please, Alexander. By all means."

"Faye," he said. "We need you to do us a favor."

I swallowed. Here it was. They knew, I thought. They were about to get me to fess up. The time had come. The games were over. My neck was on the block now, and my head was about to be removed.

"We need you to go on a mission," Dabertrand suddenly chimed in.

64

I turned and stared at him.

"A—a mission?" I said.

"Yes, Faye," Aiken said. "As it turns out, there's a problem. As you know, we offer the clients' families kidnapping insurance, right?"

I nodded.

"That kidnapping insurance itself is offered by one of the big multinational insurance and underwriting groups, the so-called insurance company of insurance companies," Paulina said.

"Diplomat Global International," Dabertrand said.

"Yes," Aiken said. "And well, we looked at our paperwork with the Haynes family and as it turns out, they never got around to signing all the proper documents."

I squinted at him.

"It turns out the Haynes family never technically signed on for the kidnapping insurance after all," Paulina said.

"I don't understand," I said.

"We handed over the kidnapping money without knowing this," Aiken said. "We jumped the gun."

"It's really just a glitch, a paperwork oversight," Paulina explained. "The Hayneses have even been paying the premiums for the insurance through us. The family doesn't even know they didn't sign the paper."

"But the bottom line is that Diplomat Global International makes its bank on paperwork oversights," Dabertrand said. "And they are sending an investigator from Switzerland as we speak."

"And once they see that the paper is not signed, they'll deny the claim—" Paulina said.

"And GBH will be on the hook for the money," I suddenly said.

They all looked at me then at each other.

"That's exactly what it means," Paulina said.

"And this is where you come in," Dabertrand said.

I took a deep breath.

"What we need you to do, Faye," Aiken said, "is to go up to the Haynes home and get Robert Haynes to sign the kidnapping insurance document."

"Me? Why me?" I said in genuine surprise.

"Because you're young and innocent looking," Aiken said. "And the best play is for you to, as innocently as possible, go in person with GBH's condolences of course, but also to ask Mr. Haynes to sign a group of documents among which will be the kidnapping insurance document that he forgot to sign."

The *backdated* insurance document, I thought but didn't say. They must have really been in a bind here. What they were trying to get me to do was illegal.

"Whatever you do, avoid any lawyers if they are around. We don't need his lawyers involved in this," Dabertrand said.

"Exactly," Aiken said. "You will show up at the home and talk to Mr. Haynes directly to acquire his simple signature."

My eyes went wide.

Face Gareth's heartbroken father! The one I'd already tormented?

I wanted to do this like I wanted a hole in my head.

"Won't Mr. Haynes be really upset right now?" I said. "Can't this wait a little?"

"No," Paulina said. "The investigator from Switzerland is going to be here at nine tomorrow. Sharp."

"We know this is asking a ton, Faye," Aiken said. "Especially with all of the duties and responsibilities we've already leveled on you."

It sure was asking a ton, I thought, peering at him. If it ever got out that I conned a dying old man into signing a backdated insurance document, I'd probably be brought up on charges.

"That's why with the success of this mission," Dabertrand said, "we will be offering you the analyst position."

I looked at him.

If that didn't take the cake. I guess there was one more slot they could create this year after all. It just took Dabertrand's personal ass being in a sling to create it. Once he was going to look bad, well then, change the rules—three analysts this year it is. Move the goalposts.

What a glittering piece of shit, I thought.

But there was no way out of this "mission," I knew.

Boy, was I in for a pound now, I thought.

Of course, I had to face Gareth's father, I thought. Of course, I had to look at what I had done. Up close and personal. My nose needed to get rubbed into the mess I made.

"Okay," I found myself saying. "Give me the paperwork. I'll go right now."

65

The Haynes residence was a quarter block east of Central Park off Fifth Avenue on the south side of 78th Street.

As the town car slowed in front of it, I really thought for once the formal word "residence" did a place justice. The five stories of ivory limestone decked out with elaborate cornices and balconies and tall deep-set windows looked more like a small private school or a foreign consulate than a private home.

Across from this marble wedding cake on 78th was what looked like an actual museum. When I noticed the heap of men and women with long-lensed cameras lounging on its steps, I didn't think they were tourists. As if that weren't bad enough, across the sidewalk down the street, I saw the call signs of a news van.

How do you like that? I had the hottest ticket in town.

I can't believe this is happening, I thought, numb with the enormity of what I had set into motion. *How can this be happening?*

"This looks even worse than the last stop," Mark the driver said. "You're bowling three hundred today, huh, Faye? Who did you screw over?"

Me, I thought. I screwed me over.

"You don't have to wait," I told him. "I'll get a taxi back."

"They told me to wait for you, Faye. I'll cruise around and get a cup of coffee and find a spot. Just text when you're ready to go, and I'll peel around the corner with the door open so you can jump in."

But when he let me out and rolled down 78th, I didn't go directly to the house. Not yet.

Instead, I crossed to the other side of Fifth and got into the Uber I had ordered from the back seat of the town car.

"Eighty-sixth and Lex," I told the driver, some thirtyish white guy wearing glasses.

When we finally got there, I asked the driver to wait for me. I took out the insurance contract I was supposed to get Mr. Haynes to sign as I ran into the Staples on the corner.

Then ten minutes later, I was back in front of Robert Haynes's door.

It was an impressive one, wrought iron with glass side panels obscured by curtains. There was a huge knocker in its center, but I pressed a camera-eyed buzzer attached to the stone jamb of the door instead.

"Yes?" said a voice after I pressed it.

"I'm from Greene Brothers Hale. I have an appointment with Mr. Haynes."

The man who opened the door a moment later was a sleek, little white guy of about fifty. His hair was slicked back over his widow's peak and he had on a white dress shirt and black waiter's pants.

"Come in, come in. Quickly," he said with a German accent.

He closed the door and stood motionless, looking out at the press across the street through the side panels.

"They are just heartless," he said, shaking his head. "There are more of them now. Look at them. Jackals."

He rotated around on a heel.

"This way," he said.

We walked over a black-and-white tiled floor past an elaborate staircase. Then the butler opened a narrow dark leather-covered door on our left.

"This is the...?" I said, squinting into the closet-sized mirrored space.

"Yes, the elevator. Mr. Haynes is on four. Please, after you."

We slowly ascended and then stopped. He opened another door into what looked like a living room, and I followed him out along the rich furnishings and oil paintings and Persian rugs into a hall and around a corner. At the end of it was a pair of French doors that he opened up for me.

"Mr. Haynes is out on the balcony," he said.

66

The fourth-floor balcony of the Haynes residence was a covered one, and the view it gave to the northwest over Fifth Avenue was breathtaking. You could see the rambling lawns of Central Park over the treetops, and in the distance, the Greek columns of the Metropolitan Museum of Art looked like a temple in an English garden.

The next thing I noticed as I turned to my right were the flowers. They were all over the place, along the balustrade and hanging down in baskets. They were red and white roses, and along with them a bunch of other flowers I didn't know the names of. School-bus-yellow ones and ones that were peacock blue. The amount of them was staggering. It was like a florist shop had been airlifted and emptied out onto the balcony.

"Please come over. There's nothing to be afraid of. Mr. Haynes is sleeping," said a voice as I wandered along the primrose path.

I found Robert Haynes at the other end of the balcony, sitting in a wheelchair, with a woman in a blue nurse's uniform sitting on a bench beside him.

He was older than I thought. The very wrinkled skin of his face was yellow, jaundiced. He looked like a dying man.

You did this to him, said a voice in my head. *You did this to him*.

"Where are you from, young lady?" said the nurse, standing and coming over to me.

She was a stout blonde middle-aged woman with the hint of an accent.

"Greene Brothers Hale. The bank. I have some papers for Mr. Haynes to sign."

"Ah, more papers," she said. "A lovely young girl like you shouldn't have papers on a nice summer day like this. You should be doing something else. On a date or something."

"I wish," I said.

"This is a nice view, huh? Mr. Haynes's favorite. See there? The dog run? He really loves that. Mr. Haynes loves dogs, but he's become allergic with his illness now. See his binoculars? He's like a bird-watcher but with dogs."

"Is that right?" I said.

She leaned closer to me.

"Mr. Haynes is very ill. He's been near death even before all this. He's on heavy painkillers. It won't be long now. But he doesn't know that... Gareth won't be coming home. The family doesn't want him to know. So please don't say anything."

"Of course," I said. "I'm sorry he's so sick."

"They have a DNR on him now," she said. "I've seen it before. I do hospice care for these rich people. It's like a wrestling match when they are near the end. The doctors want to keep him alive for the fees, but the family wants him to expire for the will."

Robert Haynes stirred and suddenly began to cough violently.

"I have to get out of here," he suddenly cried.

Me too, I thought.

"Marie?" he called out. "Marie?"

"Here, give me the papers," the nurse said. "Let me handle it."

"It's just the top one that's important," I suddenly said. "You can ignore the others."

"Here, Mr. Haynes. Drink, drink," said the nurse, sticking a strawed water bottle in his mouth.

I watched him suck at it like a toddler at a juice pack. He began to lick his lips loudly as he shifted in his seat.

"Who are you?" he suddenly said staring right at me.

There was a relaxed look in his eyes. Probably from the painkillers. I wished I had a few.

"She's asking to sign a petition for cancer research, Mr. Haynes. She's from the hospital."

"The damn hospital," he cried. "I hate that place."

"Here's a pen, Mr. Haynes. Just sign it now. There you go. That's it," the nurse said, holding up the clipboard.

I rushed over and took the clipboard from her and looked at it.

Well, that had been easy enough at least.

"Anything else?" Marie said, ushering me away.

I wanted out of there badly. But then something held me.

It was a memory. I remembered my mother. The hospital room. My father crying in the corner. She had looked just like that right before she died, too.

"I just want to say I'm sorry. I won't mention why," I said. "Would that be okay?"

"I guess so," the nurse said, peering at me. "You're a real nice girl, eh?"

She didn't know how wrong she was.

I walked over.

"Mr. Haynes?" I said. "I'm sorry."

"Sorry for what? Who are you?"

"I'm a friend of your son," I said quietly.

"Of who? Harrison?"

"No," I said. "Gareth."

"Oh, Gareth. Poor Gareth," he said, his eyes welling with

tears. "I had the worst dream. There was a monster. A monster had taken my Gareth."

My eyes filled with tears as well.

Because I was that monster and it wasn't a dream.

"You really are a nice girl," Marie said, and I felt like puking as she led me away.

When I went back inside from the balcony, I avoided the coffin-like elevator and walked around until I found the staircase.

I was at the top of the last landing when I heard the voices from the lobby.

"How is he, Franz?" a man said by the open door.

I halted in my tracks.

"Not well, sir," said the butler. "Not well."

"Is my sister here?" the voice said as the door closed.

"No, Mr. Haynes. I believe her plane just landed."

"Where is my father?"

"Up on the balcony, sir."

I waited until I heard the elevator door close to peek around.

That's when I saw it.

From the elevated angle, looking down through the porthole-like glass door in the elevator, I could see a man's wrist.

It was thick and pale and on it was a Rolex.

A gold Rolex with a black face.

67

"So," Aiken said as I pushed through his basement office door at BGH fifteen minutes later.

I shook my head slowly as I handed back the folder with the blank kidnapping insurance form that I had copied at Staples.

"No dice, boss," I said. "I tried. I really did. I almost got to him. He was with the nurse and I thought I had a chance, but then a lawyer or someone showed up and they told me to leave."

From the second I had been sent on the "mission," I had no intention at all of ever getting the form signed. GBH being on the hook for the money and eating it was ideal for me.

Because if I *had* gotten the form signed, I'd have a brand-new problem, wouldn't I?

Instead of Tweedledee and Tweedledum of 26 Federal Plaza tripping over conductors and their Mexican brothers-in-law up in Cold Spring, I'd have a Swiss insurance company going over the whole thing with laser beams and a fine-tooth comb.

Aiken held his head in his hands.

"Dammit. Dabertrand is not going to like this."

"I'm really sorry," I lied.

"It's not your fault. It's just that he has a board meeting next week and explaining a three-million-dollar loss due to a paperwork oversight is not going to go well with the board. He even said he might just cover it himself if it comes down to it."

I stared at him.

"Dabertrand will just take it out of his own pocket?" I said.

"Of course," Aiken said, leaning back with his hands behind his head. "Be a drop in the bucket for him. You know how much he makes? I'd do it if it were my job on the line."

I held my breath so as not to smile. Because despite the maelstrom of insanity I was swirling around in, the deliciousness of it was exquisite. That Arthur "Intern Diddler" Dabertrand was going to have to pay personally to cover the kidnapping loss meant only one thing.

I had literally picked the pocket of the Master of the Universe.

There had to be a swindler-of-the-year award for something like this, I thought as I left Aiken's office and happily found my cubicle and sat down.

If only I'd known Dabertrand had to pay for it, I thought, I would have stolen the whole thing.

I mean Newman and Redford from *The Sting* couldn't have done it any better.

Yeah, but Newman and Redford didn't get their partner killed, did they? I thought as I pictured Gareth dead on the strip club's kitchen floor.

Wait a second, I thought as I sat there. Obviously, I felt terrible about Gareth. Certainly, I had used him but had I put a gun to his head? I had asked him to partner up and he had agreed.

And I hadn't killed him.

But I now knew who did.

His brother.

How I was going to play that card I wasn't sure.

Yet.

68

As I was coming up the stairs for the lobby at five, an unexpected elbow hooked into mine.

"I'm taking you to Stella's for our drink, Faye," Priscilla said. "No cutting out on me this time. No ifs, ands, or buts."

At first, I really felt like knocking her effortlessly stylish slim butt back down the stairwell. Or maybe breaking her perfectly tanned arm draped in Cartier and Burberry.

But then I noticed her red eyes. She'd been crying.

Over Gareth, I realized. I remembered the way they had looked at each other at Stella's what seemed like a thousand years before.

I recovered myself and smiled.

"Twist my arm, Priscilla," I said.

"Two lemongrass daiquiris, Tommy," Priscilla said as we found our booth.

"Actually, Tommy," I said as he turned to leave, "you got any Noah's Mill Small Batch?"

His eyebrow raised. He nodded.

"On the rocks?" he said.

"Neat," I said.

"Noah's Mill?" Priscilla said.

"Best Kentucky bourbon on earth," I said. "What my daddy always drank at weddings. For some strange reason, I'm feeling like a taste of home."

"Wow, Faye. You've changed. I really like this new confident you," Priscilla said, sounding like she really didn't like it.

I smiled.

"I have you to thank for that, Priscilla."

"Me? Really? How so?"

You've taught me far more than you will ever know, Priscilla, I thought as I looked into her eyes.

"How not?" I said.

"I feel honored," she said, rolling her beautiful blue eyes. "Cut the bullshit, Faye. Why are you so mad at me? What did I do to you?"

"You know. Don't play stupid," I said.

"I don't know."

"You're getting the job. I'm not."

Her beautiful lip quivered as she stared at me. I could see pain in her eyes. Pain for how she had betrayed me. Pain for what she had to pay.

"It's okay, Priscilla," I said quietly. "I was mad because I thought it wasn't fair after all the hard work I'd put in. But you know what? It's just a job. I know that now. And life isn't fair, is it? Look what happened to Gareth."

Tears suddenly leapt in her eyes.

That was funny, I thought as I touched my cheek. In mine, too.

She covered her mouth as she began to sob.

"I'm so sorry," she said.

"I know. I forgive you," I said.

"The night Gareth came in," she said, weeping. "Remember? How sad he looked. I can't forget his eyes. When he left. Remember?"

I nodded.

"I loved him," she said. "When we were in high school, I loved him. I really did. My first crush. I should have broken my other date. Oh, why didn't I?"

I reached out and patted her hand.

"I was there the night of the accident when Gareth destroyed his knee. We all went up, Gareth, and Scarlet, and me, with his brother, Harrison, for the Yale-Harvard homecoming game. Harrison had been a linebacker for Yale. Scarlet and I stayed over with friends, but Harrison and Gareth headed back to the city. Harrison was drunk and wrecked the car. He came out without a scratch but Gareth was almost killed. That's when he started to go downhill with the painkillers. It was during the rehab."

As she said that, I pictured the gold watch on the big arm hanging out the window of the Range Rover.

The gold watch through the window of the elevator.

Then Gareth, broken and bloody, on the floor of the strip club's kitchen.

I winced as I suddenly remembered what I'd said to Gareth when I first laid out the plan.

Nobody gets hurt.

Because my calculation had been wrong, hadn't it?

Dead wrong.

And it wasn't over yet, I knew.

I turned and looked out from our booth at the darkening avenue.

"To Gareth," I said, lifting my glass.

69

After my drink with Priscilla, I was out in the street on Madison in front of Stella's trying to hail a taxi when I noticed someone running along the sidewalk behind me.

"There you are," said Cavan when he reached me. "I've been looking all over for you."

I stopped in my tracks as I looked at his face. There was an expression on it I'd never seen before. Anger.

"Cavan?" I said. "What? What happened? What is it?"

"This," he said, showing me a phone.

Holy shit. It was my burner phone. The one I'd texted Gareth with.

"What's that?" I said.

"It's a phone. You know, for talking to people on. Not just any phone. It's your phone. Your *other* phone. The one I found in your hoodie when I was painting your apartment."

I stared at him. He stared back, his usually smiling, gentle blue eyes now half crazed, half wounded.

My mouth opened but no words came out.

He looked down at the sidewalk.

"Why do you have another phone, Faye?" he said very quietly.

I stared down at the sidewalk with him.

Here it was. All my craziness, my clever plan come back right in my lap. I was in trouble up to my eyeballs. A man was dead. And for all my mad scrambling, I was still probably going to get blamed for it. Which wasn't even such a stretch as I had used Gareth, had pretty much helped set him up.

And now Cavan was involved?

No. I couldn't have that. I shook my head. Not now. No way.

Besides, maybe there was still a way out of this, I thought as I stared at the incredible hurt in Cavan's eyes.

A clean way out was still available. Wasn't it?

I couldn't involve him, I decided. I couldn't do that to him. I had to try.

"It has to do with work," I lied.

"Your project? The late nights, the you never calling me anymore? That project?" he said.

I could see he was crying.

"Cavan, no. Listen to me. I swear—"

"Don't," he said, pointing at me. "Don't. See? I knew it, Faye. I knew it. All those fancy people you work with. I knew they'd get their hooks in ya eventually. And once they did, where was someone like me in all that?"

"I—"

"Who has another phone, Faye?" he said as he slapped it into my hand. "Do you think I'm a schmuck? I guess I am. All this time me telling you to wise up. Imagine? Well, you did, it turns out. Seeing somebody else after everything between us? It turned out you're more dog-eat-dog than I gave you credit for. Congratulations. You'll go to the top with those killers you work with. Because you took my heart, lass. Like a pickpocket. I never even knew what hit me."

"No, Cavan. Stop it. It's work. I swear."

"Then give me the code," he said. "Give me the code for the phone so I can see that it's work."

I stared at him. The tears were running down his cheeks.

"I can't," I said. "Cavan, I can't even explain it to you. It's a proprietary work thing. I swear. You just have to trust me."

"Sure. Whatever you say," he said as he turned. "Well, good luck to you, Faye. Maybe one day you'll come by the statue if you and your billionaire friend want a romantic carriage ride. I'll give you a discount. And maybe if I do a real good job, he can leave me a good tip."

"Cavan, please. I swear to you. It's not that."

But it was too late. He was already running away.

70

Oh, what a stupid freaking idiot! I thought as I sat in a taxi back to my apartment trying to call Cavan and only getting his voice mail.

Why hadn't I just told him! I was going to have to tell him anyway. Hadn't I done all this crap to keep him? Now he thought I was cheating on him! And I had just stood there like a fool and let him run away.

"Dammit, dammit, dammit," I said as I tried to call him again.

I'd done all this for him—for us—and now I had completely screwed things up. Cavan had looked obliterated. Running around crazy and heartbroken. Who knew what he was capable of.

I got out of the taxi and headed toward my building, and through the glass doors, I saw there was someone there. A tall figure standing in the foyer by the buzzers.

"Cavan, thank God," I said as I rushed inside.

Then my mouth dropped open and I stood mystified as if spellbound.

It wasn't Cavan.

"There you are," the large man said, grabbing my arm.

The fraction of a second it took for him to violently yank me toward him was all I needed to realize it was Gareth's brother, Harrison.

Even though I had never even seen his face, the resemblance was unmistakable. He had the same brown eyes and reddish hair but he was taller, heavier, stockier. If Gareth was the runner on the track team, Harrison would have been the shot-putter.

"Stop! Wait! What are you doing? Get off me!" I said, trying and failing to push the barrel-chested man away.

Something suddenly poked in my ribs. I looked down. It was a gun, a little black semiauto.

"If you scream, I'll kill you right here," he said as he opened the door. "You're coming with me now."

The next thing I knew he was dragging me outside. I saw his Range Rover parked by the fire hydrant around the curve of the building.

When we arrived at it, I tried to pull away a second time, but when he placed the cold barrel of the gun he was holding under the soft of my chin, I immediately stopped. He opened the driver's door and shoved me inside and we peeled out.

As we screeched around the corner, I felt myself freeze up. My nerves and panic must have reached some sort of limit, I guess. Because though one part of me thought I should be trying to open the door or something, I just sat limp and immobilized with an almost out-of-body feeling of disconnectedness.

We made another turn after a bit, and after another three or four blocks, we slowed. When I glanced out the windshield, I saw we were now beside a construction site. It was almost like something out of a dream as he pressed a garage door remote and the gate on the construction site's driveway rattled sideways.

We pulled in and parked beside a white trailer as the gate behind us rattled back.

"In the trailer, now," he said, squeezing my arm painfully as he pulled me out of the SUV.

"No, no, no," I said.

"Shut up or I'll kill you," he said, practically lifting me up by the back of my shirt as he bum-rushed me in through its door.

There was an office inside with desks and office chairs and computers. I lost a shoe as he suddenly, violently, flung me forward. My chin bounced painfully off the plywood as I went sprawling facedown across its dusty floor.

"Leave me alone!" I said, turning and throwing my arms up.

"Relax," he said after he calmly closed the door.

He kicked a rolling office chair at me.

"C'mon. Get up. Have a seat," he said.

When I still lay there staring, he came over and seized my arm and almost pulled it out of its socket as he hauled me up and sat me down in the office chair.

"Relax," he said again, showing me the palms of his big hands. "I just needed to get you off the street, okay? Because we need to talk, Faye. Boy, do you and I need to talk."

The arrogance in his voice as he said all this reminded me of how snotty Gareth had sounded when I first spoke to him at the Third Avenue bar.

I looked up at his meaty face and beady eyes. He did seem calmer now.

But what in the hell was this?

"What do you want?" I said. "Who are you?"

"Stop it, Faye, would you?" he said, clicking on a small desk lamp and lifting a flat black bag.

He dropped his phone into it.

"Put yours in, too. So we can talk frankly without fear of recording each other."

"Who are you?" I said again as I handed over my phone.

"This is who I am, Faye," he said, showing me the gold-and-black Rolex on his wrist.

He tapped at it.

"You remember this. I know you do. This is me. Right here."

"What does that mean?" I said.

"It means my father's house has an extensive video surveillance system, Faye," he said as he smoothed his dark polo shirt over his beefy chest. "When my father's butler said you had been there, I went through the footage and I watched the video of you on the stairs very closely. I saw the expression on your face when you looked in through the window of the elevator. The hand that went to your mouth. I checked the angle and realized what you were looking at. Your expression was one of recognition. Like a light bulb went off in your head."

He suddenly lunged at me and poked me hard in the chest with his big finger.

"You saw me on Sunday night, didn't you? While I was sitting in the Range Rover by the Bellaire. Where were you? By the hot sheets motel?"

I stared at him.

"Stop playing dumb, Faye," he said.

I watched him fiddle with the gold band of his watch as he sat on the desk right beside me. I noticed his longish hair was actually more blond than reddish and had a floppy prep school look to it like Gareth's. He had huge forearms and his neck was like a bull's. He still looked like he could be a linebacker at Yale.

"I know you were partnered up with my stupid drug addict brother. He told me all about it. Funny the secrets you can get out of people when you have a gun to their head. That's why I set you up to take the fall. It was perfect really since you were already involved with the kidnapping. It would just look like a falling out. And I thought I had you. I saw you go in, down the one-way street. But then you got away somehow. How did you do that? The cops were there in like two minutes and it was a dead-end street. I was watching from the shoulder of the

Deegan so you didn't come out that way. You're a slippery one, aren't you, Faye? How'd you wriggle your way out of that one?"

I sat up straight and looked into his beady eyes again. I didn't know how I was going to get out of this, but playing dumb obviously wasn't going to be it.

"You're on a roll, Harrison," I said. "You tell me the rest of your side first."

"Now that's the spirit," Harrison said with a little laugh. "Who says there's no honor among thieves? Even after you escaped, I was going to rat you out anyway. Who would believe after all your crimes that you wouldn't just double-cross Gareth at the end? But when I heard the FBI had a lead on that conductor meathead and his brother-in-law, I decided to let things play out a little. You had to be laughing your ass off when you heard about that. Am I right?"

"Go on," I said, blank-faced.

"That was some great luck there, Faye. That's the only reason you're not in jail right now."

"Is that right?" I said.

71

Harrison nodded as he folded his big forearms.

"If that played out, I was seriously thinking of letting you off scot-free. But you had to go and figure out who I was, didn't you? You're too clever by half, Faye. You never should have gone back to work. And you never ever should have come to my father's house. That was just reckless. You should have just taken the money and run."

He played with the gold band of his Rolex some more.

"This damn thing," he said. "Should have left something this distinctive at home, huh? You know, you forget the little details in something like this. But I don't have to tell that to a master swindler like you, do I?"

He laughed again.

"I tip my hat, Faye. That was quite a plan you cooked up. Steal the money first then get the Feds to haul out the evidence. Would have worked, too. You just didn't realize someone else was already using my stupid worthless brother to get at some money. Me. But the money I aimed to get at made your paltry three million look like chump change, June bug. Like a Starbucks tip."

"The Haynes family fortune," I said.

"Yep," he said. "The old family fortune. And it is a fortune, Faye. A Fortune 500 kind of fortune. My daddy didn't go on all those trips down to the Caymans to work on his tan. I thought I was going to bag it clean, just me and my little sister. Then I saw the will."

He sighed.

"My father was one hard-ass. You don't get to where he did in Manhattan real estate without learning the art of cracking nuts. That's why when Gareth started putting a needle in his arm, Pop chucked him into the gutter faster than you could spit. He was dad's favorite. I so admired my father for that. One of the few things he ever did that I actually did admire. But I guess cancer softened him up or something."

"He was going to give Gareth an inheritance?" I said.

"No," Harrison said, glaring at me. "Not just an inheritance. *A third*. As in 33.333-to-infinity percent. That lucky little son of a gun. Even after everything—chicks throwing themselves at him, plowing through life like a rock star, even after humiliating our family by becoming an actual heroin addict street bum and knocking up strippers—he was going to end up on his feet with as much as me? After all that? *Really?*"

Harrison held his big head in his big hands.

"Oh no," he said, waving a thick finger. "I wouldn't have it, Faye. No way. Not after all I had to do for my piece of the pie. All the work I had to put in being daddy's step-and-fetch-it. A hundred hours a week for a decade. Shit work, too. Not being a fancy broker like golden boy Gareth. No, for me, Dad said, 'Be a building district manager, son. You let Gareth lunch at the Four Seasons with movie star clients. You, on the other hand, sweat it out in a backroom office on Third Avenue, helping to hire and fire all the scum-of-the-earth supers and doormen.'

"That's why I put my foot down, Faye. I said, no. The family fortune goes to the good son. Not Gareth. Gareth didn't have to learn to live with the taste of daddy's boot on his tongue all day long, did he? Didn't have to get humiliated by him regularly in front of the whole office when he started screaming his head off about the smallest thing. And make no mistake. Dad was a screamer. So, I saw that will and I said uh-uh. You can take that prodigal son shit and stuff it right up where the sun don't shine. Not on my watch."

Harrison took a deep breath.

"So, I decided to follow Gareth's every move once he returned to the city, hoping maybe he might meet with that destruction he's been egging on with his poor lifestyle choices. I thought I might even be able to help him over that edge he liked to skate on so dangerously. Especially, if no one seemed to be looking. The least a brother could do, right?

"But then all of a sudden, a few weeks ago, he starts acting funny. Cleans up his act. I knew he was up to something. So, I watched and I waited and when I finally figured it out and saw you guys get the ball rolling on your scam, I paid my little bro a surprise visit. A surprise final visit."

"At the Bellaire," I said.

"Yep. That's the place. Real swank, don't you think? The fricking south Bronx Taj Mahal. Did you know his squeeze, Sylvia, was a dancer there? That's how the two little lovebirds met. Sylvia was one of the Bellaire's premier ballarinas de nudistas back in the day. That's Spanish for stripper if you're not down with the boogie down lingo.

"Isn't that a funny way of saying stripper? Why, my brother's common law wife isn't a stripper! How dare you insult her like that. She's a ballerina of nudity. Makes it sound kind of nice, doesn't it? Artistic. Like that dirty slut's all-nude bump and grind pole dance for another line of coke is worthy of a recital at Lincoln Center with the Philharmonic or something.

"Which finally brings me to the elegant little solution to all of our problems. Miss Sylvia."

"Sylvia?" I said.

He nodded his big linebacker head.

"Yes. Sylvia."

"Why her?" I said.

"Well, as hilarious as it would be, I figure even an MTA conductor and his brother-in-law aren't stupid enough to actually take the rap for a kidnapping and murder they had nothing to do with. After that the Feds are going to come sniffing around again, right? Do we want that? No. So, if you didn't do it. And I didn't do it. Somebody had to have done it. That leaves Sylvia. She's already connected to the Bellaire, connected to the Cuban mafia dope dealer who ran it. *They* were the ones who did it obviously."

I watched as he opened a drawer and clunked something onto the table.

It was a clear Ziploc bag with a gun inside of it, a chunky black one. It was a revolver.

"And look see here. What do you know? We even have the evidence. Here's the murder weapon right here," he said. "Once the Feds find this gun in Sylvia's apartment, we'll be right as rain, Faye. Which is where you come in."

"Me?"

"Yes. We're going to take some of that money you robbed your bank of, say a hundred grand of it. Or it could be fifty, if you want. Your call. Sylvia's done much more for less, take it on good authority. And what we're going to do is drive over to Sylvia's there at Château Vernon Boulevard, and you're going to go up and give the money to her and plant the gun. Then the Feds are going to get a phone call. Voilà. Sylvia takes the pinch. You get your money. I get mine. We both walk away."

I thought about that. This crazy son of a bitch would let me walk away with me knowing that he killed his brother?

There was no chance of that. No chance in hell.

But I didn't have a choice.

"What are we waiting for?" I said, standing. "Let's just get it done."

72

"Pretty slick, huh?" he said, hitting a clicker on the site's rolling gate as we left. "Only the poor park on the street. That's what my daddy used to say. One of his favorite witty expressions. Daddy broke his ass building his real estate empire, and now I get to spend the rest of my life wallowing in it. Now I get to be the screamer-in-chief and I can't wait."

I tried to think of a way out of things as Harrison raced us down the street, but I was coming up with nothing. My mind was still a blur as he pulled up back in front of my Morningside Heights apartment.

I stared at the empty lobby, the empty sidewalk.

I was all out of plans now.

"Now, go up and get the money, Faye," he said. "And don't be stupid. Don't make me come up there. You don't want me to meet little Caitlin, do you? Yeah, I know about her. I know about everything. So don't even think about screwing around."

When I arrived upstairs, Caitlin was in the shower. As I hurried for the bedroom, I noticed how the hallway was only half painted. I stared at the roller hanging off the almost full tray of paint. Cavan. I still didn't know where he was. He must have left in a hurry when he found my secret phone.

What an idiot I am, I thought. How could I have let him stay so hurt? Why hadn't I just come clean?

But I didn't have time for should haves.

I went into my bedroom closet and kicked a hole in the Sheetrock and grabbed ten packets of hundreds and put them into my bag.

"Let's see it," Harrison said when I rushed down and got back in the Rover. "Went with the hundred thou, huh? What a magnanimous gesture."

I was completely silent and stayed that way as we drove back down to Midtown. When we took the 59th Street Bridge into Queens, I looked around for the Roosevelt Island tram that I had ridden while following Gareth what seemed like a thousand years before, but I didn't see it.

What the hell now? I thought as we finally parked just south of Sylvia's small run-down apartment building across the street on Vernon Boulevard.

As we stopped, I saw there was a brick wall on my right and behind it, some kind of industrial plant with smoke stacks.

I wondered if this would be the last view of New York I'd ever see. Or view of anything else.

"Deep breaths, Faye. Deep breaths," Harrison said as he put the plastic bag holding the gun into my purse. "Good. Now go set her up."

I pulled myself up on the soft leather of the Range Rover. We eyed each other in the silence. We were close enough that I could smell his crisp aftershave.

"Listen to me," he said. "I get how rattled you must be feeling. And even burnt out with all the crazy stuff you've been through. But do you honestly think this is tough or something? This is about as easy as it gets. I'm offering you a get-out-of-screwing-up-your-life-forever free card here, Faye. I don't even want your embezzled money. You can have the whole thing. Stop having a canary."

I pictured Gareth on the bench by the Hudson River, the tears in his eyes when he talked about his daughter. I couldn't get the image of it out of my mind.

"What about the baby?" I said.

"Baby? What baby?" he said.

"Gareth's daughter. Your niece. Won't she go to foster care or something?"

He laughed.

"Baby?" he said. "Who gives a shit? I'm my own baby. You're your own baby. Let babies baby themselves. Just go bell the slut so we can get out of here."

I looked out at Vernon Boulevard. The traffic gliding past.

Harrison was right about one thing. By that point I really did feel mentally and emotionally burnt out. I was complete toast.

"I don't know," I said.

"Don't know?" he said, suddenly cocking his head at me as if I were a misbehaving child. I saw there was a cold look in his amber eyes, a look of anger there, flaring.

He slapped me then. So hard my head slammed back and bounced off the headrest.

I felt dizzy and grasped the armrest, trying not to black out. I tasted something metallic in my mouth. It was blood. I'd bitten my tongue.

"How about now? Do you know now, Faye?" he said.

I had been merely scared before. Now I was petrified. Numb. I started crying then.

"Don't start with the crying," he said. "Don't even. That shit you said to my father? You terrified him. *You did*. Not Gareth. I heard the tape. An old dying man! Made his last moments on earth pure torment. You wanted to play with the big boys, Faye. Swim with the sharks, right? Well, be careful what you wish for."

He opened the door for me.

"It's feeding time at the shark tank now, Faye. So, if you don't want to be the chum, wake up. Wipe those crying eyes and bag that bitch upstairs. Because it's her or you."

I stumbled out.

"And Faye?"

I turned back.

"Don't you even think about messing around or pulling one of your patented slippery moves on me. I know where you live. I know what your sister looks like. And that donkey boyfriend of yours, those horse and buggies have medallions like taxis. I'll get his pulled before you can blink. Because I know everybody. The DA—everybody—in this city. After I get through with you, I'll make ruining everyone you know my lifetime hobby."

73

Dazed and devastated, I zombie walked across the street to Sylvia's building. Inside the foyer, the lock on the door was broken and the fluorescent light was flickering in the dingy lobby.

I remembered Gareth had told me he lived in 5B so I went up the stairs to the top.

"Who is it?" said a woman's voice a second after I rang the doorbell.

"Sylvia?" I whispered. "You don't know me, but I'm a friend of Gareth's."

The door opened a crack. Behind the safety chain, a pretty Asian woman stared at me.

"Who are you?" she said, sizing me up. "Friend of Gareth, my ass. Don't bullshit me. What are you? The press or something?"

"No, Sylvia. It's a long story. Listen. You and your daughter are in a ton of trouble. In about five seconds, they are going to try to frame you for Gareth's kidnapping and murder."

"Me? What!" she cried.

She closed the door, unlocked it and opened it all the way.

"What are you talking about?" she said, whispering herself now. "I didn't do it. I didn't do anything."

"I know you didn't," I said. "The kidnapping was fake. It was a scam just to get the ransom money. He must have told you. Didn't he tell you?"

She shook her head.

"I knew he was into stuff, but I didn't ask. When I saw he was kidnapped and then dead, I was stunned. I didn't know what to do. I've been sitting here like a crazy person since. Who the hell are you?"

"It doesn't matter. Can I come in?" I said, glancing down the stairs. "Just for a second."

She waved me in.

"It's a long story but the short of it is that his brother found out about the kidnapping scam and killed him for real."

"No! His brother, Harrison, did it?"

"Yes," I said, nodding vigorously.

"Gareth hated Harrison!" she cried. "Hated him!"

"Not as much as Harrison hated Gareth," I said. "That's why he killed him. He didn't want Gareth to get his inheritance."

She stared a laser-beam-like hole in me.

"Oh, now I get it. The inheritance. Gareth did say his dad was very sick," she said, nodding. "This is so crazy. But I actually believe you. Why are you here?"

I stared at Sylvia. I still had no clue what to do, but she was an ally, I saw suddenly. We needed to help each other here.

"Harrison is downstairs."

I took the plastic bag with the gun in it out of my bag.

"This is the gun he killed Gareth with. He wants me to plant this on you, but I can't do it. I'm not going to hurt you or your baby. I won't. Not even if he kills me, which he might because he's freaking out-of-his-mind crazy."

"We need to call the cops," Sylvia said.

"No," I said, suddenly realizing it. "We can't."

"Why not?"

"Because we look more guilty. Plus Harrison knows the DA. He's so rich he'll just hire million-dollar lawyers and they'll arrest us is why."

I took out the hundred thousand and started dropping it on the mail table.

"You need to take this money and get out of here with it. Get your baby and, I mean, get out of here now. When I leave, just grab a diaper bag and go. Get a hotel room or something."

"What then?" she said.

"I have no idea, but this nut is downstairs and he is dangerous so the both of us need to get away from him."

"Wait," she said, picking up one of the packets of money. "This is happening? Like really happening?"

"It's happening, Sylvia. Get out of here with your daughter."

"Maybe I should go with you."

"No, it's better if we split up," I said. "Harrison needs the gun planted on you. I'll run in the other direction with it. Is there a back way out of the building?"

"Yes. In the lobby, there's a side door that leads into a garbage way between the building and the soul food place. They usually keep the kitchen door open. Go in and through the kitchen and you should be able to sneak out on the other side onto 36th Avenue."

"Thanks," I said as I pulled open the apartment door.

"But I don't even know your name," she said as I stepped back into the hallway.

"It doesn't matter. Just get your daughter out of here. Now," I said.

I hurried down the steps. The restaurant's kitchen door was open in the alley just as Sylvia had told me. The kitchen was empty, and I walked past a prep table and into the little restaurant itself.

Past the restrooms, I saw there were Spike Lee movie stills

and headshots of Denzel Washington on the walls above the booths and beyond was the open front door.

"Those shots are great, aren't they?" Harrison said as he turned from where he was standing ten feet away to my right by the counter.

I lunged back but not fast enough. He bolted up beside me and grabbed my arm.

"I'm a real sucker for defining film moments, aren't you?" he said.

I gaped at him.

"Going somewhere, Faye? You were, weren't you? I can tell by the look on your face. Glad I decided to stop in to get a bite. Told you your luck is running out."

He was hauling me out through the front door of the place by my arm when I played the last card in the deck.

I broke away and suddenly reached into my pocket for the gun. The one I'd taken out of the bag when I was coming down the stairs.

He figured out what I was doing at the last second and seized at my wrist, but I slipped his iron grip this time.

Then I had my hand around the pistol and it went off with a muffled bang.

Harrison let me go immediately, and I watched as he bolted across Vernon Boulevard in a frantic zigzag like he'd just caught an interception and was heading for the end zone. A moment later, I heard the screech of tires.

I was feeling almost happy about making the bastard take off so quick when I felt the warm liquid pouring into my palm.

It was blood, I saw as I looked down.

My blood.

I'd shot myself.

74

I didn't look at it. I couldn't look at it. I stuffed the gun back into my pocket and clapped a hand at the wound and ran back into Sylvia's building and climbed the stairs two by two.

"Sylvia! Help! Please, it's me. Help!" I said, leaning on her doorbell.

I looked down at my blood dripping on the dirty marble hallway tile. As I waited, from one of the apartments downstairs came the blare of a TV, the infuriating happy singsong of a drug commercial slogan.

Sylvia flung open the door.

"What now?" she said.

"I'm shot," I said, tilting inside.

"He shot you?"

"No," I said as I caught myself in the kitchen doorway. "He was in the restaurant when I got down there. I shot myself when he grabbed me."

"Where is he now?"

"He took off. But who knows where. Please help me. I need to stop the bleeding."

She brought me inside to the kitchen sink and ran my arm under the cold water.

"I can't look. How is it?" I said.

"Not that bad. The hole is small. It looks like it just went straight through and came out the other side. It's all swollen, but the blood seems to be slowing at least."

"Can you bandage it? We need to go."

"Bandage it? I look like a nurse? You need an ambulance," she said.

"No. No hospital. I'll end up in jail. It'll be okay. Just bandage it up. Please."

She did. At her kitchen table, she wrapped it tight with paper towels and a couple of layers of duct tape. I swayed a little getting up but when I took a step, I was semisolid on my feet.

Beyond the doorway of the living room, I saw Sylvia and Gareth's daughter in pajamas sitting in a stroller sucking on a binkie. She had the biggest cupcake eyes I ever saw. She looked like a doll.

She'd never see her daddy again, would she? I thought. All because of me.

Seeing her blink back at me so innocently, I wanted to lie down and cry but there wasn't time, so I just shook my head instead.

"I need a coat or something," I said to Sylvia.

"Here," she said, rushing to a closet.

It was a man's raincoat. I slipped it on.

"You need a hospital, Faye," Sylvia said.

"No. I'm not sure what I need, but definitely not a hospital. It doesn't matter. Just get out of here, Sylvia. Get out of the city with the baby. Promise me."

Sylvia was nodding, and I started for the door when I thought of it.

The last place I could go.

PART FOUR

IT'S LONELY AT THE TOP

75

That was how I ended up back at the MetLife Building.

Shot.

The first thing I did after I left Sylvia's was to call Caitlin and tell her to go up to Cavan's place in the Bronx.

"What? Why?" she said.

I needed her out of there as Harrison could be on his way to get her as we spoke.

Or was he now onto a different plan? I thought. Maybe calling the cops and telling them that I was one who killed Gareth? Was there an APB out on me now?

I didn't know what the hell was going on. Only that none of it was good.

"Because Cavan is coming over and he says he has something he wants to ask me," I lied.

"What? You think he's going to pop the question?" she said excitedly.

"Who knows?" I said, smiling through the pain in my arm. "Just take the credit card I gave you and leave now."

Then I went across the car bridge into Roosevelt Island and took the tram back into Manhattan.

And now I was here, I thought, staring down at Park Avenue.

Back where the beginning of the end began.

I stared down at the city. I couldn't figure out what to do. I couldn't go to the cops. Couldn't go home.

As I lay by the window mystified at what I had done and what I had gotten myself into, I went in and out of consciousness a few times. I didn't think it was from blood loss but rather the sheer exhaustion and stress and shock.

I was obviously having trouble thinking clearly. I could hardly even move. I felt like I was stuck to the floor.

As the pain in my arm radiated up to my shoulder and back, I finally realized I had to stop hiding. That being shot was more serious than I was willing to admit. That I actually might die.

That's when it occurred to me.

Cavan, I thought.

I needed to call him. He would help me. Help me figure this out. I hadn't wanted to involve him, but that didn't matter now. He hadn't done anything wrong, and if it meant jail for me, so be it. Jail was better than being dead, I decided.

As I fumbled my phone out of my bag, I looked at the battery bar and saw it was on its last legs.

Like me, I thought as I texted Cavan.

At MetLife building 5412 need help

Then I hit send.
And the phone went black.
Then so did I.

76

When I woke up, maybe an hour or so later, there was a disquieting stillness in the empty office. As I lay there aching, I thought I caught the smell of money from the shredder. But maybe I was just imagining it.

The first thing I did was check the bandage. My arm still hurt like hell, but there was no visible blood so that was good.

I looked back at the shredder again. I remembered how jazzed I was when I had come in from the money drop. How proud I was, how cocky about outwitting everyone.

"You and your big plans," I mumbled.

I'd just remembered that my phone was dead now and that I didn't have a charger when I heard the sound.

It was the rolling sound of the elevator door opening down the hall.

As I lay there, I stared at the beam of corridor light at the bottom of the office door as I listened to the approaching footsteps. Then there were two black lines in the light beam. Someone's feet.

Cavan.

I was waiting for a knock, ready to call out, when it happened. A key went into the lock and the tumbler turned.

Huh? I thought as the door opened and the lights flicked on.

I must be dead, I thought as I saw what was in the fluorescent glare.

This is hell, I thought. I've died and gone to hell.

"There you are, Faye," Harrison said, smiling as he kicked the door shut behind him.

"Small world, huh? It's funny. I've been looking all over for you and here you are."

77

He raised the gun he was holding, the little semiauto, as he flicked the lights back off.

"Guess whose company manages the MetLife Building, Faye. One guess is all you'll need. Didn't I warn you about those slippery moves?"

I reached into the raincoat pocket.

"I'll shoot you. Don't do it," he said.

But I kept reaching. What choice did I have? As I finally fumbled the gun out, I saw him gesture futilely with the gun he was holding. He was shaking it.

"Work, dammit! Work!" he yelled at the gun.

He stopped advancing as I came out with the revolver and trained it on his face.

"Shit," he said as I somehow stood.

I clicked back the hammer.

"It's called a safety, Harrison," I said. "Semiautos have a safety. But revolvers like this one—you know this gun here, the one that you used to kill your own brother with—don't have one. You city boys think you know everything, don't you? But I guess there's still a couple of lessons for you to learn."

He screamed then as he rushed forward. I fired, but the shot went just over his shoulder as he dove. Then the gun I was holding went flying as he crashed into my ankles.

I stumbled but was just able to keep my feet as he slid facedown across the floor underneath me.

And then I ran for the office door and threw it open, and I was running out down the hall.

78

I found the stairwell, and scared I would get caught between Harrison and the security guard downstairs, I did about the stupidest thing possible.

I ran up the stairs to the roof.

The second I hit the door to the roof and ran out onto it, I realized what an incredibly bad move I had made. Where could I go now? Into a waiting helicopter? Outer space? Office buildings didn't have fire escapes.

But I was rattled with sheer terror now. I had about as much reasoning ability as a chicken with its head cut off.

The floor of the roof had gravel on it for some strange reason, and as I crunched across it looking for a place to hide, I saw that the moon had come out. Above the West Side it loomed, a full moon, ivory-colored and glowing. There was a wind up as well. It made a whistling sound as it blew around the maze of metal service boxes and electrical equipment I was quickly heading toward to hide behind.

One of the metal corners of the boxes beside me suddenly blew apart as I heard a gun go off behind me.

"Safety off! I got it now, June bug," Harrison cried out behind me.

I dove around a steel cabinet as another gunshot sounded out.

"I thank ya real kindly for the tip, country girl."

I was running along the side of the box I was behind when I tripped over an electrical cord and went facedown into the gravel with a jarring hard bang. Sparks of pain shot down my arm as the bandage came right off.

There was another larger piece of machinery to the right up on small stilts that seemed like it had just enough room to crawl under. When I wriggled beneath it, I could hear the gurgling of water. It was some kind of air-conditioning unit or something.

I was going to die here, I thought, wanting to cry. Why had I been so stupid?

"Full moon tonight, Faye," I heard Harrison call out as he crunched closer. "Just you and me and the man in the moon now. Come out and have a look. I'll let you have one last look."

I remained motionless then, curled into a ball, a ball of anguish, panic, and pain.

"You understand what has to happen now," he said. "You bet and you lost. What do you Wall Street wizards call it? Margin call? It's margin call time, Faye."

There was the wail of a siren far below in the street, the volume slowly gaining.

Was it for me?

Then I screamed as a hand seized my ankle.

"There she is," Harrison said. "There's my pretty little slippery catfish girl. Here we go. Last call for a square dance."

That's when I heard it.

"Faye! Faye! It's me. It's Cavan. Where are you?"

I kicked out as Harrison pulled harder.

He yelled as I caught him in his kneecap, and I scurried back under the air-conditioning unit and began crawling on my hands and knees for its other side.

"Cavan, run! Get back! He's got a gun!" I screamed as I heard a shot.

"Faye, where are you? Where are you?" Cavan screamed as I came out under the other side of the unit and started running around its other side.

I almost tripped again over a little metal stepstool that was there in the gravel. I started running again but then turned back and grabbed it up and ran around the next corner.

Harrison had his back turned and his gun extended back toward the open stairwell door when I smashed him in the back of the head with the square-edged stepstool.

I caught him good and hard right in the back of his big skull with the sharp aluminum edge of it, and the gun fell from his hand as he went down on one knee. He was pawing around, trying to retrieve the gun when Cavan burst from the stairwell door at a run.

Harrison had just found the gun and was up on his feet again when Cavan, leaping off his feet, caught him flush in the chest in a tackle. The gun went flying again and they both went down spinning, and I screamed as I saw them both roll and then get up by the roof's edge, swinging at each other.

"You're as good as dead," Harrison said as he got Cavan in a headlock.

And then I ran up and brained Harrison in the back of the head with the stepstool again.

He released Cavan as he went to the ground for a second time, and then Cavan snatched the stepstool out of my hand and proceeded to beat the living shit out of Harrison with it.

He smashed it across his temple and smashed him in the mouth with it and then Cavan cried out with a tennis player *ugh!* sound as he crisply broke the lunatic's nose.

Still Harrison got up on his feet. He spit out a tooth. As he finally regained his legs, I could see that his jaw was broken. He lunged at Cavan.

Then Cavan bodychecked the big bastard in the chest with the stepstool as he pivoted.

And Harrison fell back and off the edge of the roof and was gone.

79

The moon went down over Manhattan, and then the sun came up.

And when it did, I was where I always was on Tuesday mornings that very memorable summer.

Walking off the freshly hosed Madison Avenue sidewalks into the hallowed halls of Greene Brothers Hale.

My boss, Alexander Aiken, was there just inside, waiting for me. He was standing next to the new security guy with the mustache.

"Alexander," I said, smiling brightly.

Aiken seemed less bright-eyed and bushy-tailed. In fact, by the dark glare he was giving me, he seemed pretty pissed off.

"Walker," he said coldly. "Straight up to five for the interns' farewell breakfast."

Five was where the executive dining hall was.

We had to go there today because this was it, the day everyone was waiting for.

The breakfast was where they would announce who was getting the job.

On the other side of the golden elevator on five, I saw the

dining room was packed. I thought it was just going to be us, but it looked like half the company was there. I found my basement crew sitting at a big white-linen-covered table in front.

"Faye, Faye, Faye," they all chanted like they had at the dinner Priscilla had thrown for us.

Instead of wanting to kill them like last time, I put a hand to my ear and then laughed and handed out high fives before I sat between McPhee and Priscilla.

"Whatever happens, it was fun working with you guys," I said to them. "I'll never forget it."

After I gave the white-jacketed waiter my poached egg order, I saw Paulina across the room stand up and approach the podium.

Just as this happened, I suddenly saw that Aiken was behind me. And he still looked quite pissed.

"Actually, Faye, you have another meeting this morning," he said in my ear. "Come with me, please."

"A meeting?" I said as he led me back to the elevators.

"Yes. Mr. Dabertand asked if you would head up to speak with him. He is up on twelve waiting for you."

"Is that right?" I said as he stared at me none too kindly.

Because he knew what the meeting was about.

And so did I.

"Just go up to twelve, Walker," he said.

I noticed that the pity I had seen in his eyes once was nowhere to be seen now.

"Aye, aye, sir," I said, giving him a salute as I walked to the golden elevator.

80

I thought our final tête-à-tête would take place in Dabertrand's office, but he had chosen GBH's penthouse suite on twelve instead.

Like Shangri-la and other places of legend, GBH's penthouse suite was a place only whispered about and never actually seen. It was said that it was like a hotel suite instead of an office. One that top staff like Dabertrand, and other VIP bank clients and dignitaries who came into New York, sometimes spent the night in.

And as I came out of the elevator, I saw that like mostly all rumors, it was completely true.

It looked like a residence, a lavish one with Moroccan arches and Persian rugs and intricate red silk wallpaper. I stepped past the foyer into a two-story library rotunda with a painted mural on its domed ceiling. On it were depictions of American industry, steam trains and airplanes, muscular men hauling steel beams, muscular men behind plows.

"I'm in here," I heard Dabertrand call out.

Past the mural, through pocket doors, Dabertrand sat at a beautiful varnished writing desk, waiting for me. There was a globe on his right and a brass telescope on his left to take in the panoramic view of Central Park behind him.

"Please have a seat," he said, gesturing at the one opposite.

As I took it, I smiled as I spotted the Simon Bolivar statue above the treetops.

Because it reminded me of Cavan, saving me only hours before.

After Harrison had his great fall off the MetLife Building, we went back down to the office where I confessed everything to Cavan as he patched me up again. Then we took the stairs all the way down and went out a basement door. There weren't any cops so we looked around.

We found Harrison on the Park Avenue viaduct. Or what was left of him. He'd fallen into a rectilinear planter that had large trees in it. One of trees was snapped in half. And so was Harrison's neck.

Cavan and I had decided to not call the cops or do anything yet, but to wait and see how things rolled out.

I watched as Dabertrand drummed his perfectly manicured fingers on the inlaid antique desktop.

Now apparently, I was about to find out.

81

As I turned my gaze away from Simon Bolivar, I suddenly noticed the chessboard in the corner.

"Anderssen versus Kieseritzky," I said, scanning the board. "That's a classic. I love that game. Anderssen's combination finish was stunning."

"You play, do you, Faye?"

"A confirmed addict," I said.

"Why does that not surprise me? Nice view, isn't it?" he said.

"Not bad," I said, looking at Simon Bolivar again.

"Faye, is there something you wish to share with me?" Dabertrand said.

"Share with you?" I said. "I can't think of a thing."

"That's disappointing," he said.

He took a breath.

"I've seen a video of you, Faye. A curious video."

"A video?" I said.

"From that Saturday morning. When we bumped into each other."

"Oh," I said. "I remember now. Was that the morning you wanted to take me to the Hamptons in your fancy car?"

I smiled.

"But I wouldn't let you?"

"Yes, that very morning," Dabertrand said without missing a beat. "I thought you said you had just dropped by to say hi to Marvin but that's not actually true, is it?"

"Well," I said calmly. "I think I recall that Marvin said that and that I went along so as to not get Marvin into trouble. Co-workers can be like that, you know. They can have loyalty to one another."

"Well, bad news on the Marvin front."

Dabertrand tsked.

"He doesn't work here anymore."

I stared at him.

"That's a shame," I said.

You bastard.

"And yet there it is," he said with a snarky little smile. "So you didn't just drop by then?"

"No, I went downstairs to the office to wait for my friends."

"What did you do downstairs?"

"I forget exactly. Let's see," I said, tapping at my lips with a finger. "Perhaps, I played with my phone. No, wait. Do you know what I did? I took a look around the basement. I'd never seen the other side of it so I did a little exploring."

"A little exploring," Dabertrand said, cocking his head. "Is that right? That's kind of strange. How long did you explore for?"

"Oh, about an hour or so," I said.

"That's a long exploration."

"I found a paperback book in the janitors' break room, a Stephen King one. The one about the car. *Christine*. That's the one. So, I sat and read some of that."

"*Christine*. Are you sure?"

"Pretty positive. Stephen King is like potato chips. Once you start you just keep going. But by all means, verify. Heck, if the book is still there, you could check it for fingerprints."

"Instead of reading, did you instead perhaps happen to steal three million dollars out of the vault?"

There it was. Out in the open.

"No," I lied. "Why do you ask?"

Even I was surprised at how cool as a cucumber I was able to say this.

"Because I think you stole three million dollars out of the vault," Dabertrand said, sitting up. "I think you put it in your suitcase and taped it under your dress and walked right out the door with it."

"Do you really?" I said. "That's a very strange theory, Mr. Dabertrand."

"How so?"

"Because the FBI left with the money. I was there. I was the one who handed it off to them. You know, during the kidnapping of Gareth Haynes? Didn't I read in the paper that the three million was lost to the kidnapper? Which it seems, if you've read this morning's paper, turned out, in a shocking tragic twist, to be Gareth's brother, Harrison."

"Yes, I did read the paper," Dabertrand said. "Gareth Haynes's brother leaping from the MetLife Building in a quote, unquote suicide is quite shocking and tragic. With the murder weapon found by his side and everything. And a packet of the money, too. Right there in his pocket. What a dramatic story."

"I'll say," I said. "The FBI sure seems to like it. And the *New York Post* and the *New York Times* and the *Wall Street Journal* and—"

"But would a jury like that story, Faye?" he said, peering at me. "If we started digging—really digging—would a grand jury buy the story the way it's been laid out? Or would they find instead another, even more shocking truth? One about a clever little intern who robbed an investment bank and *almost* got away with it."

"I don't know what they might find out," I said with a smile. "It's hard to say what a jury might or might not do. Anything can happen in a courtroom."

He stared at me.

"Oh, and by the way, Arthur," I said, going into my bag.

"Arthur, is it suddenly?" he said, stunned.

"Yes. That is your name, right?" I said, smiling again as I fished something out of my purse. "I forgot something in all the running around. I misplaced some paperwork."

I slid the envelope across the glass-like varnish of the desk.

82

I could tell by his puzzled face that Dabertrand had no idea what was in the envelope.

"Some paperwork that you may find possesses some *personal* interest," I said.

He opened the envelope and shook out the backdated kidnapping insurance policy I had gotten signed by Robert Haynes.

After he read it, he looked back at me over the top of it.

"You little bitch," he said.

"Arthur," I said. "Such sexist abusive language is most unbecoming. Most un-CEO-like, frankly."

Dabertrand bit at his lower lip and dropped the paper and then held the edges of the desk with an expression on his face that made me think that he was close, very, very close, to flipping it.

Instead, after a moment he lifted the paper and tore it in half. And tore it in half again. Slowly.

Then it was his turn to smile. It was a great smile, like the kind you see on a toothpaste commercial.

I knew what that meant. That he was willing to eat the three million that he was personally on the hook for in order to nail me.

"Anything else you have, Faye?" he said with a yawn. "Any other, um, paperwork?"

"Why, Arthur, now that you mention it," I said as I took the tablet out of my bag, "I do have something." I hit play on the cued-up video Cavan had taken. "But paperwork, it is not."

The expression on his face while he watched himself and Priscilla exiting the hotel capped off with the ear bite was something to see.

If it were a portrait, it would have been called *Man in Shock*.

He took in a loud breath and held it, and then he let it back out even more loudly.

"Who are you?" he said. "Who do you work for?"

I smiled as I sat there. Then I looked at Simon Bolivar over his shoulder.

I'd known Cavan was the luckiest thing to happen to me that summer.

Because in the end, Cavan had done it. Not me.

Not only had he come to my rescue when I most needed it, but in the end, it was Cavan's video that was the straw that broke the jackass's back.

"I'm just an unpaid intern," I said as I stood. "One waiting to know if I got the job or not."

"You got the job," he said as I was lifting my bag.

I gave him a puzzled look.

"I mean it," he said. "In fact, I'd like that, Faye. No bullshit. You win. We could use you up here. Take the trader course, but after that I want you up here. Because I've never even heard of anything like this. You've outwitted the FBI, all of us."

"I got the job? Really?" I said happily.

He nodded with a smile.

"Yeah, well, I don't want it anymore," I said, dropping the smiley act. "In fact, for what you did to Priscilla, you can shove the job up where the sun don't shine, you disgusting creep. Ram it as far as it will go."

I stopped one last time at the door and didn't even turn this time.

"Oh, Arthur. One more thing. Marvin gets his job back."

"Marvin gets his job back," Dabertrand repeated like a sad, defeated little boy.

83

As I walked out the doors of Greene Brothers Hale for the last time, I saw the prettiest thing ever around the corner on 60th.

Miracle on East 60th Street, I thought as I saw Cavan and Caitlin and Lily all waiting for me.

I hugged my sister then I hugged Lily, and then I saved the last and longest one for Cavan, my hero, my top-hat-wearing lucky Irish Prince O'Charming.

"How did they take it?" he said after I reluctantly let him go.

I laughed thinking about Dabertrand's face. I couldn't stop laughing.

"That well, huh?"

"Even better," I said. "I'll tell you all about it."

We got up in the jockey box with Caitlin in the carriage and set off west down 60th and made the turn onto Fifth toward the Plaza.

"So where to now, Gordina Gekko?" Cavan said.

"Let's go to the airport," I said.

"The airport!" he cried.

"I hear Dublin is in dire need of a new fireman this fall," I said.

"What! Now she agrees?" he said, almost dropping the reins. "You'll come with me now? What about your blasted plan? The city and the apartment. All of it?"

"Skip it. I think leaving New York might be fine for a while," I said.

"For a while would be good. And forever even better," Cavan said, giving me the same wink he gave me after we planted the evidence on Harrison.

"That settles it then," I said. "Ireland it is. We have a new plan."

"Plan C?" he said.

"No. Plan D," I said.

"Women!" Cavan cried. "I can hardly keep up. But you'll come with me now? You're not kidding?"

"From here on, wherever Cavan goes," I said, hugging his arm, "Faye goes."

"And me too?" Caitlin said from the carriage.

"Yes, and you can come too, Miss And-Me-Too," I said.

We all broke up laughing a second later when Lily turned from where we stopped at the light with a pleading look on her face as well.

"And yes, you too, Lily," I said through the tears of laughter. "I don't know how we'll get you on the plane—as a comfort horse maybe—but you're coming too."

"Hey, move that nag!" said a honking cabbie as he passed.

"Nag? How about I move your nose to the other side of your ugly face instead, you rat bastard. So help me, I will!" Cavan said.

"Cavan?" I said. "Does Aer Lingus have first class?"

"Of course, but it costs a fortune."

"Well, you only live once and it's only money, right?" I said. "And I did get a pretty good severance package after all."

"I'll say," he said.

I laughed, remembering the look he gave me when I showed him the money stuffed into the hole in my bedroom closet.

"Whoa, whoa!" Cavan suddenly cried, pulling hard on the reins.

Horns honked all around us as we came to a dead stop in the intersection of 59th Street and Fifth Avenue. One of those red double decker tour buses making the left onto Fifth stopped right in front of us with the driver screaming.

Cavan had blocked up the entire box.

"What is it?" I said to Cavan as he jumped down. "What's wrong?"

"It's Lily. Her hoof," Cavan said. "I need your help."

I hopped down and rushed to where Cavan knelt by Lily's feet when he turned.

In the box he held in his hand something glittered. But his sparkly blue eyes glittered more.

"Will you marry me?" he said.

Talk about a jaw-dropper! Through the shock of sudden joy and tears in my eyes, I looked over at the Plaza, the Central Park trees, the halted, blaring yellow taxis.

Then I looked back down at Cavan.

Unable to speak or hardly breathe, I nodded vigorously as he leapt up and hugged me.

I'd gotten it. The full fairy tale, I thought, as the happy tears dripped off my cheeks and the horns kept honking on and on.

★ ★ ★ ★ ★

Discover more pulse-pounding thrillers by Michael Ledwidge ...

Hiding out off the grid on a trout stream in the middle of rural New England, the last thing Mike Gannon is looking for is any more trouble. But then he bumps into an old girlfriend who is an investigator up from New York City looking into the mysterious death of a student at a nearby prestigious college. And soon, what Mike wants and what he's about to get become two very different things.

First a whistleblower comes forward with evidence of a deadly scandal. Then shortly after arrives a group of dangerous men who will do anything to keep secrets buried.

Then the lights go out ...

Available to order

When Terry Rourke arrives at his brother's luxurious wedding on the east coast of the USA - summer home to billionaires and Hollywood stars – his biggest worry is the best man speech. But this isn't the first time Terry has been to the Hamptons.

As the designer tuxedos are pressed and the flowers arranged along the glittering surf, Terry can't help but revisit an unsolved murder that scandalised the town – and tore his own family apart. He soon learns that digging up secrets can be a very dangerous activity ... and quickly turn even the most beautiful beach wedding into a wake.

Available to order

When a private jet crashes into the Caribbean Sea, diving instructor Michael Gannon is the only person on the scene. Finding six dead men and a suitcase full of cash and diamonds, Gannon assumes he's the beneficiary of a drug deal gone wrong.

However, it seems one of the passengers was the Director of the FBI – despite the official story that he died of natural causes in Italy. Suddenly pursued by a shadowy cabal of the world's most powerful and dangerous men, Gannon will only survive if he unravels a terrifying conspiracy.

But those determined to kill him will learn that Gannon's past holds its own deadly secrets ... and the hunters soon become the prey.

Available to order